CW01498549

COVEN COVE

The Secret of the Blood Charm

David Clark

1

Lightning crashed, and rain pelted down on my head with the impact of an avalanche of boulders on my already crushed soul. Each drop rolled through my soaked red hair and down my face, creating a constant sheet of water mixed with the tears that already blurred my vision. Though I didn't need to see where I was, the putrid odor and the unevenness of each step told me all I needed to know about the garbage filled cobblestone alleys my mother and I streaked down. While my body kept up stride-for-stride with her, my mind was several blocks back in a similar alley, where a dark figure struck my father down. His body crumbled down into a pool of his own blood before turning to ash. It was an image I couldn't shake as it played over and over in my mind. The only thought in my head that stood a chance against the replay of torment was the realization that the same dark creature was following us. The weight of its presence increased at an alarming rate.

We stumbled out of the alley and into the street. My mother paused in the middle of the road. I stood by her side with my head on a swivel, looking around for our pursuer, but he or it was nowhere in sight. The pause was brief before my mother yanked me down the street and into oncoming traffic.

"Move!" she yelled, but she wasn't yelling at the drivers. She was yelling it at me. I had slowed up to look behind us to see if I could see our pursuer. My head didn't have a chance to turn for a look before she yelled her order. I complied in an instant.

Cars honked and swerved as they tried to avoid us. Those that didn't get out of the way, we leapt over; our feet only grazed the top of them before we landed back on the road behind it. I was raised with very few rules, but the one that wasn't to be broken was never to show your abilities in public, and before now, I never had. With the dark, whatever it was, chasing us, that rule seemed to have lost its importance for the moment.

The sensation of how close it was threatened to freeze my body in its tracks. Without even touching me, its tentacles of fear wrapped around me and squeezed, but before they tightened, my mother pulled me by the hand into another alley. Behind us, something large crunched into a car and then careened off and into the glass window of a storefront.

It took a few blocks down the alley to find a door that wasn't locked. My mother opened it and threw me inside. She followed me in and locked the door behind us.

She then rushed around the corner toward the stairs. A quick wave of her hand insisted that I followed. But instead of going up, we ducked into the dark gap under the first set, along with the mops, brooms, and other cleaning supplies that were stored there. The momentary pause let the emotions that had been trailing behind catch up with me. They produced an uncontrollable sob. My mother asked me to be quiet, but I was inconsolable no matter what she tried. Even her rubbing my shoulders didn't work, and it always had before.

"Need to be quiet, baby," cautioned my mother. Her head jerked up, and she peered through the gap between the steps of the stairs.

"I... am... trying," I whispered between sobs. "What was that thing?" My body trembled, along with my voice. I tried to wipe away the tears. A truly futile action with the pace at which new tears replaced the ones I had cleared from my vision just moments ago.

"Later. There is something more important we need to do now."

I watched as my mother reached up and removed the necklace she wore. It was a simple gold chain that had a small tear drop shaped vial hanging on the end. The vial contained a clear liquid. I wore a similar one, except mine was red. I didn't remember when I got it, or who gave it to me, and no one really ever told me anything about it. It was something I always had that she insisted that I always wore.

When I reached up for my own, I watched panic fill her face, and she screamed, "No!" Her hand slammed my vial and my own hand into my chest with a thump. "You must protect that with your life." She stared into my eyes. Even though they were dark and black, I could see her intensity. "Promise me! Tell me you understand!"

I didn't answer, and my hesitation seemed to fuel my mother's fury even further. "Promise me, Larissa!" Her hand gripped and shook my own.

"I promise," I said, but not completely sure what I had agreed to or why. She paused and watched me until I said it again. "I promise."

She popped open her vial and handed it to me. "Drink it. Hurry!" She stood up and rushed out from under the stairs and looked around while I sat there and watched, holding the open vial in my trembling hand. My mother looked back and screamed, "Drink It!"

I couldn't remember the last time my mother had screamed at me, but it didn't take long for the next time. "Now!" Her hand punched the bottom of the stairs. Its steel frame had a fist shaped dent as a memento.

"Larissa. You need to hurry. That will protect you!" This time, she watched closely as I timidly moved the vial to my lips, pausing before tilting it to drink. She nodded her approval, and I opened my lips and tilted it the rest of the way until the liquid in the vial emptied into my mouth. My body recoiled at the taste. It was salty and bitter, almost vinegary tasting.

"Good girl. Now hand me the vial." I handed it to her while my body dealt with the taste. She smashed it on the ground. "Let's go." She yanked me up by the hand, hard, sending a shooting pain into my shoulder, which was an odd sensation I hadn't felt before.

We weren't running this time, but we still hurried. Instead of going out the door we entered through, we exited through the front, which put us out on the rainy street.

People rushed up and down the sidewalk to get where they needed to be, and we blended right in. My mother reached over and pulled my black hoodie up over my head, and then pulled the collar of her own jacket up, partially ducking down below it.

We kept close to those in front of us for the next few blocks. I no longer felt the dark presence that was chasing us, but my mom still looked behind every once in a while. Each time she did, her head jerked back forward, and her black eyes were larger and blank. I reached over and grabbed my mother's hand. It felt cold, something I had never noticed before.

"There!" my mother said pointing and sounding relieved.

"The train station?"

She nodded and pulled me through the doors.

People stood just inside, partially blocking the door, while they waited for the rain to stop before venturing out. Those coming in, like us, had to squeeze past. Once through the mass of people, I saw the full grandeur of the old 1920s building. High stone arches that went up to the ceiling three stories above me. Large windows lined the front to let light in during the day, while electric lights made to look like old gas lamps provided the illumination at night, like tonight was. Even at this hour, it was full of hustle and bustle. Beyond the enormous staircase ahead of us, a train rumbled away from the station. I saw a stream of people moving in that direction. There were other trains still waiting for passengers.

We reached a row of green benches, and my mother pushed my body into one of the seats. I felt like a rag doll in her hands. "Wait here." She turned to head back into the crowd. I tightened my grip on her icy hand, but even holding on as tight as I could, she easily pulled her hand out of my grasp.

"Don't leave, mom. What if that thing comes?" I cried, beseeching her to stay.

"You have nothing to worry about now. You are safe." She then disappeared into the crowd of people.

I tried to push up off the chair to follow her, but my arms shook under my own weight, and a dizziness came over me. It squeezed my vision off to just small pinholes. I continued to search the crowd for my mother, but everyone that walked by was just a blur. Forms and figures, in an assortment of colors, moved in and out of my view, adding to the dizziness in my head. I couldn't hold on any longer and leaned my head back against the bench while the world disappeared into a void of black. I wasn't sure how much time had passed before I felt my mother's cold hands on the back of my neck, helping to lift my head up.

When I opened my eyes, she was standing over me with something paper in her hand. She pulled me up to my feet and practically carried me up the stairs toward the boarding area, over the top of two tracks, and down the ramp to a third set. We passed the side of a train. Gold letters were painted on the dark green side of the train car. My vision was too far gone to read what they said. A man in a black suit and hat helped us up the steps and on board. "She is very sleepy," she told the man.

She sat me down in a comfortable seat in the cabin and then leaned close to my cheek. The coolness that radiated from her skin caused me to shiver. "Just sit here and rest. You will be safe now," she whispered. Inside, I felt an unfamiliar thump in my chest, and then the world went black.

2

A hand shook my shoulder softly. "Larissa, it's time to wake up."

Everything around me was muted, but I could definitely feel the shake. Not that it was violent. The touch was soft, almost caring. A lot like... My eyes shot open, wanting to see the face of my mom smiling back at me, but neither of the two people standing over me were my mother. Both were complete strangers. I mean, I kind of recognized the man in the black suit and funny black hat. Not in a real personal way. He just looked familiar. The woman, I had never seen before in my life. If I had, I would have remembered her.

"Larissa, can you hear me?" she asked. She was a tall, thin woman with long white hair and eerie looking light blue eyes that stood out against her pale white complexion that matched the long white dress she wore.

I screamed my answer. "Where is my mother?" Then a sound, from inside of me, sent me bolting up straight in my seat.

What was that? That thumping in my chest. It was like a drummer playing in my chest. I felt woozy and leaned on the wall next to me.

The woman turned to the man in black and said, "This is common with new students. They miss their parents."

"Understandable," he agreed with a nod.

Wait, I recognized him, and the hat he was wearing. He helped me and my mom on the train. I looked around at the rows of tan leather seats inside the train car. The wall I thought I was leaning against was a window. The dark outlines of the dense woods outside were just visible through the window. It was still night, or was it night again? I wasn't completely sure. I had been asleep the whole time. That thought almost made me chuckle out loud at how absurd that possibility was. I hadn't slept in years. We didn't need to do such things. Then I felt a horrifying thought enter my head as it glanced up at the man's kind but only somewhat familiar face. Had he knocked me out? That had to be it. It probably contributed to the somewhat confused feeling. But why?

What was crystal clear, I was on a train. I was the only person here other than the conductor that I now recognized, and a strange snow white woman was standing over me. Worst of all, my mother wasn't with them. "Where is she?" I demanded.

"Larissa, I am Mrs. Saxon. A friend of your mother's. She asked me to meet you at the train station. Now come on, let's get off the train. We have a bit of a drive to get where we are going." She turned to the conductor. "Thank you so much." It was a proper statement of gratitude, with folded hands and all.

"Come on," she said, and held her hand out toward me. I felt a sudden trust in her. Why? I wasn't sure, but I felt it. Could she really be a family friend? Maybe someone I met once a long time ago, and just forgot. I found that hard to believe. Her appearance made her very memorable, but there was this undeniable feeling of trust and almost a desire to go with her.

Emotions flooded over me as details of the night ran through me like a runaway freight train, but even then, I couldn't deny the feeling that I needed to go with this woman. I sniffed a tear back as I stood up weak-kneed and stepped toward her. I didn't know who these two were and didn't want them to see me crying.

Mrs. Saxon let me walk ahead of her, to the front of the car and out. The terminal was rather plain compared to the grand terminal where I had boarded the train. A simple concrete pad, and a single building with a ticket counter off to one side. It took no more than ten steps to reach the front door. Strangest of all, there wasn't anyone else there. No one. No grand family reunions, or wives welcoming home their husband from a business trip. There was no way I was the only person on that train.

Out front, there was only one car. A long black Cadillac with chrome accents from easily the fifties. Mrs. Saxon walked around it with me and opened the passenger door. Inside was another scene, lost in time. Plush red velvet covered everything. I got in and sunk into the seat while Mrs. Saxon closed the door behind me. She got in on the other side, and without a word, cranked the car and pulled away.

For several minutes, the only sound was the rumble of Detroit horsepower and that of my yawns. Which was something I hadn't done in a long time. I had forgotten how wonderful it felt. After it wore off, my body tensed back up and that strange thumping in my chest raced.

Why did I yawn? Better yet, how did I yawn? I don't breathe. Then I noticed it. I was breathing.

My thoughts ping-ponged around my head at a dizzying pace before a single thought stopped it dead in its tracks. My father was dead. That single thought was enough to shatter my life. He had been our rock for years. The one stabilizing force in a world where we don't exactly fit. I was his little girl, through and through. He taught me everything. My mother told me once, I wouldn't be if it wasn't for him. It took me a while before I understood that.

I felt a sharp pain in my chest every time I tried to picture his face. Tears flowed freely, and I turned to look out the window so this strange woman wouldn't see me.

Wait! My mother? Was she still alive? I didn't know. She was when she put me on the train. That was when she told me I was safe now, but safe from what? There were too many questions. I couldn't handle it. It, combined with the grief was burying me.

"Here, Larissa. Things are going to be okay." Mrs. Saxon's white gloved hand passed me a white handkerchief.

I took it, but didn't say thank you. Instead, I unloaded the questions on her. "Are you a friend of my parents?"

"In a way of speaking, yes."

"In what way? Did you know my mother? Did she call you to tell you I was coming? Who are you?" The raw emotions I felt fueled the flood of questions. My tears and the sobs were all that stopped more questions from spilling out.

"Larissa, I knew you were coming as soon as she put you on the train." Her eyes cut in my direction briefly before they returned to the road. I sat there stern and still, or as stern as I could with how I felt inside.

"Is she still alive?" I wanted to know. I needed to know. But the fear of the answer choked my voice off to just a weak stream. I yawned again, and my eyes felt heavy.

"I honestly don't know, but," she cut her eyes toward me again. "I will help you find out. You look tired. Why don't you get some rest? We have another hour or more."

I was about to inform her that I don't sleep, but then it happened again. My body relaxed all over, my eyes closed, and the world went black.

When I woke again, I was still crying. *Can one cry while they are asleep?* Another new experience for me. There was also a deep hurt inside, like something was missing. This was a feeling I knew all too well, but why there was a rapid thumping in my chest that went along with it, I still didn't understand. At least with my eyes opened, the moments when my father fell to the ground in a pile of ash didn't play over and over in my head, nor did the moments my mother left me on the train. Though neither was far from my thoughts.

"Good, you're awake. We don't have much further."

I looked outside the window as we passed a 'Now Entering Ipswich' sign. Geography wasn't my best subject, so I had no clue where we were. It wasn't long before the highway gave way to city streets. From everything I could see in the darkness, this was a small town. A quaint little village that if you blinked, you'd miss it. Luckily, I didn't, because it didn't take long until we were through the town center and turning into a rundown residential area with some kind of bay of water in the distance. The buildings of the small town stretched around it on either side. A lonely lighthouse stood up on a rocky ledge on one side, its beacon of hope flashed in our direction before continuing on around. I didn't feel the hope of its light.

Mrs. Saxon pulled her black Cadillac into the driveway of a house that made me shudder. *You have to be kidding me? Could this day really get any worse?*

With all that had already happened, this stranger, who picked me up from the train, had taken me back to something that resembled where every horror film monster resided. Rundown and dilapidated would have been an improvement. Not a single window had glass. There were visible holes in the exterior walls and roof. Cedar shingles hung on the sides of the house by prayers, not nails. What was left was painted in the color of dirt and disrepair. I didn't even have to get out of the car to see that rot was the main feature on the front porch. When the passenger door opened, I was more than hesitant to step out and into the knee-high weeds in the front yard. Who knew what I would step on?

Mrs. Saxon said nothing as she walked up the broken brick walkway and up the steps that cracked and creaked under her petite frame.

"Um, I'm not going in there," I said from the weeds.

"Come on. You can't judge a book by its cover," she said before she disappeared through the front door, which there was no door, just a gaping hole.

"You can if the cover is rotted," I mumbled and stepped gently up on the first step, expecting it to crack and send me crashing through, but it held. The second and third steps did too. The wooden planks on the porch's floor looked sketchier. I tiptoed across them and stopped at the door.

"Hello?" I called through the opening. It was dark inside. Not just dark, as in shadows or a lack of light. There was nothing. "And this is how I die," I whispered while I stepped through.

"Wow." That is all I kept repeating. Another "Wow" chased away any other thoughts.

What the hell did I just step into?

I turned to step back out, but the large glass double door with gold handles and hinges was closed.

Where did that come from?

There wasn't a door there a second ago. Just a big gaping hole in a house that had a better chance of falling down than providing any shelter. This was beyond shelter, and it was huge.

Flames flickered inside of what looked to be brass lanterns everywhere. They lined the wall, and three large ones hung at the end of chains from the ceiling five stories up. So odd. Who uses real flames for light anymore? And what was their source? I couldn't see any sign of fuel in the ones that hung down. In fact, I didn't see any wicks inside the ones along the walls. The flames just danced in the air. I must be more tired than I thought.

The floor was some kind of marble or tile with a gloss shine that looked like I could dive into and swim. Two massive, deep red carpeted staircases led up to the floors above. Beyond the stairs was a complete wall of windows with the moon shining brightly through over the top of a forest.

"Come on, Miss Norton," Mrs. Saxon called from off to my left. Her voice echoed in the cavernous room.

I followed her quickly out of the whatever I just entered and down a narrower hall, with the same dark red carpet as I saw on the stairs. Dark, rich wooden doors and panels lined the walls on both sides. I wanted to ask what this place was, but I was scared she might tell me. Though she hadn't told me much since she picked me up from the train.

We walked for what seemed to be miles down the same hallway, which again made me wonder how big was this place? Once we stopped, it was at one of the hundreds of wooden doors I believe we passed. All with no numbers or names on them. She turned the handle, and I guess invited me in by saying, "You'll need to stay with me for a day or two. At least until you return to normal. Follow me."

I walked in. I wasn't really in a position to do anything else. If I tried to run, where would I run to?

Wow, burst in my head again after I walked in. I just left a red carpeted hallway and stepped into a white mausoleum. White marble everywhere. The floor. The walls. The stairs. The vases with pink and light blue flowers. Even the picture frames that lined the wall up the stairs. The pictures were portraits. Some were recent. I could tell that by how they were dressed. Others were really old.

At the top of the stairs, Mrs. Saxon opened a marble door. I had never seen one of those before. The room inside was blindingly white. Too much gloss for my taste. Nothing about this felt warm and inviting. Was she going to ask me to step inside and lay down on a marble slab? Maybe I was dead.

"Um, yes. Not your style, I guess," Mrs. Saxon said, and then in a blink of an eye, the room changed. Painted muted pink walls, beige carpet, and a large.. *wait. What the hell?* My bed. That was my bed sitting in the center. The carpet. The wall color. All mine. All mine from before.

"What the hell is this?" I blurted.

"I will explain in the morning, but first you need some sleep. It is late."

"I'm not tired," I protested. There was no way I was. I had never been tired a moment in my life, except.... Then I remembered the train station with my mother, and how I felt there, and again in the car. That was something I still didn't understand. What I was sure of, though, is I was not tired now. Confused? Hell yes. More confused than at any moment in my life. Even my rebirth wasn't this confusing. Tired, absolutely not.

"Are you sure?" Mrs. Saxon asked. Her eyes looked deep into mine. Mine grew heavy, and my knees felt weak again. My legs gave, but I didn't hit the white marble floor. Someone caught me and scooped me up. My eyes were closing, but before they did, I saw the face of a Greek god befitting the surroundings. Features chiseled from stone and striking blue eyes like Mrs. Saxon's.

3

When I woke up, I wasn't exactly sure where or who I was anymore. I mean, I knew I was in a bed. That was obvious, but why? Even stranger than that was the sensation of waking up. I only ever remembered doing that once before, and that was something completely different than this time. That unfamiliar thumping I heard the night before was still there. Each beat echoed in my ears, heavy with sorrow, while I laid there. The unfamiliar became familiar again, and the thumping exploded when I realized it was the beat of my own heart. This had to be a dream, or a nightmare. Whichever was only a matter of perspective.

I laid there hoping to drift away, and then wake up again, back in my own life. Ridding myself of this dream. Of course, that was an absurd hope. The real me didn't sleep, so this being some kind of dream wasn't possible.

I got out of the bed and crept over to the door. I froze there for a second and listened before cautiously opening it, not sure what I would find on the other side. Would it be my old home or the marble palace from last night? In my current state, I wasn't sure which would be comforting, and which would be disturbing. The glare of sunlight blazed off the white marble causing me to squint. I slammed the door and plastered myself to the wall. Again, the thumping pounded. This time, I put my right hand over the left side of my chest. I wanted to feel the thump. I wanted to see if it was really there, but first I had to get over feeling the warmth of my flesh first.

Two light knocks came from the other side of the door. "Larissa, why don't you come down for breakfast?"

"Um, I don't want any." I said, not wanting to explain that I didn't eat.

"Don't be silly. You have to be hungry. You will need to eat for a few days, at least until you are normal again."

"What do you mean, normal?" I demanded, as I yanked the door open.

There she stood. Long black pencil dress. Her white hair pulled back in a tight bun on the back of her head. "Well, good morning to you. How are you feeling?" Mrs. Saxon asked with a stern look.

"Okay," I started, sounding as sure as a doubt, and then corrected. "Not sure."

"That's normal, or I believe it is. I have never been around this, but have heard about it." She sounded about as sure as I did.

"Been around what?" What the hell was she talking about? My mind swam, and my head spun, and I felt cold and wet. Not drenched, just lightly moist. I was going to be sick. That much I knew.

"You are hyperventilating. Try to calm down." Mrs. Saxon came in and helped me over to my bed, where she sat me down. Her touch, firm but soft. "Let me see if I can explain things. Do you know what you are?"

"Yes, do you?" I shot back between rapid gasps for air. That was a question I wasn't about to answer freely, for obvious reasons.

"Of course, you are a vampire."

Well crap, she knew what I was. Her eyes looked into mine. This time, I saw compassion. I felt it too. There wasn't the fear that normally accompanied that realization.

"And I am a witch," she added.

"A witch?" I exclaimed before I knew what I was saying.

"Yes, a witch. A Magical. A Sorceress. Those are a few of the names we go by. But that is not important. Right now, everything is about you. We need to take care of your needs, at least until the potion wears off. Do you remember drinking a clear, bitter liquid?"

The tear drop charm my mother wore. She gave it to me and had me drink the contents. The thumping in my chest hurt while the rest of my body felt numb. "Yes," I answered, but it was more of a question than a statement.

"This will sound strange, but you should be used to strange."

Was that a shot at me? Did she really take a shot at me?

Mrs. Saxon attempted to sit next to me on the bed, but I scooted to the other end of the bed before her butt hit the comforter. She looked at me displeasingly, but I didn't care. I didn't know who she was or where I was. No way I was going to be that trusting of anyone just yet. Especially someone who just told me she was a witch. Not to mention she knew what I was. That usually sent people running in the opposite direction, and she didn't. That in itself concerned me.

"Don't be afraid." She held out her hand. There was a tingling around my neck and then my necklace lifted away from my chest. Its movement followed the movement of her fingers. "This is a new blood charm. It's a drop of your venom infected blood from the moment you turned. It will stay red until you turn someone passing on the gift of immortality to their blood. Then it turns clear and becomes the opposite, an antidote to reverse the effects."

Oh shit, I am human again.

My hands reached up and gripped the charm and pulled it back close to my heart. My own mother turned me human again. Why the hell did she do that to me? The thumping, my heart, pounded again. Tears flowed, and I gasped for air. The sobbing interrupted my gasps, and I fell back against my pillow. Mrs. Saxon reached over and rubbed my forehead, and I leapt back against the headboard, sending it crashing against the wall. My gasping increased faster with each attempt to suck in air. I might as well have been trying to suck air through a straw.

"Larissa, you need to relax. Control your breathing and listen. It only works as an antidote if given immediately after the bite. For someone who has been what you are for as long as you have, it will only last a few days, then you will re-turn back."

"But why?" The question came out as nothing but air.

"I can't know for sure. The only other time I have ever heard of its use was as a defensive mechanism to hide from something that hunts vampires. I can only assume that is the case here."

"Assume?" I asked. My father had been killed, and then the thing that did it chased my mother and me for hours. I didn't even know what it was. I saw its form when it killed my father. After that I just ran. I looked back a few times, but never really saw it. Just its shadow, but its presence was always there, driving the fear that propelled me. "My mother didn't tell you when she...," I didn't finish the question. We already went through this last night. My mother didn't call Mrs. Saxon. I took a few deep breaths, followed by a few more, and then asked, "What exactly did you mean last night that you felt me coming as soon as my mother put me on the train?"

"I did. It's one of my gifts," Mrs. Saxon said.

"So, you can see the future?"

"Some," she laughed. "Not all. It comes and goes, and I can't control what I feel or know."

"Well, that sounds like a pain."

"It can be. Now, how about that breakfast?" She got up from the bed and walked toward the door. "I am not sure what you like, but I have a variety of items downstairs. You will need to eat just like you used to until this wears off."

"This will wear off?" I asked, both surprised and relieved.

"Yes, silly," she almost laughed. "Like I told you, it will wear off in a few days, and you will be back to normal then. Until that happens, you will need to stay here with me. Now come on." She walked out the door. Her high heels clicked on the marble floor outside.

I followed. Not so much for the food. Who knew if I was really hungry or not? I had forgotten what that felt like as a human who knows when. Hunger as a vampire was more primal. It was an urge, an aggression. I never remember feeling aggressive toward a slice of pizza, though I don't doubt that I had attacked some in my past.

When I walked out, I was surprised by all the marble. It was everywhere, as was light. A huge bank of windows lined the back wall, allowing the sun to blanket every surface in warmth and light. I felt it. I loved it. Nothing inside of me told me to move away from the light. Not that I was listening as I walked right up to windows and looked out. Outside was a sight that I couldn't find a single word to describe. I was at a resort, or out in nature, or... who the hell knew. There was a lush green forest that stretched on for as far as I could see, but before you got to that, there was a huge pool in a very natural setting. Large boulders and waterfalls, and people. There were people down there in the water, and others laid out on the bank getting some sun. Off to the side was the stone lined exterior of what I had to believe was another wing of the building I was in. That brought up the next question. Where exactly was I?

"What is this place?" I asked, with my gaze still taking in the outside world.

"Well, come have a seat, and I will try to explain." Mrs. Saxon was seated at a large table in the center of the room, and she was right. She had a large variety of breakfast foods. Some I recognized, and some I didn't. I picked up an odor as I got closer to the table. It was obnoxious and also enticing all at once. The closer I got, the more enticing it was. There, right in front of the only other chair, also marble, it sat. The source of the odor, bacon. A plate piled high with bacon. I picked up a piece and took a bite as I sat at the table. The sensation was mind blowing. The saltiness, the grease, the texture. There was no taste in my normal feedings, just satisfying needs and urges. Quenching the painful burning we felt. I eagerly crammed two more strips in my mouth. Mrs. Saxon looked on amused, and I smiled back, embarrassed. "It's been a while."

"I bet it has. So, I guess I should welcome you to Coven Cove."

"Where?" I asked, with a mouth full of bacon. Talking with my mouth full in such a prim and proper setting with someone who had the posture of a statue probably wasn't giving off my best first impression.

"Coven Cove. Where to begin?" Mrs. Saxon took a sip, not a slurp, not a gulp, a sip of her coffee, with her pinky extended. Which didn't really surprise me that much. "You know what a coven is, right?"

"A home for witches. I saw it in a movie once." Referencing a movie made my answer seem more mature than the truth. I had heard that term in a pre-teen-based sitcom.

"Kind of, but not just witches. Or at least this one isn't." She put her coffee cup back down on its saucer, looking perplexed. The bridge of her nose crinkled. "I guess the only way to do this right is to start with the basics. The house you walked into was in Ipswich, Massachusetts, but when you entered the door, you stepped out of that world and into a world between the world; a kind of magical bubble where we have constructed what you saw and what you see." Her hands waved around at the room around us.

"A what?" I exclaimed. Bits of bacon sprayed out, and I reached up and wiped my mouth with my hand. I was in a bubble? My mind couldn't even fathom that. Not that it could fathom much at the moment, like the use of the cloth napkin sitting in front of me, which I embarrassedly picked up and used for the next wipe of my mouth, instead of my hand.

"Don't think of it so much as I just said and don't try to understand it. Think about it like this. It is a place that protects us from everyone else, and vice versa. A place we can be ourselves."

"We?" I shouldn't be surprised, this place was huge, but was I surrounded by witches?

"Yes, Larissa. You are not alone here. There are many like you here. And, yes, I mean vampires. There are witches, warlocks, necromancers, shapeshifters, and werewolves all here in Coven Cove. Each here to learn more about themselves, more about their ability, how to blend in with the rest of the world, and just, well, to learn. This is sort of a school."

"Okay, let me get this right?" I started, still chewing on bacon. Something about all this appeared too sensational, but who was I to question with what I had seen so far. I was me. That was who I was. I swallowed and continued. "So, this is some large magical mansion that is a school for mutants? This seems like a mash-up of some popular movies."

"Yes, I guess it does," replied Mrs. Saxon with a sophisticated chuckle. Then her smile and smirk disappeared. "Except this is real. Completely real. The world is a dangerous place. We face challenges from both sides of the world. The outside world fears us and has a history of putting our kind to death. Our own world has creatures and individuals that hunt us. Your families normally teach you about both matters. When you don't have a family, that is where we come in."

My heart beat my brain to what I thought was the truth about this place. Most importantly, what that truth said about me. "So, this is really just an orphanage?" Mrs. Saxon opened her mouth to answer, but my head finally caught up with my heart and made the next leap and I sighed, "I guess that means my mother is dead?"

"Kind of, and no." She stood up and pulled her chair around the table next to me. Her blue eyes looked into mine, and for the second time, I saw compassion deep in her. "Look, you need to stay positive about your mother. We don't know what happened to her, or what was chasing you, but we will do everything we can to find out, okay?"

I nodded. It was all I could manage to do. There was a lump in my throat, and it wasn't the bacon. It came with the feeling of being alone.

"And, while we don't use that word, yes, this is a place for those with no family. We prefer the word coven and think of it as a school."

I couldn't shake the feeling of being alone, and maybe it was just me, but her gaze had changed from one of compassion to pity, and I couldn't stand the pity. I never asked for it from anyone and didn't like receiving it. Unfortunately, there was no return policy for that gift. You had to accept it, but you could avoid it, and that was what I normally did, like now. I stood up and walked back to the window. "So, all of that is part of this magic bubble or whatever?"

"No, those woods are real. You may have entered in town, but you can step outside and immediately be out in the woods where no one will bother you. And way out there, just beyond the woods, we have our own secluded cove. It's quite beautiful."

So, if the forest and the cove I didn't know about were real, I wondered what else was. "What about the pool down there and the people?"

"The pool, no. That is part of the world we have created, but the students are."

"Students?"

"Yep."

I wasn't sure why I asked. Mrs. Saxon said this was a school, and to be a school, you had to have students. You also needed something else. "Would that make you a teacher?"

"Contemporary literature, and head mistress."

Well, I didn't see the contemporary literature coming. I wasn't thinking this was that kind of school. I turned from the window, and must have looked surprised because Mrs. Saxon added, "We are a school. We have to cover everything you will need to know. The traditional studies as well as the things more particular to your abilities. I also teach basic spells."

"Can we go down there?" With so much going on, I needed some fresh air.

"Not today. We need to wait until you are back to normal before we let you around any of the other students. For some, especially those of your kind, being around a pulse would be too much. Others are not fond of being around a normal. So, it's not safe." Mrs. Saxon appeared to think for a minute and even tapped her chin with a finger. "I can give you a little tour around. There shouldn't be any harm in that. If you want to freshen up, there is a bathroom up the stairs and clothes in your room."

That sounded like a great idea. I had been wearing the same clothes now for over a day, and even though that wasn't all that long, I felt grimy. Now, if only it were a magical shower that could wash everything away, that would be great.

With one hand on the handle of the bathroom door, I made a guess, white marble, and then opened the door. Yep, what else would it be? The floor, the walls, the tub, the sink, the toilet. The only items that weren't were the toilet paper, obviously, the two fluffy white towels, and the mirror that hung over the sink. I walked past the mirror and saw the reflection of a rosy-cheeked girl with blue eyes and long curly locks of red hair looking back at me. I let out a gasp and then a muffled shriek. I barely recognized myself without the white, ashen complexion and black eyes.

4

"I'm not even going to ask how you filled a closet with *my* clothes," I said as I walked down the stairs wearing my usual casual attire: jeans, t-shirt, which this time was white, and sneakers. Before I headed down, I spent several minutes playing with my hair in the bathroom mirror. Up or down? I couldn't decide. I think I tried every look I had ever tried before. Each looked different now for some reason. Then it hit me. The face staring back was pink and alive. I honestly couldn't remember ever seeing myself like that before. Maybe it had been so long, I had forgotten.

After spending more time than I should have studying myself in the mirror, and dabbing away a few tears as I remembered all the times my mother sat behind me brushing my hair, and putting it in a range of styles, I went with down; it made me appear older.

"Just a trick I know," Mrs. Saxon answered.

"Like the bedroom last night?"

"Yes, like the bedroom last night."

"So let me tally it up. You can see the future and read minds." I walked back to the table and grabbed another piece of bacon. I couldn't get over the taste.

"One for two," she said. "I can't read minds, but there are others that can who I will take you to. Maybe they can help find out what happened to your mother and find out what was chasing you. The bedroom and the closet are enchanted. They change to accommodate the person staying in them."

Interesting. "So, if I had been more comfortable sleeping outside..."

"The room would have turned into a forest, or beach, or whatever outside scene you liked."

"Huh," was my only reply. What else could I say? It was the strangest thing I had heard of, and if someone had just told me that flat up front, I would have screamed bullshit, but I experienced it. Twice. What was there not to believe?

"Shall we go?" Mrs. Saxon walked toward the door. Each step a measured and precise dance of elegance. Her heels clicked on the marble floor, but it was a light click. "This will just be a tour around the grounds only. We will be avoiding the spaces being used by the students for now."

"I know. I know. Until I return to normal, right?" I had already grown tired of hearing that. Especially when I felt more normal than I had in... Well... I couldn't remember when.

"Right. Now follow me."

She walked me out into the hallway and back down to the entryway we came into the night before. If you ignored the obnoxious length of it, the hallway reminded me of a hotel. One from a movie in the 1920s. Ornate woodwork that was dark, cherry I think, and dark red carpet with gold accents that I hadn't noticed last night. The grand entrance, and it was grand, had a marble tile covered floor. The walls were the same ornate wood paneling as the hallway. Each side had a set of stairs that wound up floor after floor, with the same red carpet running up the center. The view out of the wall of windows behind the stairs was similar to the one out of Mrs. Saxon's apartment, residence, office—I wasn't really sure what to call it, so I would just leave it at her residence. The vantage point was just from a different angle. I was no longer looking down at the pool from left. I was now looking straight on, dead center, but still from above. The entrance to that area had to be below us, but I didn't see any stairs down.

"This is the main entry. Those staircases are the only set of stairs in the building. All classrooms and teacher residents are here on the main floor, down these halls. The floors above are student residences. Boys on the right, girls on the left, AND, one floor, one ability." She accentuated that with a pointed finger.

"So, we are separated by our sex, and by what we are. That is very 1900s of you. Back to the days of the Old South."

"Miss Norton. Not everyone gets along so well. Separation when not supervised helps keep the peace."

"Huh? I kind of figured in a place like this will be all kum-by-ya."

Her disapproving look told me I needed to learn how to restrain my inner voice a little. Something my father often admonished me for. Every thought didn't need to be said. Or as he put it, "you don't always have to speak your mind." Of course, his warning was always focused on keeping me from hurting other people's feelings, not sounding like an idiot, which seemed to be the result more often than not.

"Larissa, there is a lot you need to learn." She looked around. "Follow me." She led me down the other hallway, which was a replica of the one on the other side.

She stopped at a room that, like the others, had no number or name on it. "Wait here," she said as she slipped inside the room, closing the door behind her. I waited, as requested, out in a silent hallway that continued as far one way as I could see as it did the other way. The pattern of door, ornate wood panel, door was so regularly spaced, it reminded me of a carnival funhouse mirror trick. "Okay, you can come in," she said through the cracked door.

Wow! I had to get over being surprised by what I saw, though it was hard not to be. Books, books, and more books. All in bookcases that extended up. Way above the five floors I had seen earlier in the entry way. This was double, if not triple, that.

How do you get a book down from there? I looked for the top of the shelves, but never found it. The books just faded into the sky above.

"This is the library. Right now, there aren't any students in here. Unfortunately, an all too common occurrence," smirked Mrs. Saxon.

"I kind of guessed. All the books." I pointed up at the bookcases that went up and on forever.

"Yes, there are a lot of books. Everything you will need to know can be found here," she said, and then led me to a row of tables.

I didn't doubt what she said. There were a ton of books. Which meant a ton of reading, which was fine with me. I loved reading, and spent most of my time at home reading any number of the books my parents had in their obviously much smaller library. "So, how do we get something from way up there?" I asked curiously. With my luck, something I needed for an assignment would be at the top. I could climb it. Not in my current form, but when I turned back to, well, normal. *I just did it to myself.*

"Well, you don't retrieve any of the books. You ask the librarian." she pulled out a wooden chair back from the wood table. Its legs screeched against the floor, and then she sat. "Like this. Librarian?"

Just then, a blue vapor appeared in the center of the table, and dissipated, leaving the head of an elderly gentleman with white wavy hair, bushy eyebrows, and a cherub nose. "Good morning Mrs. Saxon." Then it turned to me. "Good morning, Miss Norton. What can I help you two with today?"

"You know who I am?" I asked, surprised and more than a bit stunned. I wasn't sure which was more responsible for the feeling. Seeing a head float above the table and talk to us, or that it knew my name.

"Yes ma'am. I know the names of all the students who enter here. Now, what can I help you find today?"

"Larissa, this is Edward, he has presided over the library here for last three centuries."

"Indeed. I am the first and only librarian here. I have curated this collection to meet the needs of our special students," he boasted.

"How many books are in your collection, Edward?" Mrs. Saxon asked. She was looking at me with an amused look on her face. It was then that I realized that my mouth was hanging wide open.

"There are 1,447,398 books currently in the collection. Of which twelve are out on loan to a student," Edward reported.

"Can you find me Elemental Based Spells, volumes one and two?"

"Right away," he said, and then disappeared.

"See, if you ever need a book, or want to find a book on a subject, you just have to ask," explained Mrs. Saxon.

Just then, two books floated down to the table and landed stacked in front of her. Edward's head returned, and Mrs. Saxon held up both books for me to see the covers of clearly. A green-covered book with gold letters that said, Elemental Based Spells, Volume 1. The second book was a red-covered book, also with gold letters, Elemental Based Spells, Volume 2.

"Thank you, Edward. When you are done with them, you just leave them on the table, and Edward will put them back."

"Interesting," I said, while my brain screamed *holy shit*.

"Now have a seat with me, and we can talk more about what we were outside." Mrs. Saxon turned her attention back to Edward. "That is all Edward. Thank you very much."

"Always a pleasure Mrs. Saxon." He disappeared just as he appeared, a light blue mist and then nothing.

I took a seat across from her, my eyes locked on the books that still sat in front of her. They were thick books. I hadn't ever seen anything that thick before.

"As I was explaining before, when not supervised, we need to keep everyone separated. It might seem old fashioned or against some rights you feel you might have; it is for everyone's protection."

"Protection, I don't get it." Which I didn't.

"Let me explain further. Most people are fearful of your kind. I am sure that doesn't surprise you."

I nodded my agreement.

"It's the same in here. Many are fearful of you, at least until they get to know you on an individual level. Even then, we know there are times where some of your primal urges are too strong for you to resist. Like when you haven't hunted in a while. Which is why I won't let you around any of your kind right now. Just the scent of what is coursing through your veins could drive them into a frenzy, and unlike the others, you don't have any way to protect yourself at the moment. Werewolves and your kind don't tend to get along that well to begin with, and that is something we have to watch out for. Many are suspicious of shapeshifters for obvious reasons. Though a completely undeserved rap. Those like me, well, we can defend ourselves somewhat before accension, but not fully until then. Do you know what that is?"

I shook my head.

"Witches and warlocks are born with their abilities, but they are limited until they ascend on their eighteenth birthday. Then they have their full power. It is our job to teach them how to handle that, and how to use that power. It is our job to help you learn what you need to know to function as an adult in the world, while also handling what makes you different, such as knowing how to resist some of your primal urges, and how to properly deal with them when needed. Does that make sense?"

"So, you guys are worried we are all going to attack each other when you and the other teachers aren't around?"

"In a way yes, at least until you learn what you need to, but just to be safe we have segregated things, and in case you are wondering, how does being on separate floors stop that?"

She was right, I was wondering about that. One could easily sneak out and do whatever they wanted to do.

"A charm protects the entry for each floor. Only what is supposed to be there can enter. Except teachers, they can go everywhere, of course."

"Of course," I nodded. "And the boys on one side and girls on the other. Does someone's gender have something to do with power or strength?" At this point, I felt anything was possible.

"Um no. Just because we are what we are, doesn't mean we won't succumb to other urges."

"Oh," I said. My cheeks flushed.

"Come, let me show you to my classroom."

We left the library and kept walking down the hallway, passing door after door. All of them, the same, until we passed one with voices coming out of it, and an aroma. Tangy. Sweet. I paused to smell it a bit longer, and to listen to the voices, before continuing on.

"That's the cafeteria. I doubt you will have much use for it once you are back," Mrs. Saxon said without pausing. "That would be rigatoni primavera, I think, based on the smell. One of the more popular choices, but you can pretty much have whatever you want."

"Do you just ask out loud and it appears?" I asked, expecting the answer to be yes, based on what I saw in the library.

"Oh no," she laughed. "Well, maybe. We have a real chef, Rene. He has been with us for a long time now, probably since before the turn of the last century, and he is very good, but everything is cooked from scratch, no magic."

Three more doors down, she reached into the pocket of her dress and pulled out a key. Which I thought was strange. I hadn't seen her use a key before, not even at her residence. She opened it, and I entered another room of wonder. The entire room was glass, like some kind of greenhouse. Various plants, most of which I didn't recognize, hung from the wall. In front of the wall of glass was a simple wooden desk, and two old-fashioned green chalk boards, not white boards like I had seen in movies and television shows. I even had one in my own room at home where my mother helped me with math problems. I hated math, but would give anything right now to be there with her, letting her correct me.

There was no overhead light source beside whatever came in through the glass roof. Outside, it was stormy. The clouds spun and bubbled around each other. Not at all like the scene out the windows I saw earlier. Maybe a front had moved in.

Standing up by the desk, Mrs. Saxon announced. "This is my Spells classroom. While you won't ever take this class, not being a witch, I wanted to show it to you to help you understand something about this place. It is whatever you need. Like the room last night that changed into what you were more comfortable with, this classroom became what I needed to teach this subject in." She moved to the glass wall behind her and touched the glass lightly and waved around it like displaying the grand prize for a game show. "As you see, we have plants and access to the outside. So, when one of my students is working on an elemental spell that involves manipulating the weather, we can see it. The cauldron over there to the right," a big brass pot that I hadn't seen before, "provides the fire we need, and the fountain over there," a stone fountain that looked like an oversized birdbath sprung to life with water flowing, "gives us the water we need. See, it provides everything I need to teach. Similarly, the classroom I use for contemporary literature is a miniature library, and Edward keeps it stocked with what I am teaching at that moment. The reason I wanted you to see and hear this is, when you are assigned a room, it will become whatever you need or want. It is your world to live in. Understand?"

"I think so," I said, but it sounded more like a question than a statement. Which it was. I got it, but didn't. The room becomes what you need, but how does it know?

"You will see. Trust me. No need to overthink it, or even to think about it. Just trust the room, okay?"

"Okay." I agreed, sounding more confident this time, and not pointing out that I was the queen of overthinking something. This will go against all of my instincts, but then again, what in the last day hasn't? This normally cautious girl had been shipped off to a new place, who knows where, because of who knows why, for who knows how long. Way too many unknowns for my comfort. Not to mention, I had been turned back into a human, albeit temporarily, or so I kept being reminded.

"Good, now I do need to get ready for my afternoon class, and as we discussed, we need to keep you separate from everyone else until you turn back, so you will need to hang out in my place for the day. I will have them bring you some lunch. Do you know what you might want?"

I didn't have a clue, possibly more bacon. I just shook my head.

"Okay, I will pick a few things and will see you later. You can go through that door there to your left, and you will be back."

Wait! What? We walked for twenty minutes. I stood there looking at a door that I was quite sure wasn't there before. It was just to the right of the door we entered the classroom through.

"Go on," encouraged Mrs. Saxon.

I reached out and turned the handle. It opened, and my jaw hit the floor. There it was. The white marble mausoleum. I stepped through and turned. That door was its front door. The same one we came in through last night from the hall. The same one we left through earlier.

"I will see you later this afternoon, Larissa. Have a good day and help yourself to any of the books and movies. The remote of the TV is next to the couch."

The door closed, but I quickly reached down and turned the handle. It opened, but not to the classroom. It opened to the hallway. Dumbfounded, I closed it and staggered backward into the room, bumping into a white couch that sat in front of the largest screen I had ever seen. It was white, not that surprising anymore, but it was not there last night or this morning.

5

Her collection of movies and shows was extensive. Maybe too extensive. There wasn't a movie, show, or channel I could think of that wasn't available, and God knows I tried. I had no clue there was a channel of Japanese anime about pigs. After a rather creative search, I just picked a favorite horror film of mine, "Dead Break." The cliché filled typical teenage spring break spoof with silicone filled girls and brain-dead jocks running from a killer that was doing everyone a favor by killing them. It was one of my new favorites, much to my parents' disapproval. Even with all the other choices available, that was what I picked. It was familiar, and familiar felt good at the moment. Though tears still flowed when I thought about how many times either my father or mother walked in the room voicing their distaste for all the blood and gore in it. Of course, I always reminded them of the irony of their reaction.

I sat and watched it for the first twenty minutes, three deaths, before I found myself distracted. It took another death until I got up. I left it playing in the background and walked around. As amazing as everything was, and it was amazing, the windows were what pulled at me. I found myself standing at them more than once, mouthing lines from the movie as it played in the background, "*oh my god, is that Cheryl, no it's just her head, but her hair looks good.*"

Outside, the sky was a crystal blue canvas, not a cloudy blemish to be seen. The trees swayed back and forth in a gentle breeze. I could almost feel it on my skin through the windows, along with the warmth of the sun. As majestic as all that appeared, that wasn't what I kept focusing on. What pulled at me was the pool, but not really the pool itself. I didn't know how to swim, and never really felt the need or desire to learn. It just wasn't me or wasn't me then, and not something I had to worry about. I couldn't drown, or wouldn't be able to soon. No, it was the people. Kids or teens. People my own age. I couldn't remember the last time I had hung out with anyone my own age.

"*Teach you to interrupt our vacation, fuc-ah.*" Of course, they thought they killed the killer, but they didn't.

I was mostly a loner. A necessary state for someone like me. Those that visited, or we visited, were my parents' friends, but even then, that didn't happen often. As I understood it, there weren't many that were like us, and even less like me, but... Mrs. Saxon said there are others here like me. I wonder if any of them are down there. Probably not, the sun was out, but they had to be here, in the coven somewhere. I wish I could talk to them. The silence was driving me mad. Yes, my favorite movie was playing behind me, and occasionally I lost myself in that familiar feeling, but then one look around reminded me of where I was, and why.

Each time I remembered where I was and why I drowned in a wave of grief, with a hard ugly cry following. I was alone, so I wasn't afraid to let go. I missed my mother. Where was she? Was she okay? I had so many questions, and hoped I would see her one day. A hope that helped quell some of the despair I felt, but didn't chase away the black cloud completely. The thoughts of what happened to my father brought the rain and a pain deep in my core. He was gone. I would never see him again; never hear him laugh again; never feel one of his big bear hugs. Though his voice constantly echoed in my head, "*Chin up Larissa,*" and "*Stay strong.*" He wouldn't want me wallowing in grief. He never did. Though I couldn't help myself and broke down again.

The ugly cry continued through the credits and right through the sequel teaser at the end when the killer's hand broke through the ground in the cemetery they buried him in. It wasn't a child's cry, but an adult cry. A sit there with your head in your hands, staring at nothing at all, while the tears rolled cry. When I heard the door crack open, I turned and did the best I could with my fingers and wrist to wipe away my tears. One look from Mrs. Saxon told me that my red eyes gave it away. I didn't have to worry about any makeup streaking down my face, as I didn't put any on after my shower. Not that there wasn't any there. Everything I would have needed was there, and my brands too. I would have looked a real mess with my typical dark mascara running down my cheeks. I felt I looked bad enough as it was and struggled to compose myself as Mrs. Saxon stepped through the door with two guests.

Both guests were women, and both looked on at me with a wide-eyed fascination. The older of the two, what many would describe as grandmotherly, with kind eyes and salt-and-pepper hair, was quite shorter than Mrs. Saxon. Even shorter than me, and a little stout. She was dressed in a dark purple suit with pants. The other guest was younger, a lot younger. Late twenties if I had to guess. Of course, she could be anywhere from early twenties to late thirties. It was so hard to tell at times with makeup, and everything; though she wasn't wearing much makeup and made no attempt to hide her pale complexion. I had seen that same ashy complexion staring back at me for years and did the same. Never using blush or anything to hide it, just adding a little color to my lips to keep them from looking grey, and then around my eyes, to draw the gaze of those looking at me. A trick my mother taught me — *God, I hoped she was okay.*

"Larissa, I would like for you to meet Mrs. Tenderschott, and Mrs. Bolden." Each nodded their head when Mrs. Saxon introduced them. Mrs. Tenderschott was the older of the two. Mrs. Bolden was the vampire. "They will be joining us for dinner tonight, if that is okay with you," she continued.

I nodded, knowing any attempt to speak would produce a sniffle from the tears I was still holding back behind a very shaky, emotional floodgate.

"Good. I guess you know what Mrs. Bolden is."

"Yes, I do," I said weakly, struggling to hold back the tears. My gaze locked with the slender upright woman, dressed in a long black dress, and a charm, no, a vial of clear liquid around her neck at the end of a gold chain.

"Mrs. Tenderschott is a witch like me. Her specialty is potions, and she might be able to help you. I am going to go see about dinner and let you three get acquainted." She walked past the stairs and through a door I hadn't seen before. Either it wasn't there before, or the fact it was white marble it blended in with everything else.

"Deary, you can call me Michelle," said the older woman. Her voice was as friendly as her appearance. "My last name is a mouthful, and I am not one for formality, plus you might be older than me." She laughed, and Mrs. Bolden smirked. Yes, I could be, but doubted it. I hadn't been like this long, from what I remembered, and I was raised to respect my elders. Even if it was just based on appearance.

She walked over and had a seat on the couch close to where I was standing. Mrs. Bolden followed her and had a seat next to her. Her stare watched me, still locked on to mine, but as I leaned forward to sit back down where I just spent the last twenty minutes crying, my own charm fell out from under my t-shirt and dangled down from my neck.

"You still have it," she gasped. Her voice was surprising compared to her appearance. Warm and compassionate, with a rich tone that could sing jazz in a smoky club somewhere.

"I do," I said, waiting for her to explain why she seemed surprised that I did.

"Rebecca, you said she drank it," she called.

Rebecca? I would have never picked Mrs. Saxon as a Rebecca, and most assuredly she wasn't a Becky. Those names were for your favorite aunt, not a witch that was a headmistress at a school for the, well, gifted. Esmeralda would be a better name. Of course, there I was going with movie and television stereotypes. If you followed them, all of us would be from castles in eastern Europe with names that were more consonants than vowels, and an abundance of 'v' and 'z.' Of course, that wasn't me. I was a Larissa from Virginia.

"She drank her mother's," Mrs. Saxon responded back from the other room.

"Oh," she said, and then sat back against the sofa. No longer sitting upright and proper, but more slouched and comfortable. "She probably did it to protect you. Do you know what or who was after you?"

I shook my head.

"Well then, that is why I am here," interjected Mrs. Tenderschott. She turned toward me and grabbed both of my hands. "We know you have been through a lot.

Rebecca told us all about what happened. I think I can help you and would like to try."

"How?" I asked.

"I have various spells and potions that can help me read your mind and help you remember more, and then, I believe you will find this more important; I can use your imprint to find those you are connected with."

What? I screamed through my eyes at both women, looking back and forth at them.

"Dear, I should be able to find out what happened to your mother and where she is."

"Oh my god, how do we do it? When can we start? Let's go," I sprung up straight right in front of her, not knowing if she needed to put her hand on my head, or maybe grab my ears.

"Slow down," Mrs. Saxon said. She came back in and sat on the back of the sofa behind me. Again, she looked down at me with her compassionate eyes. A single hand stroked my red hair. "Look, I know you want to find out about your mother, but there is something more important. Something was after you, and it was serious enough for your mother to do what she did. We need to find out who or what it is, first."

"But why?" I cried before thinking about it.

"Safety."

"That's right," added Mrs. Bolden. "Your safety, not to mention our safety. We have to assume it is out there and still looking, and even though it can't find you right now, you won't stay like this much longer. We need to know, so we can protect you."

I searched the eyes of all three women for compassion and understanding, and I found it, but that didn't change the logic of what they seemed to be steadfastly in their agreement on. I wanted to know about my mother. That longing and hurt were clear, but there was something else. The fear that I felt that night reemerged just by the mere reminder that something was hunting me. I knew they were right. I didn't want them to be, but they were, and no one appeared to offer an alternative. All I could do was swallow my hurt, and agree, "Okay."

"Let's give it a try." Mrs. Tenderschott reached inside the pocket of her pants suit and removed a vial with green liquid in it. This wasn't just a plain glass vial. There were ornate carvings in the glass, and also around the rim of the gold cap. She removed the cap before offering it to me. "Drink, then lie back."

I gave it a sniff, and there wasn't any smell at all.

"You will feel a little tired. Go with it. Just lie back and close your eyes. This will let your mind drift, and I will come find you and guide you to where we need you to be, and then bring you back here to us."

"My mind will drift?" I asked, having the image of a few popular horror films in my mind where someone's spirit went out roaming and couldn't get back. A side effect of too many late nights watching those kinds of movies in my past.

"Yes, there is nothing to worry about. I will be there with you." Mrs. Tenderschott urged me to drink it, while the other two watched.

I took a tentative drink, just to taste it. It didn't have one and felt like water going down my throat. I went ahead and drank the rest of it, handed it back to her, and did what she said. She wasn't kidding. My eyes were already feeling heavy before I was even halfway down. By the time my head hit the cushion, I was out, but unlike sleep, I knew it. I knew where I was, and I knew what I was doing.

"Okay, dear. Let's get started, shall we?"

"Oh, wow!" I screamed. She was right there with me, in my head. I could hear her. I could feel her, and strangest of all, I could see her.

"I told you I would be right here with you."

"I know, but I thought it would only be your voice. Kind of like hypnotism or something."

"Nah, that stuff doesn't work. Here I can see what you see. So, this happened yesterday? Morning, afternoon, or night?"

"Um," that wasn't an easy question to answer. It spanned most of the day. "It was dark when my mother put me on the train, but the sun was still going down when my father was," — I couldn't make myself say it — "but it was like right around noon, when they grabbed me from my room, and we left our home."

"Okay, that is a really wide range of time. I need you to think. Do you happen to remember when you first saw it?" she asked, her hand on my shoulder.

"I am not sure I did," I said as I thought back, knowing I had lied and hoping she couldn't tell. I did see it, at least once really good, possibly a second time. The first was when it killed my father. A moment I didn't want to go back and relive. I needed another time. Most of the time, I was feeding off my mother's own fear. Her expression and the sound of her voice. How hard she urged me forward, then I remembered, and the cold icy feeling of his presence followed the memory.

"Good, you remembered," she noted flatly.

"I do. We were running." The surrounding darkness dripped away, and I felt drops of rain pelting my face.

"I got this. Just keep thinking of that moment. Bring it in as clearly as you can."

Slowly, the image emerged. I was up in the air again over the brown station wagon, drenched by the rain. I remembered we were running against the traffic down the street, which I sure got some stares to begin with. If it didn't then, it certainly did when we started skipping over the top of cars. That was the one and only moment I saw it out of the corner of my eye, like now when I turned my head. It wasn't a great view, or even a good view. The darkness that surrounded it was just in the corner of my eye, up on the roof.

"Hold your memory there, dear," Mrs. Tenderschott implored. She was there, dry, walking between the cars. She walked toward it, and out of my field of vision. I turned my head to follow. "No, don't do that. Stay still like you were," she warned. "Do exactly like you did that day."

There were a few moments of silence as I stayed there in mid-air like a statue. The presence of whatever it was, ever present behind me and to the right. Then I heard a series of curious "O's" followed by more silence. Then out of nowhere, like a bolt of lightning, my head went black, and a pain sliced through me. Like a hot knife through butter. I lost my concentration and fell down on the roof of the car. I tried to get up, but a heavy weight had me pinned, and it was getting heavier. Deafening screams filled my ears. Not just one or two. Not even a dozen. There were hundreds of voices screaming. Then as many deaths flashed before my eyes. None lasted long enough to see who or what. Just the moment of when life ended flashed, and a new scream was added to the deafening chorus. Then it all went black again, and I was in a puddle of ice cold water, under a single streetlamp. Standing over me was the dark shadow. The figure, it was human, or shaped like one. Its hand reached down toward me. I tried to stand up and run, but I was stuck to the ground. Attempts to push it away found my hands passing right through its arms, but when it grabbed my charm and picked me up by it, its grasp was real. My voice trembled as I let out a blood-curdling scream. It matched the shake that had consumed my body. My very life was being choked out of by the chain of my own charm.

"Larissa!" Mrs. Tenderschott's voice echoed in my ears, and I fell back to the street and through the puddle. Where I landed was back on the couch, with three genuinely concerned women standing over me.

"I am sorry, dear. I don't know what happened," apologized Mrs. Tenderschott as she moved closer to me and cradled my head, which felt good. The pain in my head I felt while under, whatever that was, still remained.

"I don't know what it is," she told the others. "Whatever it is, is dark, very dark, and not human."

"A vampire?" Mrs. Bolden asked.

Mrs. Tenderschott shook her head, and then she recanted. "You know, I don't know. It could be. Could be a witch. Something supernatural. Could be anything, but it is definitely not human. There is something dark shrouded over it, blocking me." She looked up at the others and explained, "Probably just the wrong potion. We can try again."

While I understood the urgency, I wasn't exactly interested in taking another trip down that memory lane, but there was one I did want to visit. "Now, can we try my mother?"

The looks the three women gave me broke my heart before the answer arrived. "Dear," Mrs. Tenderschott started with another stroke through my hair. "We can only make one attempt a day. The potions are powerful. I can't mix them."

A tear rolled down my cheek, and I turned away to try to avoid them seeing. A hand went up to brush it away, but found it had friends, lots of friends. It appeared that I had wept my eyes out while I was under her control.

"If you want, you can stop by tomorrow afternoon, and we can try then."

I agreed, "Okay."

6

I went to bed shortly after the four of us ate dinner. It was delicious, or the small portions of it I ate were. I didn't have much of an appetite, and if I did, something else filled its space. I couldn't shake the suffocating darkness from my trip with Mrs. Tenderschott. I think she noticed, asking me several times if I was all right during dinner, trying, like what a grandmother might, to get me to eat a little more. Even Mrs. Bolden, who was only partaking in the wine, made her attempts to get me to eat.

The fear of what I had experienced may have stolen my appetite, but the disappointment of having to wait another day to find out about my mother took away my personality. The three sat at the table and attempted to engage me in conversation. Telling me all about the school and the wonderful things they do here. Everything from the fall festival that they go all out with, obviously, to the holidays, which they said were no less as grand with a large tree decorating party. When neither of those topics appeared to pull me in, they moved on to the students, who to me were just random names, most of which I didn't even hear. I was already calculating how to get to my room. I just wanted to close my eyes and make this all go away, even temporarily. The one benefit of being human again.

When they started on the topic of alumni stopping by, I saw my opportunity. Again, these were names I didn't know, and eventually the three of them found themselves lost in old stories and catching up. That was when I asked to be excused from the table. The fact that I asked seemed to surprise them, but that was how I was raised.

I went up to my room and hoped for that temporary escape. Another one of life's cruel tricks. I wanted to escape, but I guess that potion and what I had experienced had made that an impossibility. Each time I let the darkness take me, the nightmares came. That presence was everywhere, and the feeling of it picking me up by my charm wasn't far behind. I could feel the gold chain cutting into the back of my neck. The pressure on the front of my neck from its hand, gripping it, and nothing under my feet but air. I dangled there, choking, trembling, and whining. Each time I woke up in a complete flop sweat and cold. Then, almost like a routine, I lay there, staring up at the ceiling above me until my eyes closed, and it happened all over again.

This happened four times before I said enough was enough and got up and walked around. It was more like I snuck around. There wasn't a clock anywhere I could see, but if I had to guess, it was late, very late. It was completely dark except for the rivers of moonlight splashing off the white marble floor below. I snuck down the stairs, which you had to. Even barefoot, every step sounded with a muffled thud on the marble. Once at the bottom, I made my way across to the windows and just stood there. It was beautiful. The moon used the trees to cast long majestic shadows, like the masterstroke from the brush of an artist. I loved the night, especially if I was outside. There was something about the cool night air that always relaxed and cleared my head.

I looked down at the pool area again. It was empty. Which, of course, it would be. It was night, but that also meant it was perfect. I remembered the warning from Mrs. Saxon about running into any of my kind in my current form. There was no one out there. If only I could figure out how to get down there. I leaned as close to the window as I could get. There had to be a path or walkway that led out there. There had to be, and there was. Right in the middle, a bit of beige concrete stamped to look like stone, surrounded by boulders on either side. It went back toward the building. Okay, but how do I get to it?

I leaned forward, pressing my cheek against the glass. My left eye tried to see the door on the outside of the building. My right saw something that wasn't there before. Right there, in the wall next to the large windows, was a door that I hadn't seen during any of the several times I stood in front of the windows. Could it be? There was only one way to find out. I walked over and turned the handle. As soon as it cracked open, I felt the cool air of night rush past me. When I stepped through and out, I was standing on that beige concrete walkway maybe twenty feet from the pool.

Walking out there felt great. For the first time all night, the dark veil that was over me lifted. It's amazing what the night air could do for you, or at least what it always did for me. Throw in a few minutes with your feet dangling in the pool, and you feel like a new person, almost. There was a sense of freedom out here, but that didn't mean everything was all right. My life was different from what it had been just yesterday, and there was nothing I could do to pull it back.

I stepped off the patio a few steps and felt the damp grass under my feet and between my toes. A reminder of all the nights I went outside in our backyard and walked around, looking up at the moon, and strolling through the woods. Sometimes I even brought a good book with me and read under the moonlight. I didn't have a book now, but I had some woods right out in front of me. I strolled in, and just like home, these were tall pines. Discarded needles covered the ground. The wind moved between the branches and caused a light rustling; something I called tree-talk. The nights outside were so solemn, and even though the solitude was what I was looking for, it felt good to hear the signs of something else alive around you. All I had to do was just stop and listen. Trees. Wind. Small animals, which most of the time I heard scouring around trying to get out of my way. If I were lucky, I would hear the sound of a bird. Maybe the hoot of an owl, or the song of a whip-poor-will. There was a nest of them close to our backdoor at home.

I continued out, wanting to find the cove Mrs. Saxon told me about, but had to stop and sit down next to the closest tree. I was feeling… well, tired; I think. What I knew for sure was I didn't feel right. My breathing was fast and labored. Had I pushed myself too hard? Maybe I should have eaten more at dinner? Those were the questions that I wondered about. Being mortal was not something I was used to, nor did I remember much about the care and feeding instructions that came with this form. It's not like I could turn around and look at the label on my neck. I figured I would rest here for a moment, and then head back in. I hoped getting back into the coven, and Mrs. Saxon's residence was as easy as getting out was.

I sat with my head leaned back against the tree and focusing on making each breath smooth and slow, but that was a battle I was quickly losing. They were fast, and each breath left me feeling like I was out of breath. I needed more. I was concerned, but not worried about the breathing. The worry kicked in when the still strangely unfamiliar beating of my heart joined in with its own frenetic pace. I stood, but my legs didn't fully cooperate, forcing me to use the tree to help me up. The first few steps back were an effort. The remaining were an exercise in forcing myself to move. Every muscle in my body had forgotten how to work together. A few times, I had to use my arms to pull a leg forward. It took a while to get that arm to understand what it was supposed to do, though. At the edge of the woods, I felt some relief. I was almost back. Then I looked up and ran into my worst nightmare. There was no pool. No boulders. No building. Just an open space in the woods.

"Oh crap!" I panicked, but that wasn't the worst of my problems. Standing was a problem. I wobbled a lot. Where was it? It had to be there. Then I remembered it was magic. Probably hidden from view, and if I kept walking, it would probably appear as soon as I stepped back on the patio. It had to. It wasn't far, I knew it. But with the way my body was working, ten feet might as well have been ten miles. Then things got worse.

I heard a sound behind me, one I had heard before many times. The sharp pop of a large foot, or paw, breaking a stick. The loud, deep pants from a cavernous chest accompanied it. I turned, hoping not to see what I saw. Two yellow eyes in the distance. How stupid I had been. I wasn't what I was before. I was not the hunter. Out here, there were things that would make me their prey, and right now, a large wolf was moving in to make me his. In my panic, I tried to run, but only flailed around and fell to the ground. I knew the laws of nature. I was a wounded animal, and that would attract the alpha predator more.

It walked out of the shadows slowly, stalking me. My instincts were right. It was a wolf. One of the largest grey wolves I had ever seen. My arms attempted to pull myself forward on the ground, hoping once I reached where the pool had been, there would be some kind of protection. Then I heard the first growl and snarl, and I wasn't sure it was the fear of that sound or my situation that caused my arms to stop working. All I could do was lie there, face down on the ground.

I had seen wolves before, many times, but they usually ran away. This one circled around me. I pushed myself up the best I could and tried to crawl again, and it growled again. A shudder went through my body at the sound. Then I thought about the irony. I was about to be eaten by something that had fangs like I used to have. My arms pulled me forward about two feet more, which all that did was bring me closer to the wolf. Its hot breath blasted my face. Maybe it was instinct, something from who I used to be, that prompted my next action. I swung at it and expected the impact to send it flying through the air. Instead, my hand hit its fur, stopped, and flopped to the ground. It let out a loud howl that was echoed by at least three others from deeper in the woods. Its fierce yellow eyes looked back down at me. I felt the pads of its paw whack me across the face. Then nothing.

7

"Mom!" I screamed, running in through the front door. I stood in the entry-way and screamed again, "Mom!" There was no response other than the echo of my own voice. I ran into the library, which was right off the main hall. It was the normal hang-out for my mother. She wasn't in her comfortable chair, and there weren't any books stacked on the table next to it to indicate she had been there reading. She always had two or three there when she was reading, even though she was only reading one of them. She called it giving-herself-options.

I yelled again, "Mom!" Then I walked through the library to the kitchen, but no one was there. I ran around the large white marble island, my feet thudding on the tile floors. The sound changed to a slap when I hit the hardwood of the hallway, which I followed to the stairs. I ran up and yelled again when I reached the top. She wasn't in her and dad's room. She wasn't in my room. That was where I panicked, but before I lost it completely, I caught a glance of her through my bedroom window. She was outside in the backyard, with dad.

Down the stairs I rushed, and back down the hall to the kitchen, where I paused in the bay windows to just look at them. My mother, her raven hair flowing in the breeze, along with the skirt of the blue sundress. Her favorite color. My father stood next to her, laughing. I thought to myself, *what was laughable was that outfit he wore.* Who actually still wore a sweater tied around their neck anymore?

I rapped on the window, and they both spotted me. The expressions on their faces while they both rushed toward the back door warmed me. I waited, feeling something familiar about this. I knew what this moment was, but unlike the moment I remembered, they never came through the door. Instead, they vanished between the back screen door and the kitchen, leaving me staring at a single reflection in the window. My own ashen complexion with black eyes that were as empty as I felt.

"Oh crap!" I exclaimed as I woke up again, wondering when the effects of that potion would wear off. These dreams were nuts. Then I realized I didn't remember how I got back to bed. Was the entire episode outside a dream, too? Did I ever make it outside to the pool deck? What about the woods? The wolf? It had to be a dream, or a nightmare. How else would I explain not being able to walk or even crawl? A nightmare would be the only way to explain that. I gathered my thoughts and looked around the room. It was just as it was the last time I woke up in it, well, almost.

Someone had closed the curtains on the window, and sunlight leaked in around the edges. I had opened them before I went to bed, the night before.

Not knowing what time of day it was, other than it was day, I got up and headed to the bathroom. Downstairs, I heard a cacophony of conversations. All of which ended when the door of the bedroom closed with the lightest of clicks.

"Larissa, you feeling okay?" Mrs. Saxon asked from downstairs.

"Um, yea. Just slept in late," I said and then slipped into the bathroom. It was an odd question. Maybe she knew about the dream effect of the potion. I felt fine. I actually felt better than fine. I was rested and energetic. Wanting a shower, I turned the water on, and then undressed. I turned to head back to the shower and caught a glimpse of my image in the mirror. Then I went back and caught more than a glimpse. What I saw would have made my heart skip a beat, if it was beating. I leaned forward and blinked my eyes a few times. Each time, I saw my own black eyes staring back at me. My beautiful cheek bones covered by pale white skin, offset by my flowing red hair. I was ravishing, but best of all, I was me.

I rushed through my shower, fixed my hair, and then put on my classic red lipstick to give me a bit of color, and then hurried back to my room. It happened again when I passed from the bathroom to my room. The conversations stopped. I slowly closed my bedroom door and then stood there with an ear to the door, listening. Right on cue, they all started back up. That was odd. I listened a bit longer and could pick out three distinct voices. Two I recognized: Mrs. Saxon and Mrs. Bolden. The third was new, and male.

"She seems fine," said Mrs. Bolden.

"I am going to give her a few minutes, and then go check," said Mrs. Saxon.

"Are you sure that is safe?" asked the unidentified male.

They were talking about me, and what was that last question about? Of course, it was safe. Then I remembered. I quickly went to the closet, feeling a bit unnerved that I was *the* topic of their conversation, wondering what else they had talked about while I slept. Of course, the closet showed me exactly what I wanted to wear. Nothing fancy, just casual. Black jeans, and a black tank, and a comfy pair of Vans.

Dressed and ready, I headed back out and stopped at the top of the stairs to admire the pink and orange hues created by the last bit of sun still above the horizon in the west. An interesting contrast to the midnight blue that was creeping in from the east. I had slept longer than I thought, but I already knew I hadn't slept. What I went through took some time. I was told the first time it happened to me took two full days.

I stepped down the first step, and for the third time in a row, the conversations downstairs ended. Now they were watching me. Three sets of eyes followed my every move down the stairs. The three of them were seated on the white couch. Mrs. Saxon, Mrs. Bolden, and the unidentified man between them. He was a muscular man with dark hair and brown eyes. I could tell that thanks to the skin-tight t-shirt he wore. I could also tell he was human. Halfway down the stairs, I felt the first sensations of two hearts pumping blood through veins, and I knew Mrs. Bolden wasn't one of them.

"Larissa, how are you feeling?" Mrs. Saxon asked.

I didn't answer. I just stopped one step from the floor and did a quick spin and strutted the rest of the way to them.

"Welcome back," Mrs. Bolden said.

"Thanks. I feel like me again."

"Larissa Norton, I would like for you to meet Mr. Spencer Markinson, advanced science and math teacher."

The man stood up. He was taller than I thought. He held out his hand towards me, but he was tentative, almost afraid. A big strong man like that, afraid of a little girl like me. How odd. I took it. His hand felt warm in my cold grasp. I felt the liquid of life flowing through his veins just under his skin. The heart that pumped it forward produced a rhythm that was in tune with my world. Perfect synchronicity. Maybe I held it too long. He pulled it back rather quickly from my grasp, with a nervous smile on his face. The others watched me, ready to pounce.

"I am fine," I said, looking at both Mrs. Saxon and Mrs. Bolden. I believe I saw Mrs. Saxon exhale.

"I am glad. Sorry about last night," apologized Mr. Markinson with the rich dulcet tones of a Vegas lounge crooner. I just wasn't sure what he was apologizing for.

"Last night?" I asked, confused, not sure what he meant.

"Outside," he said, timidly. "When we first met."

"We met?" I asked, more confused than ever. Since I had arrived, I only met three people, and none of them were male. Well, if you didn't count the floating head librarian, Edward, and the mystery arms that caught me the first night.

Like a lightning bolt, it hit me. My little trip outside wasn't a dream, but I damn sure didn't meet him out there. There was nobody else out there with me. Just me, the wind, trees, and that wolf —

"Yep, last night. I kind of hit you. Really sorry about that. I didn't know who you were. Just thought you were another local that had gotten drunk and stumbled too close..."

He kept talking, but I stopped listening. Several million synapses fired all at once, putting two and two together, or in this case, putting paw and face together. I exploded into the man, picking him up, and ramming him across the room into a marble wall. The impact sent a large crack up the full length of the panel. I felt all the air leave his lungs and rush past my face as his body impacted the wall. Behind me, two voices shrieked. "No!"

The whole action took less than a second, and within another half second Mrs. Bolden was there grabbing my arms, pulling me back. "Larissa, remember how strong you are now, not to mention you are a newborn again, so you are even stronger. Let him go."

I released my grip, and he fell to the floor like a rag doll. "The wolf?" I asked.

"Yes, Spencer is a werewolf," Mrs. Saxon explained. "Mr. Markinson, and several other members of our staff and some of the students routinely go out to patrol the grounds to check for anyone stumbling in someplace they shouldn't."

"Yea," he interrupted, and then continued the explanation. His voice pained. "Usually, it's just a local that had too much of a good time at night staggering around. We knock them out and take them somewhere safe and a long way from here to wake up." He attempted to stand, using his legs to push while his body slid up the wall. His arms wrapped around his ribs to lick the wounds that I had given him.

"Oh my god. I am so sorry. I guess I lost control," I apologized, and extended my hand to help him up, but he waved it away.

"It's okay. Not my first rodeo, and I heal quick. Those that aren't so inebriated, we just scare off with some growls and howls. I didn't know who you were, so I figured you were just a drunk local with how you were falling all over the place."

Falling all over the place? I remember doing that. It was like my body stopped working. Oh god, they thought I was... "I wasn't drunk. I don't drink," I explained, flustered. Now it was my turn for my voice to shake and sound weak. I couldn't have them thinking that I was like that.

"Larissa, we know," Mrs. Bolden explained. "You were turning back, which first you must die. That is what you were doing."

"What a horrifying experience," I snapped.

"It's terrifying," agreed Mrs. Bolden. Her hand reached out and touched my shoulder. "Larissa, why don't we go introduce you to the others, and get you settled in."

I looked at Mrs. Saxon, who agreed and told me, "Go ahead. I will see you around and see you in class."

"Oh, okay," I reluctantly agreed, while being led toward the door by Mrs. Bolden's touch.

I turned once more and apologized to Mr. Markinson. "I am really sorry. It won't happen again."

"It's fine Larissa." He was now standing up on his own, and no longer appeared to be in any physical pain. "Next time I will try to go a little easier on you." He flashed me a big smile, which made me giggle a little inside.

8

Fifth floor, which was where we were, and being a girl meant I was on the left. Finding another long hall of deep cherry wood paneling and red carpet behind the door wasn't a surprise. Like the others, it appeared to go on forever.

"Now, there are only three other girls in your class here, so here you are," Mrs. Bolden said, standing at the fourth door. "You should have everything you need in there." Then she stopped and asked. "Rebecca explained about the rooms in this place, right?"

"Yep, they are what we want them to be."

"Good. If you ever need anything, I am right next door, but first, let me show you something else."

"What is it?" I asked curiously.

"Well, it's night, no classes, and we don't exactly sleep, so..." She opened my door and walked straight through my room. It was setup exactly like the room I had in Mrs. Saxon's residence, which was exactly like the room I had back at home. She went straight for my closet and yanked it open. I stood and watched her step in and disappear behind the clothes leaving them swaying on their hangers. When I reached in and pushed the clothes aside, I was shocked to find a set of stairs. Why I was surprised by anything appearing around here where it shouldn't, I didn't have a clue. I guess it was something I still needed to get used to.

I heard her walking up the stairs, and I followed. It was dark, but that was fine. I could see perfectly without light. At the top, there wasn't a door or flap, or anything, just an opening, and as I walked up the last few steps, my head poked up through the opening and out into the night. At the top, I stepped out on to a wooden deck built into the large, peaked roof. There were spots with outdoor couches, chairs, and tables everywhere. Mrs. Bolden continued across the deck. Beyond her, people sat and talked. People. People like me.

"Hi guys," Mrs. Bolden called out as she approached. "I have someone I want you to meet. Please welcome Larissa Norton" She moved aside, and there I was, out in the open, and exposed with six sets of eyes looking at me like the new kid at a school, which made sense, since I was. And, like any new kid in a school, I used my opportunity to set a first impression, the most important impression, to completely dork it up by holding up my right hand waving with all five fingers.

The embarrassment caused me to yank my right hand down and put the appendage of betrayal behind my back as I stepped closer. No one had said a word, nor had they moved. They just looked.

"Larissa is going to be staying with us for a bit," Mrs. Bolden announced. Then, as if that were his cue, a man, slightly older than the rest, but no more than late twenties in a red sweater with the collar of a white shirt sticking out, a look I thought only my father attempted, got up and walked my way. The wind played with his dark hair, and the moonlight danced along his pale, chiseled features.

"Welcome, Larissa," he greeted me with an extended hand. I let my right hand out of the jail I had put it in and took his hand. "I see you have met my wife. I am Kevin, Kevin Bolden. Welcome to our little night club."

"Thanks," I said, not wanting to say too much and take a chance of adding to the damage already done.

"Why don't you take my seat?" he offered, motioning to the wicker chair he just stood up from. I moved toward it and watched as he and Mrs. Bolden settled into a small wicker loveseat together. His arm around her. She leaned into him with one hand on his thigh.

"So, Larissa, where are you from?" asked a strange voice that sounded like it belonged more in a cornfield than a magical school.

My head swung around from looking at the Boldens to see who asked, but I was greeted by five people looking at me, with no idea who asked. "Virginia," I answered, watching for a reaction.

"The state for lovers," a dark-haired teen, probably my age, in a flannel shirt and jeans, said in the same voice he asked in. "I am from Wichita. My name is Jeremy Phillips."

I nodded in his direction. The girl to his left, tall with long blonde hair, and like me, opted for the bright red lipstick for some color, looked around at the others. Then she spoke. "I guess we should probably introduce ourselves. I am Apryl Stewart. Not spelled like the month, a 'y' instead of an 'i.' I am from East Lansing."

"Michigan?" I asked.

"Yep."

"Mike," said the male next to her with a simple wave. He sported a goatee and wore a wife beater that was several sizes too small. The bulges of flesh where his shoulders and base of his neck hinted at the existence of a gym in this place.

"I'm Laura Webb, from Florida." The rather striking girl with dark hair that sat next to Mike. She never looked in my direction as she spoke. Her focus was on Mike, and only Mike. One of her hands constantly massaged his arm. From the looks of it, he liked it.

"Pamela Marco, from Mexico."

"If you couldn't guess," Mike interjected, and then took a playful slap from Laura.

"Anyway. I am Pamela, but you can call me Pam." Her accent, as well as her features, the full lips, and long dark hair did make it obvious.

"And I am Brad Cone from New York, both the city and the state," the last teen said. He flashed a bright white smile. His blonde hair was perfectly slicked back, as he sat comfortably in the chair, but unlike the others who were dressed rather comfortably in jeans, or in a long black skirt like Pam wore, he was in slacks and loafers, with a button-up shirt and something puffed out of the top of it. I think I remember hearing it called an ascot. "So, what is your story?"

"My what?" I asked.

"Your story. How did you come to be here?" clarified Apryl.

"Oh, well," I started. This was only the second time I have had to tell my story, out loud. The last time almost made me cry. I had to hold it together this time. This was no time to show any weakness. I paused, cleared my mind, and told myself, *here we go.* "Something was chasing me and my parents. It killed my father and kept chasing my mother and me. So, she had me drink her charm to temporarily turn me back into a human and put me on a train where I fell asleep. Mrs. Saxon woke me up on the train and brought me here."

There was silence and a stunned look on every face. Laura had even stopped stroking Mike's arm.

"Um, yea. That's my story," I added, hoping to break the silence myself.

"Larissa, you will have to excuse them. I am sure they were expecting your story to match their own," explained Mrs. Bolden. "Each of them was one of mine or Kevin's finds. Children and teens that were turned and abandoned with no one to guide them. Something that is heavily frowned upon in our world. We take them in to teach them what they need to know to cope with the real world, and they can leave once we all agree they are ready."

"Of course, they are welcome to come back anytime they want. Once they are a member of our coven, they are always a member. It's a family." her husband added.

"Yep, our door is always open."

There was a question in my head I had to ask. It was something I had been wondering since Mrs. Saxon told me this was a school. I could understand what the others must learn, but what about those like me? We didn't learn any spells or skills. "Learn what?"

"Wait," Apryl exclaimed. "Let me get this right. Your mother had you drink her charm, the clear liquid, and you turned back." She looked around at the others, who were all still staring in my direction. All the attention made me more than a little uncomfortable. "Am I the only one here who is curious what the hell that was like?" she asked.

There were a few nods and jerks of heads, but no one spoke.

"Okay fine. I know I am." She got up and moved to the chair directly to my right and leaned against the chair arm we shared. "What was it like?"

"Confusing, and hell," I said, which was the truth.

"I bet, but what did it feel like? I mean, was it instantaneous? Was it like of the reverse of when we turn?" she asked.

"I didn't really feel anything when it happened except sleepy. Right after my mom had me drink it, I started getting tired."

"She gave it to you right before the train?" Apryl interjected.

"Yes, and I fell asleep on the train. When I woke up, I was, I guess, human again. Beating heart and all," I said, and then added, "and breathing." I remembered my fascination with how good the yawn felt.

"So weird. That would freak me out," Laura said.

"It freaked me out," I said and barely finished before Apryl interrupted.

"How long did it last?"

"About a day, maybe a little longer. I turned back earlier today." I explained. I knew what would be next from the woman of many questions and went ahead and answered. "That felt like I was dying. First my legs stopped working, then my arms. I was left on the ground flailing around trying to pull myself to safety."

"She snuck outside for a walk and was in the woods when it started. She was lucky Spencer found her," added Mrs. Bolden.

"You had a run in with a werewolf and survived," Pam asked. There was a look of fear on her face. Something I made note of and would have to ask her about later.

"She was never in any danger. At first, he just thought she was a drunk local, then he noticed what was happening. He was aware that Rebecca had a new arrival and put two and two together."

"He actually saved me, in a way," I added. I didn't feel it necessary to mention the swipe of his paw, or how I put him through a wall. "When I woke up, I was back to normal."

"You poor girl," Apryl said. Now Pam had moved over to the chair directly to my left.

"I made it," I said, trying to sound strong.

"So, Larissa, you asked what they learn while they are here," Mr. Bolden said. He got up and walked over to where we were all sitting and took the seat Apryl had vacated. "Well, think about everything you found odd when you turned back to human. Your heartbeat and breathing. Probably eating." He motioned toward me looking for agreement.

"Definitely."

"You ate?" Pam asked.

"Yes," I said. "Some bacon for breakfast and a cheeseburger and fries for lunch."

Apryl came close to climbing over the chair arm, and if there had been room in my seat, I was sure she would have tried to squeeze in. "What did it taste like? Did it taste like you remembered?"

"To be honest. I don't remember how it tasted before, but this time it tasted good. I really liked the bacon." Which was the truth. Of all the tastes I had tried, bacon was my favorite. Then I confessed, "The taste was great, but chewing was something I had to relearn." That brought a laugh from everyone.

"Oh my god, I remember bacon." Laura exclaimed. She was practically drooling.

"It's things like that," Mr. Bolden said to bring the conversation back to his original topic. "We have to blend in, which means being conscious of what others take for granted. Things like how we move. Our speed and strength causes us to stick out, and not in a good way, so we have to adjust and move slower when others are around. Slouch a little"—his shoulders slouched in the loveseat — "when sitting or standing. Humans don't sit up as rigid as we do. Actions as simple as blinking and breathing, we need to imitate to appear like everyone else."

"Yes, everyone. Let's do our breathing exercises," interrupted Laura. "1, 2, 3,"

All at once, everyone, including the Boldens, raised their shoulders up just slightly and then let them drop. It gave the appearance that they each inhaled and then exhaled.

"Oh geez," I said.

"Yep, I am sure you will be starting with classes tomorrow," Mr. Bolden stated, "Not to mention there is still the normal things like Reading, Math, Science, etc.... that you need to learn to get into college and get a decent job."

"Another way of blending in?" I asked.

"That and a way of supporting yourself. House, clothes, that kind of stuff. In case you choose to leave the coven."

"Makes sense," I replied, and it did. My father had a job. He was a carpenter and built custom cabinets. It made a nice living for us. While we didn't need to buy food, we still needed a place to live, a car, clothes, and money to take trips, see shows, or anything else that was just part of life. If we didn't have a way to do that, we would just have to sit inside some hole in the wall all day, and I had no intention of living life like that. I wanted a good life. Anything else just wouldn't do.

"Enough shop talk!" Mike hollered. "It's Thursday night, which means the club is Apryl's. Eighties music night. Let's get this party going."

9

It was eighties and early nineties music until the first light of the new day. Everything from the Eurythmics and Duran to Depeche Mode. Not to mention the hour of the Pet Shop Boys. We all danced, and a few sang. I didn't, or at least not loud enough for anyone to hear. I don't have much of a singing voice. Not that it mattered. No one was shy about it. It was just a way to pass the time and enjoy each other's company. It was nice, and for an hour here and an hour there, I felt as normal as I could, considering the circumstances. Reality only slapped me across the face a few times. When it did, I took a break and walked to the edge of the deck, allowing myself to stand and stare out into the darkness as the sorrow of the moment took hold. I would stand there until it passed. Once it did, I returned to the group.

Most let me go by myself, but they all noticed. A few watched me with a look I could only call pity. Which I hated, but understood. My story was heartbreaking. The thing great novels and movies were made of, but lord knows I felt enough pity of my own inside, I didn't need anyone else's adding to the heap. I wanted them to see who I was trying to convey, the confident and sassy girl. The *IT* girl. That was how I saw myself. That was how I wanted them to see me. More importantly, that was how I needed them to see me. My misery didn't really want any company.

That was why my entire body cringed when I heard footsteps approaching me. These were male, a little heavier than what I would expect one of the girls to produce; Mrs. Bolden barely made a sound when I followed her across the deck earlier. That left four possibilities, and none of them were any more welcome than another. I stood there like a statue, leaning on the glass railing, focused out in the darkness, and the woods that were just beyond it.

It was Brad. He leaned against the railing right next to me. So much for personal space. If I shifted slightly on my right leg, I would bump into him. I had a few options. Move to the left, which would scream to him and everyone else who watched that he bothered me, probably not setting the best impression then. Being friendly and starting up a conversation was another, but that was completely out of the question. I just wanted to be alone at that moment, so I ignored him, hoping he would take the hint.

The glances that I caught Brad making in my direction were not signs of him taking a hint. Inside, I started imaging myself a character in one of the romantic comedies my mother used to force me to watch with her, a fair trade considering all the horror movies she sat through for me. I was the lonely girl standing out under the moon, away from the large crowd, lost in her thoughts and upset. He, the annoying guy who walked over with hopes of delivering a few cheesy pickup lines and then walk back to the crowd with the girl on his arm while cheesy music played in the background. Probably a power ballad.

"How you holding up?" Brad was staring a hole in the side of my face.

"Okay, just enjoying the night," I said, adding that last bit hoping he would take the hint.

"It is nice. I always like this time just before daybreak. It's beautiful."

Oh god. I braced myself for something corny like—*not as beautiful as you.*

"I can't imagine what all is going through your mind. I would be a complete wreck. If you ever need anyone to talk to..."

Oh, so he isn't trying the corny pickup line. He is going for the sensitive friend, with the hopes of not being friend-zoned. Obviously, he hasn't watched a lot of these movies and seen how this method usually ends.

"We are all good listeners. Everyone has been through a lot here, and we are all here to help each other."

Huh! Interesting. "Thanks," I said, trying to hide any hint of curiosity from my voice.

"I have been here just shy of three years, longer than everyone else. I don't have to tell you the first few nights are the toughest, but I have to say you seem to be doing quite well."

"You think so?" I sniped back. Dang my bad habit of speaking my mind. The irritation of being under his microscope might have been my trigger. Of course, if you asked my father, I didn't need one.

"I do. Most of us come in a little...," he paused and finally diverted his eyes off of me, but only to check around us for just a split second before they returned. My skin crawled when it did, and the impulse to tell him I just wanted to be alone grew. "Most come in a little wilder," he concluded.

"Wilder?"

"Most are newborns that were turned and left to fend for themselves. That is how it was for me." He turned toward me and again leaned against the railing, bracing himself on his right arm. His expression serious, almost somber. "When Mr. Bolden found me, I would have rather fought him than respect him. I was angry and fed all the time. When I look back on how I was then, I will admit, I am a little embarrassed... and a lot shocked. I was animalistic, hunting and killing everything in sight. Partially from the thirst, but mostly out of anger for what had happened to me. Everywhere I looked were people that would live a normal life, and I was cursed to be this." Brad paused and looked back toward the group across the deck. His lip curled up on one side. "Mr. Bolden broke me, and I do mean broke me. Physically and spiritually, but once he did, I realized what I had become and how wrong I was. There is so much more this life can offer. I just had to get past the anger to see it. So just give them time, though I don't really think you will need it. You seem to have things rather controlled."

"Thanks, I guess." I had nothing else to say. Mostly because I still wanted to just stand there quietly by myself. I had hoped that would have been the end of his little visit, but he settled back in, again facing forward. At least he wasn't staring a hole in the side of my head with his eyes anymore.

We stood like that for quite some time, and I was the one who finally broke the silence. It was my silence, after all. "So that is why the rules about the doors and such?"

Brad laughed, "Yep, never know when the urge gets too bad. They say it takes years before you learn to control it. You know what I mean?"

"Um, yea," I said, but in truth, I didn't have a clue. I had never felt a thirst I couldn't control. Not even close, except the first time.

"Here they come," he said, and pointed down at the edge of the woods. Six of the largest dogs emerged and walked up to the pool deck. I watched and my jaw dropped when one at a time they stood up right on their hind-legs and became men and boys.

"What are they?" I gasped.

"Werewolves, doing the last sweep of the woods before daybreak."

"Sweep of what?"

"The woods. To check for intruders and threats. They are our protectors. You didn't think we were top of the food chain now, did you?"

It was a point I had never really thought of before.

"You better than anyone else up here understand that there are things out there that want to do harm to us... the witches, shapeshifters, and even the werewolves. Our enemy is everyone and everywhere, but that one with his shirt off can protect me and I will be just fine." Brad leaned into me, bumping my shoulder, and then turned around and left, leaving me alone with a set of surprised eyes, fighting the urge to laugh. I hadn't seen that coming.

Once the sun came up, we all went down our own flights of stairs to our rooms. Apryl told me she would meet me outside of my room in an hour to walk me to class. It didn't take me the full hour to get ready, but I sat and admired my room, and even changed a few things to be more to my liking. The lamp that was in the room was the one that was there the last time I had seen my actual room, but it wasn't my favorite. I had one before it, with a pink shade with ribs that flared out with miniature tassels dangling from the bottom. I loved that lamp, but it broke, and my father couldn't fix it. Here, I could think about it, and it was back on the nightstand where it always sat, and it worked perfectly.

At an hour, 8:00 AM, I opened my door, and there she was, just like she said. Her appearance differed slightly from what I had seen the night before. Her long blonde hair pulled back in a ponytail, white button-up shirt, long white flowing skirt.

"What, no uniform?" I asked, half serious, though I didn't find one in my closet, when I picked out my usual t-shirt and jeans look.

"Keep your voice down. We don't want to be giving them any ideas now," she cautioned, and handed me a notebook with a pen and pencil sticking out of the metal spirals. "I wasn't sure if they set you up with stuff or not."

"Will I need books?" I asked.

"Yes, but you will get those in class. Let's go."

We started down the hallway toward the door leading out to the stairs. Before we reached the door, she turned and asked, "How are you feeling?"

I looked at her inquisitively. I felt great. In fact, I can't remember ever feeling better.

"Let me be more specific. Any urges? Feel like everything is under control? Morning classes are in mixed company."

"Oh, that. I'm fine."

"You sure?" she asked. "I know newborns usually need to feed immediately, but since you are," she paused and looked at the wall behind me for a second. "Since you are a born-again, I am not sure if you still have that same need."

I remember what she meant. Just hours after I woke the first time I turned; I felt the back of my throat ignite. It was a burning unlike anything I had ever felt before. Though at that moment, I couldn't remember much of my life before. It was like everything began when I opened my eyes. With the burning came an awareness of everything alive around me. The small field mouse running under our house. The birds overhead. The squirrels in the woods behind us. All of them. I smelled them. I felt the blood coursing through their veins. I could even hear every thump of their hearts. It was overwhelming. As much as I tried to resist, I wanted them. I needed them. Nothing would stop me, except my parents. My mother grabbed me and sprinted out into the woods, miles away from anyone. Once we were there she told me, "Do what nature intended," and I did. A buck that any hunter would have been proud to put on his wall was no match for my speed and strength. When I was done, I felt better. No more burning. No more all-consuming thoughts and cravings. All of that was quieted down. It took me a while to learn the pattern. If I hadn't fed in a about a week, the cravings started. If I kept putting it off, it progressed to those like a dieter walking past a cabinet with cookies inside; strong with a little justification going on in their mind, trying to convince them to give in, but in the end, still able to control it. I never let it get beyond that before I went out and safely hunted, but as the years passed, I found I could control it more and more, and at times went months without feeding. Though I felt it those times too. I was weaker and felt sick when I let it go that long, and my parents could tell. My mother constantly pled with me to do what my body said I needed to do.

"No cravings. I'm fine," I said, and she turned and opened the door, and I felt it. The thumping of several hearts. The flowing of that sweet liquid. I am fine, I told myself and I followed her out.

We walked down. I saw Mike, Brad, and Jeremy coming out of their door on the other side. Each gave us a quick wave. At the bottom of each set of stairs were others, that on the outside looked like regular teenagers like us, but different. All of them watched me as I walked down the stairs. *Dang being the new kid.*

Another group of girls waited at the bottom. Each looked me over as I descended and walked past with Apryl to join Laura and Pam.

"Who's the new blood sucker?" asked a voice from the boys' stairs.

The comment caused a chorus of groans and sighs from everyone.

"What?" the same voice asked. This time I could see the redheaded freckle faced kid who smiled like he was the funniest person ever.

"Just ignore him. That is Jack Ass," said a girl behind me.

"Jack Nash. It's Jack Nash," the freckled faced jerk corrected.

"Hi, I am Gwen, you must be new." I turned around and ran right into a walking and talking life size Barbie doll. Blonde, pink, with way too much make-up and sparkles.

"All right everyone. No gawking. This is Larissa," announced Laura. "She's new, so go ahead with the awkward stares and all." Before I could be embarrassed, she threw her arm around me and said, "We need to get to science. Let's go." I looked around as the other students parted, and we walked right through toward the hall with the classrooms.

The science classroom itself wasn't like the one Mrs. Saxon had showed me yesterday. This honestly reminded me of every high school science classroom I had seen in the movies. Tall tables with black tops, stools, a center aisle down the middle of the classroom leading to a larger table at the center and two blackboards behind it. What was standing in front of the blackboards caused me to hide my face a little as I sat at a table in two rows back. Laura, Apryl, and Pam joined me at the table. Brad, Mark, and Jeremy were on the other side.

"Nice to see you again, Larissa," Mr. Markinson said, and put a Modern Physics volume 2 textbook on the table in front of me. I looked up past the hand that I was using to block my face from seeing him. "We don't use it often in class, but you will need it for homework and studying." He then walked away from the table with a mild limp. After a few steps, he turned to laugh, and then went on walking normally.

"Oh god," I muttered.

"You really threw him through a marble wall?" Laura asked. I had confessed to my little indiscretion during a moment of levity last night, somewhere between U2 and Michael Jackson.

"Yep, I didn't..." I tried to come up with a good excuse, but I couldn't. Not one that made it seem like mistaken identity or something explainable, but that wasn't it. I did it because he hit me. "Let's just say not my finest hour."

"Well, there are a few here I wouldn't mind putting through a wall. Like Jack Ass, for example," Apryl muttered. "He is rather trying."

"What is he?" I asked, more out of curiosity as I looked around the classroom. Other than our dark eyes, nothing about the others made it obvious what they were.

"Guess we need to give you the lay of the land here." Laura scooted her stool over closer to me and then whispered, "So, that table in front of us. Tera, witch, just a normal spell caster. Lynn, elemental, which means she can control the weather and stuff easier than others. Marcia, I am not sure, but she can do this weird trick where time stands still that none of the others can do. Next table over, you already met Gwen, just a spell caster, but she does have a bit of ergokinesis in her. That means she can absorb and control energy. That dark haired little witch next to her, Lisa. I would stay clear of her. She is a necromancer."

"Wait, what?"

"There are many types of witches. Some are only normal spells and such. Others are called elementalist and can control things like the weather, fire, and water naturally without a spell or incantation. Jack Ass back there," she turned to look at the table behind where the boys were sitting, "he is both empathic and telepathic. So far, he can read thoughts, and I am willing to bet he has tried to plant a few thoughts here and there, so watch out for him. He might have you walking out of your room to class in your birthday suit." She then giggled. "I am joking. He is a harmless jerk. Then next to him, you have Stan and Steve, two of the sweetest people you will ever meet. They are shapeshifters, and then there is Cynthia, Steve's younger sister. She is one too, but still pretty standoffish. They have only been here a week or so."

"Oh," I said. My mind was trying to absorb everything and remember all the names, but I still had a question she hadn't answered. "You never told me what a necro... whatever you said is?"

"Oh, yeah. She can reanimate the dead. Real dark magic stuff."

"The dead?" I gasped. My mind going back to the zombie movies I used to watch on television with my father.

"Yep, like corpses, ghosts, and stuff. I heard a rumor she can even talk to the dead. Just weird," Laura whispered hollowly. Then she turned to look behind us, at the empty table. "The dog pack is late."

I looked back at her. I was sure the information overload was clear in my eyes. If I were a cartoon, my eyes would be meters that would be flashing full right now.

"Werewolves," Pam whispered. "They are unruly mutts."

Just then, the three boys I had seen earlier burst in through the door, pushing and shoving each other. Each a muscular brute with dark hair. They crashed into their table, causing the stools to squeak against the floor, and then each took their seat. When they noticed we were looking at them, they smiled at us and waved. Then all three of them set their focus on me. "You must be the new girl."

Apryl shot back, "Yes she is. Larissa, the dog pack. Dog pack, Larissa."

They met her introduction with a look of disdain, but the one closest to me, and the one that captured Brad's attention this morning, ignored her and addressed me directly. "Larissa, I am Martin, and I am at your service." He winked.

"Knock it off Casanova. You know the rules," Laura warned sternly.

"I can look."

"I am sure she doesn't want you drooling all over her," added Pam.

"Jealous?" Martin sarcastically asked.

"All right everyone. Eyes up here. Let's get started," Mr. Markinson announced, and then started today's class.

As I turned toward the front of the class, I saw one last person walk in out of the corner of my eye. He sat on the last stool at the table behind us with the werewolves, but there was something about him. Something about the quick look he made in my direction, which caused me to turn my head instantly, told me he was not one of them. He was different. Tall, and slim, with almost model like facial features that should have been on a fashion magazine or a mall clothing poster. Not to mention the perfectly groomed head of brown hair with a wave through it. Not a single strand was out of place.

"Who is that?" I whispered to Laura. She made a quick look behind, and then turned back to the front of the class.

"Someone to stay away from," she whispered back.

After a full morning of science, math, and Mrs. Saxon's English class, the afternoon was split into specific disciplines. Witches went to classes around their specific area of expertise. Same with shape shifters. Of course, my mind wandered on that topic for a few moments. I imagined a classroom full of shapes and statues that they practiced mimicking. What werewolves did, I didn't know. Maybe house training, I thought, and giggled softly to myself.

Our classes were broken into the physical and the emotional side of blending in. I kind of understood the physical side after the brief description they gave me last night, but did not know it was as detailed as it was. We spent hours watching videos of humans and then trying to emulate them. It went beyond remembering to look like we were breathing and blinking. There was also situational awareness. If we were lifting something heavy, we needed to appear like we were straining, and then, of course, there was heavy breathing as we recovered from the exertion. There was nothing we could do to force ourselves to sweat, but that was really the only limitation.

What I hadn't given any consideration to were the emotional reactions to things like pain, stress, loss, and what Mrs. Bolden said was the hardest of all, empathy. She said as immortal creatures, we took things for granted and didn't respond the same way humans do. I wasn't so sure about that, at least not now. I still felt the loss of my father and knew if everything else that had happened in the last two days hadn't distracted me, my own world of depression and loss would have drowned me. Not to mention the concern about my mother always had a place in my mind.

At the end of the day's classes, I sought out Mrs. Tenderschott's classroom. If you ignored what surrounded the room, you would think you had just walked into a chemistry class in any high school. Tables with burners, beakers, vials, and tubing were set up for the next lab, but a quick look at the shelves made the room look more like a pharmacy. Well, that might be stretching it a bit, unless the pharmacist's client was The Munsters. Vials of various colored liquids filled the shelves all along the walls. Some of the liquids just sat there while others bubbled. Each labeled with a simple handwritten white label.

I stood at the back of the classroom, while Mrs. Tenderschott was head down, appearing to grade papers. There was a smell in this place. I couldn't quite put my finger on it. Smelling an odor here made some sense to me, considering all the mixing that happens here.

"Larissa, don't be a stranger. Come on up here, dear," Mrs. Tenderschott called from her desk at the front. Her head never looked up, but I walked up toward her.

"Here for another go at your reading?"

"Yes ma'am," I said, and put my books down on the table to my right.

"I imagine you are quite eager to find out about your mom." She finally looked up at me this time. "I would be too." Mrs. Tenderschott pushed back from her desk and stood up. "Let's get to it."

She walked over to the shelves on the left and searched up and down. Some of the vials were turned to their side, making them hard to read. As she reached them, she took the time to turn them and then read their labels. Her hand stopped on one, and she asked, "Are you sure we can't have another go at what is chasing you? We really need to find out."

We did. I knew that. Like Mrs. Saxon said yesterday, we needed to know for my, and everyone's, safety. And, I wouldn't deny having some answers about what or who might help explain the why, something I had thought about many times over the last two days, but I really wanted, needed, to know what happened to my mother. One way or the other, it would fill a hole in my soul. My worry had been eating away at the edges of that hole since I woke up on the train. If I had to wait much longer, it might join with the larger hole caused by my father's death and consume me. "Can we do that tomorrow? I really need to know," I replied as calmly as I could, but my voice came out with a quiver.

"Sure dear. I completely understand." Her hand left that vial and kept searching, but stayed focused on that shelf until she hit one with a yellow elixir in it. She pulled it down and brought it back up to her desk. "Pull up a chair and have a seat. This one has about the same punch as yesterday."

I pulled the chair from the table and sat while she went and retrieved a small skinny vial and then rinsed it out in the sink before returning to her desk and placing it in a stand. She opened the vial of yellow fluid and poured it slowly into the smaller vial. I watched as her eyes focused on the marks on the side of the vial and stopped just as it reached the third from the top. She sat the larger vial down and recapped it. When she placed it down, I tried to read the writing on the label. It was legible, but in a different language, which I didn't speak. She handed the smaller one to me, and warned, "Unlike the stuff yesterday, this isn't going to taste too good. Family related things never do." She gave me a look like I would know what that means, but I didn't.

Like yesterday, I tipped it back and drank it, choking and gagging at the taste. It reminded me of vomiting in reverse: putrid and acidic. Even my throat protested, and my stomach turned.

"I am sorry, sweetie. It's bad tasting stuff. Now try to relax. This will be like yesterday. Just let yourself go, and I will join you..."

I was out, and then alone in the darkness before Mrs. Tenderschott finished her instructions, but I knew just to wait, and just like yesterday, she was there. She walked forward and grabbed both of my hands. I could feel her, the warmth of her skin against my cold flesh, just like I would have if I were awake.

"You ready for this?" she asked compassionately.

"Absolutely. Tell me what to do."

"I will need you to latch hold of a memory of your mother. Once you have it, hold on to it with everything you have. Don't let it waver at all. Don't think of another memory. Once you are locked in, the potion will let me slip out and use the connection you share as mother and daughter to find her, but you will be the link. Without you I won't be able to find her."

"I understand," I replied eagerly, and I did. I already had the memory in my head.

"Okay, tell me when you have it."

"Got it," I said.

"Okay, in that moment, think about how your mother looks, how she smells. If she hugged you or touched you, think about how that felt. The stronger the memory, the better."

"Okay." I focused in on the memory. My mother and myself sitting in our library on a rainy afternoon just two weeks ago. We were on the couch, sharing the same blanket. My legs were over hers, leaning against opposite ends, reading, having one of our typical lazy days. I am not sure if she did the same, but every time I stopped to turn the page, I looked up at her. Seeing her raven hair, her kind expression. My father had told me, take away my red hair and we would be twins. Each of us had read the book the other was reading, and throughout the afternoon we would debate our own interpretations. I think my mother thought she was being rather clever in these moments, but I knew what they were. These were not only a fantastic way for us to bond, but they also gave her a way to teach me how to appreciate literature.

"Still have it?" Mrs. Tenderschott asked.

"Yes, she is right here with me."

"Hmmm," she said in a concerned tone.

"Is something wrong? Is she okay?" I asked.

"Nothing to be too worried about. Let me try pushing deeper. This might get a little weird, just stay with me."

"Okay," I said and hung on to the dream for a few seconds longer, and then things got weird, just as she said. The shelves of books in the library dissolved into a black void. Then the floor, followed by all the furniture except the sofa we were on. It turned cold around us, but my mother didn't seem to notice. She kept reading. I pulled at the blanket to cover my arms. Finally, she disappeared.

"What is happening?" I screamed.

"Hang on."

The couch was gone, and I was lying on the ground: cold, wet, and covered in something red. Agonizing pains shot through my body. Everything hurt, and I couldn't move. Nothing held me down, but my legs hurt when I tried to move them. I tilted my head up to look down, and all I saw was blood covering every inch of me. Some of it still spurting up from down around my legs, but I couldn't see anything beyond that. Trees swayed above me.

"Help! Help! Mrs. Tenderschott!" I screamed.

I turned my head to look for her and saw a woman lying beside me in a long black wool dress covered in blood, and red hair.

I screamed again, and a hand touched my neck. I came out screaming back into the classroom. Mrs. Tenderschott hugged me close. "You're okay. You're okay. I got you."

10

It was a good half an hour before I left Mrs. Tenderschott's classroom. I hoped she had the answers I wanted. The ones I needed. What I found were answers that I didn't have any idea I needed when I walked in. I wanted to find out if my mother was still alive. That was the only answer I truly wanted. After the walk through my mind, not only couldn't Mrs. Tenderschott tell me she was still alive, but there was more, so much more. She wasn't even sure that the woman I thought was my mother was really my mother at all. That potion had never failed her, she said. It was foolproof. Guaranteed to bring you to those you had a genetic connection with. For me, it did the opposite. My mother, or the woman who I thought was my mother, disappeared, and another woman who was dead and covered in blood appeared.

"What the hell was that?" I asked as soon as I was lucid, but Mrs. Tenderschott didn't have an explanation. She called Mrs. Bolden down to her classroom, and it was no surprise it only took a minute or two before she appeared through a door. They talked out of my earshot for several minutes while I alternated between weeping and screaming. Normally, I could hear anything anyone said within a few hundred feet of me, but this time I couldn't. Either there was some magic at play, or my emotional state interfered somehow with my ability. That or I just couldn't hear them over my own crying.

When they were done, Mrs. Bolden came and sat next to me, and Mrs. Tenderschott took her seat across the table from me. I was nothing but a mass of tissue crumpled down on the table. A hand rubbed my shoulders. "Larissa?"

I lifted my head up and looked at Mrs. Bolden. "I am sorry. This won't help any, but sometimes when we go searching, we find things we didn't want to know."

She was right, it didn't help. "I don't understand. What was that? How could it be so wrong?" I asked, crushed, still holding on to hope that something went wrong with the potion.

"It's not wrong dear," Mrs. Tenderschott comforted. "What you saw is what there is."

"What does that mean? What was that?" I demanded. Tears flowed down my face.

I heard the world's largest sigh coming from Mrs. Tenderschott as she and Mrs. Bolden exchanged a few looks. Neither of them appeared comfortable at this moment, which made three of us. Then I saw it. I saw Mrs. Bolden put into practice some of those human responses she was teaching us earlier. A tilt of the head. A focused softening of her brow. "Larissa, there isn't any easy way to say it. What you saw was a deep memory that had been suppressed a long time ago. That woman was your mother."

I buried my head in my hands. My fingers attempted to rub the emotional pain from my head. Like an eraser trying to remove an errant answer. Except in this case, the eraser was running out, and the answer was getting darker and clearer with every moment that passed. Another image flashed in my mind of the woman. This time, she was alive, and for the split second I saw her, she was smiling in a chiffon yellow dress. Her hair pulled back, and she wore a hat. Then the image was gone as soon as it arrived, but a familiar longing stayed. "How?"

There was another sigh, and I saw Mrs. Tenderschott had joined me in the tear production business. My factory was working a little harder than hers appeared to be. It had only produced a couple of stragglers escaping the sides of her eyes. She got up and walked away.

"Larissa, look at me." I turned and looked at Mrs. Bolden. "We don't have a lot of answers, but we will try to help you find them. Chances are, the people you thought were your parents either took you in after they found you like Kevin and I do, or they turned you."

It didn't take long before my mind made a major leap. Of all the directions it could have gone, why I went this one, I didn't know. Well, maybe I did. I had a bit of a temper and always jumped before thinking. Just ask Mr. Markinson.

"They were who attacked me and my mother," I blurted out. It made sense. We were both covered in blood. Blood means a violent attack. I was now a vampire. I just put two and five together and came up with that conclusion.

"Larissa, you don't know that," warned Mrs. Bolden. "We don't really know anything at this point, just that your parents aren't your biological parents. That is all."

"If you want, I can help you find the truth," Mrs. Tenderschott offered. "When you are ready, of course."

I wanted to scream yes now, like I did the night before, but instead there was a question there. Did I really want to know the truth? Then another question, would I be able to handle the truth? I loved my mother, or I mean the woman... Oh god I had to stop that. If I kept that up, I would drive myself crazy. Of course, it was probably way too late, anyway. I was already on the verge of being totally and completely nuts.

After I settled down a bit, I left the classroom with Mrs. Bolden, and we walked back up to our floor. When she dropped me off at my door, she asked if I was going to be okay, and I lied. I needed to be alone for a bit.

"Relax for a bit. I will send someone for you in a bit. We have something special planned for tonight after dark."

"Okay," I said, and then let the door close. I guess that meant it was 70s night up on the deck. Not that getting lost in some music right now wasn't that bad of an idea. Right on cue, music began in the room. Modern rock, Bad Wolves I think. It didn't help, but gave me something other than the ear ringing silence. I sat on my bed, listening, and watching out the window. The light of the day faded, and the light of the moon rose. With it, several more memories of that woman emerged. Nothing solid or substantial, just flashes. I wish I knew her name. I guess I did. Her name was mom, or mother. My other mother, or the woman I thought was my mother, there I go making myself nuts again, was Marie, Marie Norton. When did my life turn into something that would put an afternoon soap opera to shame? Well, viewers, that was about thirty minutes ago.

My memories oscillated back and forth for a while. I lost track of how many times Marie and Thomas Norton went from loving parents to murdering monsters, and back, before there was a knock at my door. I opened it and found Apryl standing there. "Ready?" she asked eagerly.

"For what?"

"Come on, you will find out." she grabbed my hand and yanked me out of my door and down the hall. I wasn't in any emotional shape to fight it. We hit the door, and the boys were running down the stairs on the other side, hooting and hollering like out-of-control teenagers, which they were. Apryl dragged me down the stairs at a pace that was not only difficult to keep up with but also dangerous. I could have fallen. Of course, we couldn't die, so who cared. At the bottom, I about got whiplash as she yanked me around the newel post, and toward the windows, where a door I hadn't seen before stood open to the outside. Pam and Laura were out there waiting for us.

"What is this?" I asked, looking around. There were a few adults I hadn't met yet standing along with Stan, Steve, and Cynthia.

"Our night," Laura cheered. Her eyes were wide and twitching.

Behind me, I heard heels clicking on the concrete of the deck. Mrs. Saxon walked past us and continued toward the others. I wondered if she ever dressed casually. She wore another pencil dress, grey this time. She nodded to the adults and then to Stan, Steve, and Cynthia. All five of them took off out into the woods. Then she turned toward us. "Just to remind you of the rules. You are confined to the woods. If you try to leave, one of the shapeshifters will fence you in. Do not attack them, they are off limits. Get too out of hand, and myself and the others will have to intervene. Understood?"

"Yes ma'am." Everyone but myself and Mike responded, and Mrs. Bolden noticed.

"Mike?" asked Mr. Bolden.

"Got it," he seethed.

"Good. Laura, Pam, Apryl. Show our girl a fun time," Mr. Bolden said with a smile. "Let's go," he yelled and took off into the woods with his wife. Mike, Brad, and Jeremy followed them, running at full speed.

"Go where?" I asked.

Apryl looked at me with an animalistic sneer. "Let's hunt."

Off we went into the woods. Apryl, in the lead, and I was nothing more than anchor until we reached the edge of the woods. The others went on.

"Every Friday, they clear the woods of anyone from the town, and we have free rein from dusk to dawn to hunt. There are only a few rules you need to make sure you follow." She held up a finger. "First, you cannot go past roads to the east or the west." Then she held up a second finger. "Second, the shapeshifters are out there to make sure we follow the first rule, and to keep anyone from stumbling into our party." The third finger came up on her right hand. "Third, if you run into anyone, whether it is a member of the town or Steve, Stan, Cynthia, or any other shape shifter, you cannot harm them. Got it?"

I nodded.

"Good, then let's have some fun. If you get lost, we will find you."

Before I could respond, she was gone. Just a blur running into the woods. I wasn't expecting this, but I wasn't one to turn down the opportunity, and ran after her, thinking I could get used to weekly hunting.

At first, I found myself just enjoying the run through the woods, not really paying any attention to what was around me. It was freeing, so was climbing up a tree, and then leaping from treetop to treetop. God, I loved this feeling. Flying up above with each leap. The wind. The moonlight. The stars. This was my world. Always had been.

I was sitting on top of the tallest tree in the woods when it hit me. The beating of its heart echoed in my ears. I let myself fall down to the forest floor, landing on both feet, ready to run. It was close, but where? Standing still at the bottom of the tree, I let my senses take hold. The perfect tools for nature's perfect hunter. Both smell and sound turned way up past their limits. Everything amplified. Everything clear. Every beat of its heart betrayed it and told me right where it was. The chase was on.

My four-legged target was fast and had a head start. The closer I was, the louder the beat. The more I could hear the fluid running through its veins like water in a pipe, and a thirst built up in me that only this special elixir would quench. Ahead of me I saw it hop over a bush. Did it know it was being chased? It sure ran like it did, but I didn't care. I had to catch it. I had to have it. I had to satisfy this burning in the back of my throat.

There was a clearing ahead, and I knew I could catch it with straight on speed. I entered the clearing and only saw a glimpse of the road the doe hopped across before I ran into a stonewall that wasn't there half a second ago.

"Sorry Larissa. You need to turn back," said the wall.

I sat on my butt rubbing my head, staring at a talking wall that just slowly morphed into a Steve, one of the three shapeshifters. "Good lord, you can turn into a stone wall?" I asked, surprised.

"Yep, one of the more challenging shapes, but I like a challenge. You all right?"

"I'm fine. I didn't hurt you, did I? I was running..." His laughter interrupted my question. I had hit him full speed. That had to have hurt or at least taken the wind out of him. I know it did me, but yet he was standing there laughing, showing no worse for wear.

"Not a chance. We don't feel pain," he said after he stopped laughing.

"Huh." Then I thought about it. This actually made some sense. "I get it. If you did, just changing would hurt."

"You got it," he said with a wink and a point. "I saw a few others closer back to the campus. Why don't you head back? Let me see if I can locate them." Then poof, the six-foot teenager was an eagle soaring above me.

I followed, noting how fast the bugger was. Eventually, I picked up the trail and took off. Above me, Steve screeched, and I looked up, then he headed off in another direction. I heard three hearts beating in different rhythms. I knew which was the largest before I even saw the group. I hit the largest buck in the herd before the others knew I was there. While I did what nature created me to do, I felt the others scatter away. I drank until my thirst was quenched, and I felt strong, renewed, and invincible. At least my body did. My mind was still a wreck, and I stayed out in the woods until the first light of day to see if that would help renew my spirit.

11

After my feeding, I walked further out, deep into the woods to find the cove Mrs. Saxon had said was out there. I found it under the moonlit night. It was beautiful. A rocky cliff surrounding a small sandy beach. The sound of the waves crashing into the rocks offshore was hypnotic. At first, it was soothing. Then the torturous images that had played in my mind like the slideshow from hell followed the rhythm of the waves. The images came in, and then they left. In again, and then out. The pause before they rolled in again was my only reprieve. It was short, but appreciated. It was in those moments I could admire the beauty of the spot, and the shimmer of the light on water.

When I spied the telltale green flash of sunlight over the watery horizon line, I headed back. Surprisingly, I was the last one to emerge, and Mrs. Saxon had considered sending someone in after me, but Stan had monitored me all night and relayed to her that I was doing okay. I guess that meant I wasn't getting into, or causing, any trouble, but I was far from okay. I couldn't clear the images from my mind, and now others had joined them.

Eventually, I realized that wasn't necessarily a bad thing. Every image could be one step closer to the truth, but was it a truth I wanted to know? That was something I wasn't sure of, nor did I feel I was in any position to even consider. My emotions still had a firm hand on the wheel and steered me from hating my mother and father, the Nortons, and calling them murderers, to remembering how wonderful they were and back again, over and over again. I just couldn't make myself accept they could do anything so horrible, but there was a fact I had to accept. They could have lost control. Overtaken by the hunger so much that they weren't thinking. Then, they realized what they did, and saved me out of guilt. Then the mental and emotional rollercoaster reloaded and started again, picking up a new image on the way.

I was in the shower, with a pool of pink water circling the drain below me, when the most confusing of all images came into my mind. This was the first one with any kind of movement. I was running toward my mother. She was in a dress I could only call huge. Big skirt. Lots of frilly lace. She stood up on a big white porch with wood scroll work everywhere I could see. The memory stopped when my foot hit the second of three steps. This has to be a special moment with how my mother was dressed. Maybe Easter and that was her Easter dress. Then I wondered where that thought came from. I had never in my life ever thought of an Easter dress. It did seem warm out, so spring or possibly summer. I tossed it around and around until the water ran clean: no more blood, no more soap, just water. I got out and toweled off and headed to the closet. Again, wouldn't you know? I found exactly what I wanted to wear. Jean shorts, black tank, and flip flops. Amid everything else, a thought came into my head. *I could get used to this.*

There were no classes on Saturday, and I couldn't go back for another reading until later that afternoon. Not that I hadn't asked a few times already. Something about not wanting to do too many of these potions close together to avoid causing long term harm. There wasn't really anything else to do, and I didn't want to be stuck in my room with my thoughts. I headed up to the deck, hoping to find the others.

When I stepped out into the fresh air of the overcast day, there wasn't a soul on the deck. Just me. On any other day, this would be fine, but every moment I was alone was another moment my mind was free to roam into thoughts I didn't even want to consider. The absolute last thing I needed right now. I already felt like an emotional nightmare coated pretzel. I just hoped no one else could see it. I had to put on a brave face, then it hit me. That was something my mother, Mrs. Norton, had said to me many times when I was feeling down. To be honest, now that I think about those times, I can't remember whether I was really feeling down, and if I was, why.

Up on the deck, I walked all the way to the glass railing with every intention of just taking a few minutes to look out at woods or the sky before returning to my room. The prospects of spending an afternoon with my thoughts wasn't that appealing, but the voices I heard below me seemed like an attractive alternative. The pool. Talking, squealing, and laughing. I needed that. I needed anything that wasn't just me right now. Seeing Mr. Bolden and Mike diving off the waterfall in the pool was a surprise. Not sure why, but I kind of had a feeling we wouldn't be allowed down there, but not only were we, we were everywhere. From up here, I saw everyone. Seeing the crowd, and hearing the music, sent me racing down the stairs. A quick check of my dresser found a bathing suit, a black bikini, just my size and style. No surprise now. All changed and ready. I headed down the same way we did last night for the hunt.

When I hit the deck, I heard Pam's voice summon me, "Larissa over here."

The girls had a row of chairs all to themselves. Each laying out as if they were getting some sun, a fruitless act for us. We can't tan, and we can't burn. Not that either was an option on this day. It was overcast. I found an empty lounger and dragged it over next to Laura, laid out my towel that just happened to be in my room, and stretched out. The four of us laid there with shades on. A rather normal picture if I had to say so myself.

The boys were in the pool doing what boys did, horse playing, but not just with themselves. Steve and Stan were right in the middle of it all, throwing a ball back and forth as hard as they could. Those two were probably the only others here that could do something like that with one of us, and not get hurt. Cynthia probably could, too. On the other side were Gwen and her witchy posse. That was what Laura and Apryl called them.

"Looking good ladies, getting some color?" Jack Nash commented as he walked past. It almost appeared as if he was leering at us.

Laura responded with a display of a single finger to point him in the direction he needed to go. Of course, it started out pointed up before she turned it sideways.

"Oh, that hurts," Jack whimpered as he walked on by.

"There goes the nice quiet day," muttered Apryl.

I wasn't exactly sure what she meant, though. He seemed to have moved on to annoy Gwen and the other witches. I continued to watch as the banter between them continued, almost like siblings.

Further around the pool, I saw the teachers I knew. *Wohoo Mrs. Saxon*, I said to myself, seeing her laid out like all of us. Next to her were Mrs. and Mr. Bolden. Seeing them like this made me wonder. They looked no older than we were. Physically, they might not be. There were others, teachers I assumed, that I hadn't met yet, and then there was the dog pack. Martin had introduced himself, but the others didn't, and then there was the mystery boy. He was tall, slender, and familiar; even though he was there with the other werewolves, there was a little separation between them. I had to know. His face, and body, were mesmerizing. I had to know who he was.

"That boy, over there next to the dog pack?" I asked, almost not believing I used that term. "Is he a werewolf?"

"Absolutely not," laughed Laura.

"Who is he?"

"I already told you, he is someone to stay away from," Laura reminded me.

"She needs to know," interjected Apryl. Now my curiosity was up. Was he dangerous in some way?

"Fine," resigned Laura with a huff. "But, you tell her."

"Not a problem," Apryl agreed smugly. "That is Nathan Saxon."

She leaned up and looked at me with a smile. It didn't take me more than a second to make the connection. "Mrs. Saxon's son?"

"Yep, now you know," Laura tersely said. She looked annoyed at the whole conversation, which made me even more curious.

"So, he is a witch," I concluded.

"Uh," Apryl said wide smiled and shaking her head.

"Jesus," Laura huffed. "He is a nothing. A blank. A big fat zero. Now, can you guys stop?"

Every protest she made just fueled my need to know more. Apryl was still looking at me and I shrugged my confusion.

Pam then leaned forward and across Apryl's chair, and whispered, "Mrs. Saxon was married to a mortal at one time, but he died. Nathan was her son, but he didn't inherit any of her abilities. He lives and goes to school here so she can stay in his life and help protect him."

"Oh," I said, leaning back in my chair.

"Laura is just a little touchy because Mrs. Saxon got on to her once when she caught her flirting with Nathan," blurted Apryl.

"Was not," she screamed and slugged Apryl on the arm. The impact sounded like a gun shot and got everyone's attention. Laura just waved at everyone, and they all picked up doing what they were.

We laid there. Four teens, assumed friends, enjoying the music and the sounds. Under my shades, I couldn't take my eyes off of Nathan. He was striking. Not in just a cute way, but in a not-another-like-him-in-the-world kind of way. A you only see in the movies kind of way. Modern day style, with the jawline of Rock Hudson or Cary Grant, and Brad Pitt's smile. Those images were better than what had been flashing through my mind. The reprieve was nice, but short lived.

"So, don't know which are your *real* parents?" I looked up and saw Jack Nash standing up on the edge of the pool right in front of me. He had that annoying smile on his face that I had seen on others before. I had seen it on him just yesterday morning. The one they make when they are trying to be funny, but are really being annoying, and they know it.

"What?"

That was when he pointed to his head, and I remembered what his niche was. That god damn bastard had read my mind, and worst yet, he had the nerve to say something about it. To say that burned me, would be calling the caldera of a volcano a little candle. It erupted in me, and Jack flew backwards into the pool with a large splash. I am not sure who was more shocked, me or Jack.

He sprang up and immediately looked toward Gwen and her posse and screamed, "Who did it?"

One by one, Gwen, Lisa, and Tera all denied it. Then Gwen pointed the suspicion in our direction. "It was probably one of them, you know how fast they are."

He turned toward us and leveled the same demand. "Who the hell did it?"

By now Mrs. Bolden, Mrs. Saxon and a few of the teachers were watching. "It wasn't one of them," Mr. Bolden said from the top of the waterfall where he was preparing to dive in. "If it was, I would have seen it. Jen, did you see anything?"

"No," Mrs. Bolden agreed, "and I was looking right at them."

Mrs. Saxon then looked back at the other witches. "Okay, we know we don't use our abilities against each other. No one is going to get into trouble. It just can't happen again, but I need you to tell me who did it."

As a group, they all shook their heads and looked as confused as everyone when I raised my hand.

12

Mrs. Saxon told me I wasn't in trouble when she asked me and Mrs. Bolden to come with her inside. In fact, she said it several times. Too many times for me to really believe it. Mrs. Bolden followed me closely and then put her arm around me as we walked into Mrs. Saxon's marble palace. I immediately looked around for a door to another bedroom, a place for Nathan to sleep. There wasn't one. Just the bedroom and bathroom I used up the stairs and her own room and the kitchen downstairs.

"Have a seat," Mrs. Saxon said as we passed the couch. I plopped down, but they continued past and into the kitchen, out of the range of my hearing. This wasn't good. I kept repeating that to myself over and over again, though I did pause a few times to find the positive to this. There wasn't one. We weren't supposed to use our abilities on each other. I knew that. I just wasn't thinking about that when I did what I did. Not that I really had a lot of control over it. What had happened kind of followed my rage. Whether or not I could have stopped it was an interesting question.

Both returned to the living area after several uncomfortable minutes of me being left alone with my thoughts. They stood in front of me with that posture that everyone knows well. Two parents about to deliver a scolding. I hoped for just a scolding, but expected to be ordered to leave.

"Larissa, how long have you been able to do that?" Mrs. Bolden asked.

"A while," was all I could say. I couldn't remember specifically when I realized I could move objects. I just knew I could, and I had really poor control over it. I even spent some time practicing at it, if you could call it that. Half the time, I couldn't even wiggle the object I focused on. Other times I could send it speeding across the room and through a wall, when all I was trying to do was make it wiggle.

"Do you do it by wishing or by pushing?" Mrs. Saxon asked with a great curiosity. She took a seat a cushion away from me.

"Hard to say," I said, and then tried my best to explain. "It just kind of happens." I failed.

"Okay, um... Today, with Jack. How did that happen? I know he said something to you."

"He said something about my parents," I answered and felt my jaw clench at just the thought of his statement.

"And?"

"It pissed me off. That's what!" I snapped, more heated than I had intended. "Then it happened," I explained, more controlled this time. Which, as stupid as it sounded, was really the best way to describe it. Then I looked up to Mrs. Bolden, who looked at me oddly, almost disconnected from the moment. A single finger over her lips. "I can't really explain it. Maybe you can help?"

"I can't," she said, very shortly, returning the finger in front of her lips as soon as she spoke.

"Larissa, she can't, because she can't do what you just did. Vampires aren't telekinetic," Mrs. Saxon explained.

I looked back up at Mrs. Bolden. Her head shook in agreement with Mrs. Saxon's statement. Then I collapsed backwards against the back of the couch. Partially in disbelief, but completely confused. "I don't understand."

"Neither do we," Mrs. Saxon said. "There appears to be more to you than we know."

Mrs. Bolden broke her silence. "Larissa. We have abnormal strength and speed and are immortal. A gift we can pass on when we turn someone, but that is it. We don't do anything like what you showed. At least, I haven't ever heard of anyone like you, and definitely never witnessed it."

Then there was a knock on the door, and Mrs. Bolden quickly walked to open it. While she did. Mrs. Saxon moved a cushion closer. "Like I said, you aren't in trouble, but we need to find out what your story is. It will help us figure out how best to help you and might even tell us more about what was going on when you came to us."

"I understand." I did. Both points were clear to me. A lot clearer than what I was. All this also cast more shadow and doubts over my parents. I mean the Nortons. When I had exhibited this ability, they had told me it was normal. Though, I can't remember ever seeing them do anything like it.

"Miss Norton, you are full of surprises," Mrs. Tenderschott cooed, coming in through the door. She wore a blue and white house dress with an apron, reminding me of a grandmother that might be baking cookies in the kitchen, but I knew her kitchen, and was quite sure it was not cookies. She joined me on the couch and sat close to me.

"Here, hold this." She pushed a large yellow crystal into my hand. She watched the object, as did Mrs. Saxon and Mrs. Bolden.

"Grip it tightly." She reached over and squeezed my hand around it.

Then it happened. A blue light emerged through my fingers, and Mrs. Tenderschott let out a loud giggle. Mrs. Bolden gasped, and her hand shot up over her mouth. Mrs. Saxon, for the first time since I had met her, looked on with a wide, pleased grin.

"That explains everything," declared Mrs. Tenderschott. Her hands reached over and opened my own. The light stopped, and she took the crystal back.

All three women shared a knowing look among themselves. Which I looked upon with a great deal of jealousy. It must be nice finding an answer. That was something I didn't know the feeling of yet. I was confused as hell.

"It does, but now what?" Mrs. Saxon asked, sitting on the other side of me.

Mrs. Bolden paced back and forth. Her bare feet slapping down on the marble. Each slap added to the tension I felt. I didn't know why, but I had a feeling this was bad, very bad, and I did the only thing I knew to do. "I am sorry."

"Oh no," Mrs. Saxon gushed. "There is nothing to be sorry about, Larissa. You are a very special girl."

"Very special," Mrs. Tenderschott said. Her face would break if she smiled any wider.

"Then that would mean," Mrs. Bolden started. She continued to pace back and forth.

"Yep," added Mrs. Saxon.

They were talking in their own special way, with little looks back and forth. Shared thoughts and purpose. A quick look at Mrs. Tenderschott told me she was aware of where they were going, too.

"We need to find out for sure." Mrs. Bolden stopped her pace.

"I agree," Mrs. Saxon said.

"Find out what?" I asked, completely perplexed about what the two or three knew that I didn't.

Mrs. Tenderschott took my hands in hers and stroked them slowly and calmly. I knew I was about to hear unwelcome news about how she was trying to comfort me. "Well, dear. That crystal detects magic. To be plain, it tells us who is a witch and who isn't. The color of the light tells us what your ability or strength is..."

"I am a witch!" I interrupted and leapt up from the couch.

"Yes Larissa. You are," Mrs. Saxon confirmed.

Mrs. Tenderschott cleared her throat and continued, "Yours was blue, which means you're a telekinetic. You can move things using the force of the universe, much easier than most. Chances are, you were a witch before you were turned into a vampire and kept your original ability."

"Larissa, if this is true. It might explain at least why you were being chased," Mrs. Bolden said. She pointed to the charm around my neck. "If you were a witch and maintained your ability when you were turned into a vampire, then you are now an immortal that can perform magic, which is an immensely powerful combination. Your blood charm may hold both abilities, and if someone were to drink it or were turned by you, they may become the same."

My hand instinctively reached up and caressed my charm. I noticed Mrs. Bolden did the same with hers, which was still red. I knew that meant she hadn't turned anyone. In fact, I hadn't run into anyone here whose charm was clear like my mother's, I meant Mrs. Norton. That made me wonder if I was who she turned, or if I wasn't her first. This was the first time I had thought about that. Maybe that was a bit naïve on my part. We never had the talk about where I came from. I just assumed I was theirs. It never came up if I was born, found, or stolen, I mean turned.

"I think we need to get some facts," Mrs. Saxon said. The wide grin was gone, and she was back to her firm but compassionate posture and expression.

"Well, knowing this now, I think I can whip up a magic tracker that will trace her magical heritage. We should be able to find that out," Mrs. Tenderschott let go of my hands and stood up, looking at both Mrs. Saxon and Mrs. Bolden for direction. Both seemed non-committal. Then she offered up another option. "That is, if you want to look at that. We did plan to make another attempt to find out what was after her today."

No! I cried inside. I wanted to make this next trip in my head about finding out who I really was. I turned to each, pleading with my eyes and expression. Mrs. Bolden appeared to understand and nodded toward me. I then focused my attention on Mrs. Saxon, who remained stoic, even while looking directly at me. I was about to plead my case verbally when she broke her silence. "I agree. The more we know about Larissa, the better."

"Then let's get to it. Come with me." Mrs. Tenderschott turned and walked toward the door. She paused before opening it, waiting for me to follow. It might have been a good thing too. When she opened the door from Mrs. Saxon's marble palace to the hallway, there was no hallway. We walked right into Mrs. Tenderschott's classroom.

"You are full of surprises, aren't you?" she asked as she headed toward her shelves.

"I guess so. I had no clue."

"That is not uncommon. What do you know about the process of turning someone?" she asked. So far, she had retrieved two vials of clear liquids and one bottle of some brown powder. The search continued, though, so it was obvious she needed more ingredients.

"Not much to be honest," I confessed, and took the same seat I had sat in during yesterday's visit. "My mother," I said without stopping to correct how I addressed her, "told me once it was a very personal and traumatic experience for both them and us, and I shouldn't take that action lightly. She said there is a level of guilt that stays with you forever about the life you took." As I remembered and said that, I felt a weird uneasiness as I wondered if she felt guilty about me.

"Well, I can see that," she said, her back to me. "But I was talking more about the physiological impacts of you when you are turned."

"No, I don't think so," I lied. I knew it quite well. I had been through it twice now.

"It's not a pleasant process, from what I have heard. You die, and it's a painful death. Only once you are dead can a vampire's venom infect the cells and start the transformation. That in itself can take a few hours to days to complete. It is said, some remember nothing from their life before. Everything just starts over for them. But that is just what they say. Every vampire we have had here in the coven remembered their previous life. You are our first that doesn't, but... We have had other students come here with repressed memories from traumatic experiences, and I helped them break through that wall that was hiding them. I think that is what we did yesterday. We broke through one of those walls and you saw a repressed memory. Now normally, I can't help you beyond that. It is up to you to figure out what the memory was, and what it meant. But you are lucky. If your biological parents were witches, I can trace that through your DNA. That might help us find a few more details to help figure out who they were." She returned to the table with another vial and another bottle. The vial was clear, but the bottle had a black dirt-like substance in it.

I watched in silence as she mixed the concoction. From what I could tell, it was pretty equal parts of the three different liquids. She put that over a burner and let it reach a boil. Then she added two spoons of the black God-I-hope-it-really-isn't-dirt substance, and let it boil again. The entire mixture turned a silvery grey, almost like some kind of liquid chrome. While it was boiling, she went to a cabinet in the back of the room and retrieved a relatively normal item, a coffee filter, which she spooned four full spoonfuls of a brown powder in and placed it on top of another vial, and then poured the boiling liquid over it. "Let it cool for a bit."

I smelled it and couldn't believe my nose. "Coffee?"

"Yep, not even a vampire would be able to swallow that stuff with its natural taste. The coffee covers that."

I sat there and watched steam rise from the liquid, wishing I had the power to will it cool. I wanted to get this over with; to find out who and what I really was.

"This won't be like the others. You will be there all on your own. It is a path that you, and you alone, must walk. Just let it flow around you. The answers will come."

"How will I know what's an answer?" I asked. Thinking this was going to be like some life-sized memory game where I would have to remember everything I saw so it could be interpreted later. Of course, that was because both of the last two attempts resulted in flashes of images that I had to analyze. I assumed this would be the same.

"You will know." She touched the side of the vial and then picked it up and handed it to me. "It's ready. Are you?"

"Yes." I agreed, but I wasn't sure if I meant it. My mind wasn't sure of anything. I took the vial. It was warm, but not hot. Not that it really mattered to me. I could have drunk it scalding hot with no risk of harm, but I wasn't sure if that would affect the effectiveness of the potion. Like with the other two, I sipped it at first, and after tasting nothing but black coffee, I downed the rest.

13

She was right. This was unlike the last two times. I didn't find myself in darkness. I found myself on a dirt path, covered by the shadows of the large magnolia trees lining it on either side. Their lemony fragrance was all around me. The path itself led up to a house. The same house I had seen in one of the images that had flashed in and out of my mind since my last visit to Mrs. Tenderschott. This was all awfully familiar, and I followed that feeling as it drew me toward the house. A fog of smeared greens and yellows covered the world outside the line of trees. As I came closer to the house, I noticed this same fog surrounded everything around the house, but it didn't make things eerie. This was a happy place. I knew it. I felt it. Everything about it was.

I reached the porch and bounded up the steps and almost skipped across the grey tongue-and-groove floorboards. As I did, I ignored the large swing that hung from the ceiling by two chains, the ornate banisters, and the Model-T just parked beside the house.

I threw open the screen door and screamed, "Mom!" The sound of a much younger version of my voice echoed through the interior of the house. Its sound was a sweet and warm song. All the floors were dark wood, and the walls were plaster, with wide wood trim that was painted white. A large sweeping set of stairs rose up the wall to the second floor. At the top, a stained-glass window created a kaleidoscope of color on the landing. A coat of rich, dark burgundy red paint covered every wall, most of which had paintings and photos hanging on them.

"In here," a voice called. I knew that voice, and I knew where she was. I could even smell dinner cooking.

I ran into the kitchen, and saw her, my mother. She didn't have to tell me who she was. I knew it in my heart at the first sight of her. She sat at the table as if she had been waiting for me all day. The chair on the other side of the table had been pulled out. I sat and looked across at the woman, who, like me, had red hair and ruby red lips. Her features made me believe I was looking into a mirror. The reflection was someone who was only a few years older than I was now. She smiled with her mouth, but her eyes were pained. She had been crying.

"I have been waiting a long time. What kept you?" she asked.

This had to be a dream, or a memory. Was there a time I was lost, or maybe came home very late? I couldn't remember. Not that I trusted my memories to all come back to me at this moment. I wasn't sure if that was how this would work or not.

"Larissa, are you okay?" she asked. Her words hesitated while she looked at me with a furrowed brow, tilting her head back and forth for a better look.

"Yes ma'am." My voice shook. It was a combination of excitement and nerves. I couldn't believe I was here, but was also not sure what here was.

"You seem odd. What happened? I expected you to come visit me much sooner after my death."

"You know you're dead?" I gasped as the weight of her statement and my own question hit me, knocking the air out of me. This wasn't an old memory that I had forgotten, and it wasn't a dream. This was here, and this was now.

"Yes Larissa, I do, but we really never die. We just transcend to a higher plane where we can help guide the next generation."

"Mom," I started, and then stopped out of the shock that remained from what she had said. It took a good stern conversation with myself to try to move past it and focus on what I was there for, which was problematic as it was.

I had questions, but I couldn't ask them without raising some questions for my mother, and those would lead to answers that might break her heart, which was the last thing I wanted to do right now. It was bad enough my heart felt broken sitting there, knowing who this woman was, but unable to remember anything. No tender moments we shared. There were no memories of Christmas or any of my birthdays with her. I didn't even remember a moment when we shared a silly laugh. Things everyone has with their parents. I remembered many of those moments with the Nortons.

"Larissa, what's wrong?"

Two tears streamed down, one from each eye, and I did my best to sniff out, "Mom, I don't remember anything about you."

She looked at me, concerned, and not as heartbroken as I sounded saying it. "Oh," she started. Then stopped and straightened up in her chair, and pulled at her grey dress, pulling out any wrinkles and folds. "Do you remember anything at all about your childhood, or is it just me you can't remember?"

"It's everything. I can't remember anything." I scanned the room around her for anything that might look familiar.

"Not even home?" she asked and appeared to be watching me as I looked around the room.

I shook my head.

She sat back in the chair. Her eyes, for the first time, weren't looking at me. They were staring a hole in the table. "A spell perhaps," she muttered.

"It's not a spell," I spouted, not really planning to reply, but my thought leaked out.

"How do you know?" she asked, with an inquisitive squint in her eyes.

I couldn't answer that. There was no way in hell I could tell her I was now a vampire, but there was no way to really answer that question, so I did what anyone would. I changed the subject, "Mom, what are we?"

"Oh." My mom looked around the room before her gaze returned to me. "Larissa, there is no easy way to say it, but you're a witch. Does it shock you to hear me say that?"

"No," I replied flatly.

"Good, because that is what you are, and you need to embrace it. It is who we are, and who we have been for generations," she lectured. "Don't ever forget it or take it for granted. You owe it to me, and the ones before us, to learn your craft."

"Yes ma'am," I said. "What is this place?"

She relaxed and leaned forward, took a few deep breaths, and said, "Well, I am not exactly sure what you did to get here. There are many ways to do it. Spells. Potions. Some can just drift into a trance and do it. No matter the way, they all lead to the same place, right here. A place where I exist in a place you remember me. A place where we can sit and talk, and I can guide you. I was older than you were when my own mother passed, and after a few days I made this journey to talk to her, and she awaited me in our home in Mobile. For you, I sit here waiting for you in our home in New Orleans."

"New Orleans?" I screamed.

"Yes, Larissa. New Orleans, where you grew up."

I didn't remember ever living in New Orleans. Hell, I hadn't even traveled that far south at all, from what I remembered, which, from what I was learning, was flawed. Then I had to think about it. We, I mean the Nortons, didn't travel around that much. We mostly just kept to Virginia and a few times I remember going to the coast in North Carolina, but those were rare.

A sickening spike stabbed through me like a bolt of lightning. Its source, the realization that I needed to stop considering myself a Norton. Who was I? "Mom, what is our last name?"

This again sent my mother flying backward against the back of her chair. "You don't remember your name?"

I had to open up to her about everything. Well, not everything. I couldn't tell her what I was now. "Mom, something happened. I can't really explain what, but I have forgotten everything. I don't remember ever growing up in New Orleans. I don't remember my name. I don't remember if I had a favorite doll or anything like that growing up. I don't even remember my birthday. It was only a few moments ago I found out I was a witch, and another witch helped me get to this place to talk to you. To find out who I am." Tears flowed as freely as the words.

"Well," my mother started, her hands fidgeted with each. "Then who you are with is a wise witch."

I had only known Mrs. Tenderschott for a few days and couldn't agree more.

"You need to develop a relationship with her. Learn from her. Not only to develop your craft, but to also learn how to deal with the world around you. I shouldn't have to tell you; they are not friendly to our kind."

"Mom, I know that."

"Good," she said, sounding relieved. "I am here to help you with all that, too. I always will be. Have her teach you how to come find me on your own. Once you know that, you will never be alone. You need to understand that."

"I do." I leaned across the table, my arms bracing myself up. "But Mom, who am I?"

She smiled pleasantly and leaned forward as well. Her hands reached across the table and grabbed my own. They were warm, but her expression changed. "They are so cold."

Her pleasant smile switched to a blank gaze. Both of her hands rubbed mine in an attempt to warm them up. I didn't have the heart to tell her it was fruitless. "It's fine, mom."

"You are Larissa Susan Dubois. You were born here, in this very house, on June 17, 1923. The next in a long line of witches that goes back centuries."

My mother kept going on about our family's history, but my mind stopped at the date. 1923. I wasn't sixteen. I wasn't even close. At the oldest, I kind of thought I was in my early to mid-twenties, remembering five to six years with the Nortons. I was almost a hundred. *God I was old.*

14

"Okay then," Mrs. Saxon said with her head down, and her forehead furrowed.

I had to admit there was a lot to think about. My mother had dumped a lifetime of details on me in the course of about an hour. It was odd to hear about my own life from my dead mother, and not be able to remember a single detail on my own. Nothing she told me stirred any memories. It was like reading a book, or watching a movie, about someone else's life. Beyond feeling unfamiliar, everything she told me was overwhelming.

"It's a treasure trove of information, but I think we need to do more research," interjected Mrs. Tenderschott.

"The archives," Mrs. Saxon said, and then threw her head backward.

"The archives," agreed Mrs. Tenderschott.

"The archives?" I asked.

"Larissa, the Council of Mages keeps a written record of the birth, family history, and death of every witch..." Mrs. Saxon started.

I interrupted. "Whoa wait. Time out. The what? The who?" I felt if anymore was thrown on me, I would drown. Of course, I did just ask two more questions that would probably receive answers. I better start holding my breath and learning to swim.

"Right," Mrs. Saxon started, and then looked down at me.

I smiled back nervously, wanting to say, *hey, new witch here, remember?* I held my tongue, feeling I was becoming troublesome as it was. I wasn't sure if she could read thoughts or not, and I watched for any hint that she knew what I was thinking.

"Hold that thought for a minute," she said, and I slouched down in my chair. "Edward," she called out loud. Before the sound of her voice vanished from the room, Edward appeared. While I may have gotten used to doors magically appearing, and rooms giving you everything you want, it was still odd to see a floating translucent head hovering in the middle of the room.

"Yes, Mrs. Saxon. How may I help you?"

"I need your help to research a family in the archives. 1920s. New Orleans. Last name Dubois. Can you do that?"

"Yes ma'am. It may take a bit as most archive searches do, but the covens in New Orleans are excellent at keeping written records, so the records should be complete," he replied, as polite as always.

"And I have another request," she started. Her voice wavered as she thought while talking. "I know there are some records on other covens. Can you check for any records of two vampires, by the name of Norton in the same area, about the same time?"

Edward's translucent eyebrows rose up, and he appeared to stare right past Mrs. Saxon. "Sure, ma'am, but I must remind you, vampire covens don't keep any written records." His eyes looked sideways at me, before he moved closer to Mrs. Saxon and whispered, "They prefer to hide in the shadows."

"Edward, don't worry. Larissa is not full vampire; she is part witch too. You are in the presence of Larissa Dubois. And I am well aware of the challenges. I am thinking there might be a reference about them around that time in one of our archives. Can you do that?"

"Yes ma'am. I will let you know when I find anything. Is there anything else?"

"No, that is all Edward. Thank you."

"Thank you, Mrs. Saxon. Have a good day." Edward turned and regarded me with a, "and a good day to you Miss Dubois." Then he disappeared.

The whole time she was giving Edward his orders, I sat there with my head going back and forth, following the conversation like I was watching a tennis match. Back and forth, back, and forth, and yet, like with tennis, I understood nothing they were talking about. All I knew about tennis was you tried to hit the ball over the net. At that moment, I felt like the ball.

"Okay, the council and the archives," Mrs. Saxon said as she sat on the table I sat at. Mrs. Tenderschott sat on the other side of the same table. The moment had just become as informal of an event as I had ever had with Mrs. Saxon. Her dead straight posture was more relaxed. "The best way to explain it is, there is a council that oversees everything that is magical to make sure no one misuses their ability."

Mrs. Tenderschott let out a little huff at this statement and Mrs. Saxon looked back at her.

"You probably need to know there are no stated, written, or spoken laws. It is more subjective on a case-by-case evaluation. Based on our experiences, we have some idea what gets their attention, and we can teach you how to avoid it."

"Witch hunters," grumbled Mrs. Tenderschott. This drew another look from Mrs. Saxon, a little more intense than the previous one, but she still appeared to agree.

"There have been a few times where they were, but you shouldn't worry about that. Anyways," Mrs. Saxon paused to see if there were going to be anymore interruptions. A rather irritated Mrs. Tenderschott sat back with crossed arms, and I made a note to ask her later what she meant by the witch hunter comment. "They keep written records of the birth, life, and death of everyone with any kind of ability at all. These are the archives. Some are kept by covens and contain the complete life histories of every member. Those witches that are not part of covens are detected by the sentries that work for the council. They record their birth and the death. Everything is in the central library that all covens have access to. If your family was part of a coven, we should be able to find a great deal more information about them. We may even be able to find out more about your other family, too. The more we know, the more we can help figure out what happened to them and what was after you."

"I know," I said. This was something they kept reminding me of. I just wasn't sure how much more self-discovery I could take. I was no longer the girl I thought I was when I walked in the door, and I wasn't who my mother thought I was either. "Now what?"

"Well, we give Edward some time to do his research, and I give you some homework." Mrs. Saxon hopped down off the table and held out her hands. I wasn't sure what she wanted, so I stood up and reached for hers. Before my hand reached hers, a book appeared on her flat palms, and she presented it to me. Spells and witchcraft 101 by Rebecca Saxon. "I don't expect you to spend your entire weekend reading, but I would like for you to go through the first chapter by Monday. I want to see how strong your ability really is with some simple spells. That will tell us how to proceed with you. In the meantime, why don't you go on back out and join the others and try to relax. I am sure you feel you have a lot to take in."

"Understatement of the century," I muttered before I realized it escaped past my lips. I gave both her and Mrs. Tenderschott a nervous smile and then stood up and walked toward the door.

"Should we?" I heard Mrs. Tenderschott ask from behind me.

"Oh yes." agreed Mrs. Saxon. "Larissa?" I turned around and saw both now standing. "There is something I want you to witness tonight. I will stop by and get you around eleven."

"Okay," I said, and then opened the door out to the hallway with my head already spinning and unable to handle anything else. Of course, that didn't stop anyone from laying more on me.

I rounded the corner to the main entrance, not paying a whole lot of attention to where I was going. My body was there, but my mind was in New Orleans. My face, on the other hand, was in neither of those places. It was now buried in the muscular, firm, and warm chest that I just slammed into. Two familiar hands gripped my shoulders and pushed me back at arm's length.

"You okay?" asked a voice from heaven. My head leapt back from New Orleans and rejoined my embarrassed body which had just ran smack into Nathan Saxon. He smelled of suntan lotion and chlorine. His arms were tanned, with a little pink on his shoulders.

"Yep, fine," I said, my eyes stared down at my own feet.

"You sure?" he asked. I looked up. That perfect smile was looking right at me. "You look like you just received some bad news."

"Nah, nothing like that." I pulled back from his grip, remembering the warning I had received about being around him. "It's just been a really strange, bad day. That is all."

"Jack?" he asked. "Don't let him get to you. He is just being a jerk. Every school has to have one of those." He laughed, and again that smile. Hearing his laugh soothed my embarrassment, but I still couldn't force myself to take more than a brief glance up at his face. I was afraid I might like it too much. Instead, it was the letter 's' in the tight Quiksilver t-shirt he wore that received most of my attention. A shirt that had conformed to the ripples of his body, which didn't help things much. I needed to stop looking.

"Yea, I guess," I replied, and immediately admonished myself about my witty repartee. "I can handle him on my own." I added, trying to add something of substance to the conversation.

"Obviously. I doubt he will mess with you again."

Good, I thought, but answered with a less arrogant, "Probably."

"Interesting reading for a vampire."

"Huh?"

"The book," he said, pointing to the book that I held against my chest. I let my hands and the book drop to my waist. His eyes didn't follow the book, they slowly traced its path down. That was when I realized I was standing there in just a bikini, and the guy, this guy, had just checked me out. If my heart still beat, I was sure it would have fluttered.

"Your mom's idea." I attempted to give him a smile, the one I had practiced for years in the mirror. Just slightly opened lips, enough to show teeth, but not those teeth. My body added in a little bounce on my feet as I did. A betrayal of the highest degree.

"Uh yea, I don't think we have been formally introduced. I am Nathan Saxon," he said, and held his right hand out toward me.

I pulled the book back to my chest and supported its hefty weight with my left arm as my right hand greeted his. It was warm and comforting. "Larissa Nort...," I started and then corrected myself, "Larissa Dubois, nice to meet you, Nathan."

"Nice to meet you too, especially nice to meet you while you are awake," he laughed. This time, it was a nervous laugh. He shoved both of his hands in the pockets of his swimsuit.

"Sorry about that. Not my fault. Kind of my mother's, and your mother's," I explained.

"No explanation needed. I have learned to expect pretty much anything around here. I was heading to meet my mother for lunch, so I better get going before she comes to find me. Don't be a stranger, okay?"

He moved on past me down the hall before I responded. I could sense each time he turned to look at me before I rounded the corner out of his view. I mumbled, "I won't," low enough that he wouldn't hear, but bit my own lip to keep me from saying anymore and then headed back out to the pool, trying to push any thoughts of Nathan's perfect smile out of my head. No matter what ever that was I felt, it couldn't happen. We are too different, and most importantly, it's not allowed.

The welcome Nathan gave me in the hall was a warm one. The one I received when I walked back up on the pool deck was Antarctica. Stares were plentiful as I went back to my lounge chair. Even my own were staring at me as I passed them and sat beside them, putting the book on the ground beside me, and sliding the sunglasses down back over my black eyes. All three of them kept staring as I laid back and closed my eyes under my sunglasses. Each of them knew how annoying the sensation of being stared at was, yet they were doing it. So, I said, "Yep, I am a witch too."

I said it loud enough for everyone around the pool to hear. The collective gasp in reply didn't come from those seated right next to me, but from those further around the pool. The tone of Gwen's voice was unmistakable in the collective sound. That made me smile.

15

"Okay, tell me again," requested Apryl.

"I was a witch that was turned into a vampire," I said flatly, for the I-had-no-clue-how-many-times now. Even Tera and Lynn had broken ranks to come over and sit with me for a while to talk about my big announcement. The feeling of Gwen's stare accompanied them. They were all beyond curious, and even started calling me a hybrid which at first, I didn't like, but then it grew on me. I wasn't one or the other. I was both. Maybe I was a Vitch. That sounded better than Wampire.

Lynn was interested because she was from Baton Rouge, and I guess felt some kind of kinship with me, a fellow Cajun. Of course, I hadn't told anyone how old I was, and the Louisiana that I would have known, if I could remember any of it, would have been a lot different from the one she knew.

Tera was more humorous about things and took the hybrid concept to the next level. Her question of what would happen if I turned werewolf, would they become a werewolf that lives forever that could perform magic, created an awkward silence everywhere. I wasn't exactly sure how that worked, and I asked Mr. Bolden if I would pass on all of my abilities to anyone I turned, and at first, he said I would, but then came back with a less definitive, "not sure, maybe," and looked toward his wife who just shrugged and smiled. That seemed to be the answer for most things where I was involved.

When an afternoon rainstorm chased everyone in, I sat in the window and cracked open the book Mrs. Saxon had given me. Holding it in my hands brought back the memory of running into Nathan. I couldn't get his smile, or the feeling of his hands on my shoulders, out of my head, but I needed to. My life was a hell as it was. Why make it even worse by entertaining some hopeless notion like a lovesick teen. What a complicated creature I was. A vampire, who was also a witch, who was also forever stuck in the teenage form with teenage hormones, even though I was almost a century old.

I forced the thought of Nathan out of my head, a challenging task, and opened the book to the first page. Having never seen a book on magic before, I didn't know what to expect. I half expected the first chapter to be titled, 'So you are a witch,' but instead, it was titled 'Illumination.' I flipped through wondering could there really be twenty-nine pages on how to turn the lights on, but looking at all variations, the explanations, and all the possible uses, I quickly realized there was more to this spell thing.

First, the words were just a mechanism to help you focus. The real magic was in visualizing and controlling the universe to make it do what you wanted to do. Take the simple act of lighting a candle without a match or a lighter. You look at the wick and concentrate on heating the surrounding air. The molecules in the air get hotter and hotter; moving faster and faster until eventually they dry out the wick to the perfect balance where the heat itself causes it to smolder. Then you let a little air into it, and poof, you have fire. The notes inside the book said this could take up to thirty minutes at first, but an experienced witch could do it in the flick of the wrist with the proper focus.

Great, I thought. I needed focus, the one thing my mind didn't have at the moment. The Nortons, the Dubois, that thing that chased me, and now Nathan Saxon had robbed all the focus out of my head. If only there was a spell for that.

I read through the first several pages and decided to give it a try. A candle appeared on my dresser. No longer surprised by such events anymore, I focused my eyes on the tall wax covered wick that stood up on the long white candle. Then I thought about warming the surrounding air, unsure how I would even know if the air was getting warmer, and then reminded myself about what I read was the most important step, focus. Ugh. Warmer and warmer, I thought about it, waiting for any signs that the wax covering the wick had started to melt. What I wanted to see was a waft of black smoke coming from it, telling me that it had started to smolder.

Minutes passed, and there was nothing, but I kept reminding myself what the book said. It could take thirty minutes for the first time. Thirty minutes. Thirty minutes of staring at a wax covered wick, waiting for smoke. This sounded like an odd torture instead of magic. I got up out of the window seat and walked closer to the candle, keeping my focus on the wick, thinking of fast-moving molecules of air warming everything they touched. Then I started thinking about fire itself, white hot fire. The wick remained unchanged. I let several other minutes pass and even stepped closer, never taking my eyes off the wick and my thoughts of warming the surrounding air.

After another several minutes, I was curious and passed my hand over the top of the wick. The air was cool, like the rest of the room. It wasn't working. The only thing increasing in temperature was my frustration, but continued to try, now adding the word to it, "Luxos."

I looked over at the clock and realized I was approaching twenty minutes of this and passed my hand over it again, and air was still cold. "Well damn it!," I screamed and slammed my hands down on my side. Just then, a huge flash lit the top of my dresser on fire.

"Oh shit!" I ran to the bathroom and grabbed a towel to snuff out the fire. The top of the dresser was blackened and even bubbled in some areas. Next to the damage was the candle, still untouched by fire, standing clean.

Over the next few hours, I lit the top of my dresser on fire three more times, the towel itself twice, and a few other random objects, including the book of spells at least once. Sometimes with the word, of course I was just repeating it over and over until something happened, but other times without. Each time, it was taking less time before my fire bug kicked in. I kind of felt like Drew Barrymore in that old movie.

I still hadn't managed to light the top of the candle. Each time after I put the fire out, the damage repaired itself in the room. So, there was no evidence of my incompetence. Then one time, I felt something, or more saw something. I saw the particles moving around as I concentrated. I saw them change color. They were a large mass all around the room, which explained why I was setting random things around the room on fire. In my mind, I imagined reaching out and pulling them together into a tight ball right on the top of the wick and whispered, "Luxos." Voila! The mass created a white spark on top of the candle, and then there was light. I flopped back on my bed and kicked my legs up in the air. By this time, it was already dark outside, and I knew where Apryl, Laura, and Pam would be. I had to show them.

I ran up the stairs and out onto the deck. Halfway up I heard the twang of country music. Going out on a limb, I guessed it was Jeremy's night to choose. I wasn't much of a fan of country music, but I could tolerate it for one night a week. Laura told me it wasn't a music party every night. Sometimes it was old board games, or movies. We just had to keep things down for those that were sleeping below us. I stepped out and was treated to the scene of Jeremy in a flannel shirt, jeans, boots, and hat, doing some kind of boogie to the music. Mr. and Mrs. Bolden tried to keep up, while the rest sat in the chairs and sofas watching and laughing. During one of his Jeremy's spins, he saw me and snapped to attention. "Attention! Witch on deck." He tipped his hat at me and picked up his dance right in rhythm with the song.

"Hey witchy," Mike called from his seat. Laura and Pam stood up and gave me a hug.

"How you holding up with all... this?" Brad asked and pointed at me, twisting his hand back and forth. Everyone looked in my direction, waiting for the answer. Even the Boldens stopped dancing for the moment. Jeremy watched for my response, but it appeared nothing would keep him from his groove.

"Well, it's a lot to absorb learning who you really are. I still have many questions," I said, eyeing the needles on a branch of a miniature fir tree in the planter next to Mike. "But there are some advantages." I threw my hand out, proclaimed "Luxos," and just like that, the end of the branch flickered to a flame.

Everyone who was seated jumped up. Mr. and Mrs. Bolden gasped. Jeremy dropped his hat mid-heel click. That wasn't all he dropped. His jaw dropped too, joining the others.

"Neato!" exclaimed Mike. He held his hand over the flame and watched it dance. Then I pulled my second trick, one I had become really good at with all my practicing. I pulled back my hand, pulling the particles apart again, snuffing out the flame.

"Well, that settles it. You are a witch," Apryl concluded.

"Not just a witch," started Laura. "A witch with style. Gwen is going to freak. She is no longer queen bee around here."

"She is still queen B," snickered Apryl.

"Girls!" Mrs. Bolden admonished. She looked like a disappointed parent.

"Sorry Mrs. Bolden," Apryl and Laura both said.

"So, what else can you do?" Brad asked. He retook his seat, which was just a single chair.

"Just that. It's only my first day, but the next chapter covers how to give someone a sense of style," I joked with a nod to his slacks and sweater ensemble that would have fit right in during the yuppie hell of the eighties. A nervous laugh made its rounds through the others. Brad, being the butt of the joke, smiled back at me with a point. "Actually, I like your style." I smiled, and he bowed his head.

"Well, join in with the dancing if you wish, or you can sit here with us and laugh at Jeremy making a fool out of his self. It's his choice tonight, but we will break out a movie later on," offered Mike. Apryl scooted over on the sofa she was sitting on to make room and patted the cushion.

I held up my hand to let her know that wasn't necessary. "Maybe later, I won't be staying long. Mrs. Saxon is picking me up for something around eleven." When I left my room, it was almost ten 'til, but I had to show someone. What I said drew more curious looks than it did when I set the tip of the branch on fire. Everyone, except the Boldens, scurried for the chairs closest to me. Some sat on the arms of the furniture, while others used the edges of the planters as temporary seating.

"She is letting you go to it?" shrieked Laura.

"Go to what?" I asked, befuddled, which was becoming an all too familiar feeling.

"Lisa's ascension?" asked Pam.

"Her what?" I asked and then watched everyone who had been leaning in close lean back as the sound of high heels approached from behind.

"Larissa, you ready?"

Apryl reached up, and gave me a hug, and whispered into my ear, "Tell us all about it when you get back."

16

"Any word from Edward?" I asked, as I followed Mrs. Saxon down the stairs. I was eager to hear anything, even the smallest piece of information about my past, in hopes of adding structure to the puzzle pieces that danced in my head.

"Not yet. It may be a few days, but I am confident he will find some useful information. In the meantime, we have a lot to catch you up on."

It was a good thing I was following her, or she would have seen my expression droop. This had become beyond excruciating.

We exited out through my room, and I followed her down the stairs and down the hall where the classrooms were. We walked for a long time, passing door after door. They all looked alike. As far as I knew, we were passing the same door every time. That was when the thought hit me. Like the rooms, this entire building could grow and shrink as needed. I could walk for days and never hit the end of the hall. Whoa, my mind was blown, or I thought it was.

Mrs. Saxon finally stopped at a door and placed her hand on the handle, and sternly instructed, "Just stand with Mrs. Tenderschott and watch. Say nothing. Understood?"

I nodded, and she opened the door. A large black curtain hung just beyond the door, covering the opening. Mrs. Saxon pushed through, and I followed. Now my mind was completely blown.

The room was all black. Not dark, but black. The walls of the circular room were still ornate wood, but black. They towered up for what seemed like a hundred feet to skylights where the moon shone in brightly. Candles floated in the air around the perimeter. Each of them were already lit, so I was too late to help with that. The floor was all black except for these strange symbols that were drawn around the center in bright white.

After I walked through the curtain, Mrs. Saxon left me in the creepiest place I had ever been. Not that I had ever visited a haunted house or anything like that, or at least I don't think I have. If I had, I am sure they wouldn't hold a candle to this place. I walked around for a bit, staying to the sides. Almost afraid to walk too close to the creepy symbols and figures drawn on the floor. It was just a feeling, something I couldn't explain. Then, for a moment, I stood right under one of the floating candles and thought again about a haunted house. Throw in a few floating ghosts and a couple of pumpkins and this would be perfect. The thought brought a nervous giggle.

"Larissa," a familiar voice called from the other side of the room. It was Mrs. Tenderschott, my assigned chaperone for the night. She motioned for me to join her, and I did, but not without a little apprehension. As I approached Mrs. Tenderschott, I noticed she wasn't dressed in her normal colorful and expressive attire. This wasn't even just a toned-down conservative outfit for a special occasion. She was in a gown and hood, which of course were black.

"Stand with me through this. I will try to explain what I can, when I can." She then handed me something she was holding in her hand that I hadn't seen before. "Put this on." I took it and let it fall free and then slipped into my own black robe and hood.

"Oka..." I started to respond, but she abruptly shushed me, and then quickly turned back to face the center of the room. Feeling uncomfortable and wondering what I had just walked into, I did the same and bit my lip.

If her reaction wasn't enough to give me more than a strange vibe, what happened next took it from strange to downright frightening. All the witches, and I do mean all the witches, other than Mrs. Tenderschott who stood next to me, entered through the black curtains in a single file. Each wore a black robe with a matching hood. The students entered first, followed by what I assumed were the teachers, several I hadn't met yet. The line rounded the room and walked right past me. Most kept their eyes straight ahead, but Gwen spotted me and gave me a look of sheer disgust.

After they completed a lap around the room, the students went to the center inside the strange drawings and knelt, forming a ring. Lisa moved to the center of the ring. The teachers followed suit and knelt behind the students. I freaked when I noticed how much what I was watching matched every sacrificial cult scene I had ever seen in the movies. They started chanting. The shock of the sound would have taken my breath away, if I breathed. The only thing missing was a pentagram in the center. As far as I knew, the odd drawings in white served the same purpose.

"This is an ascension ceremony," whispered Mrs. Tenderschott. "Witches have some power, but they don't gain their full strength until midnight on their eighteenth birthday. That is when we ask for their ancestors to gift them with their powers, if they feel they deserve it."

The rhythmic chanting continued. From the best I could tell, it was made up of six words or phrases that were repeated over and over again, like the Satan's favorite round. The volume of the chant swelled with the phrase, starting soft and becoming louder until they started over soft again. There was a hypnotic quality to it. I assumed this was how you asked the ancestors, and with Lisa in the middle, it had to be her ancestors they were addressing. What I didn't know was how many times you could ask, and how you knew when they answered. Did a voice say yes or no?

Over and over again, they chanted while I watched. Even Mrs. Tenderschott had joined in, but she wasn't the only one. Other voices had joined the chant. Both male and female voices, but I didn't see anyone else here. The voices echoed up above me, and out of nowhere, a light breeze whipped around the room. It gained strength on each pass around, rustling the fabric of the robes we all wore. The flames on the candles flickered, and a single ray of moonlight exploded through the sky light in the ceiling of the room. It illuminated Lisa, and no one else.

I stood there, with the breeze buffeting against me, pass after pass, watching Lisa, there in a spotlight created by the moon. It gave her a luminescent appearance, and every once in a while, I thought I saw something dancing around her, but dismissed it as just dust whipped up by the wind, and my mind that had been through quite a bit lately playing tricks on me. The dust took shapes. Shapes of people, people that floated in the air and whirled around her. They moved out around and above everyone. Gwen and the others ducked their heads as they passed over. The teachers didn't flinch as the shapes moved through them. When the shapes howled a painful and demonic sound, the room shook. None of the circle of witches flinched, but I sure the hell did. I jumped and gasped, which seemed to get the attention of one creature, causing it to rush toward me. It fell short as it smacked into some kind of barrier above the drawings on the floor. It, and it's frightening skinless skull face and hollow eyes, attempted to break through, but couldn't. Each attempt caused it to howl and screech. I put my hands over my ears to block the horrifying sound. That did nothing. The sound of it, and the dozen or more of its friends that swirled around the rings, created a deafening noise. The sights, the sounds, all scared the hell out of me. I was no longer wondering what I had walked into, and instead was concerned if I was going to walk out. I tried to look through the mass of demonic visions to Lisa. She sat there, still, illuminated by the moon. The other girls around her fought to stay still, but the teachers never moved.

More of the creatures smashed into the barrier as they spun around. They had to be after me. I felt it, and I slid to my side, putting myself behind Mrs. Tenderschott. I felt her hand reach back and grab my own. She didn't hold it, but gave it a quick squeeze. An attempt to pass on comfort that completely failed.

The chanting, the crying of the beasts, the howling of the wind, and the screeches rattled my bones and the walls. Dust danced everywhere in the vibrations. This had to be a no. There is no way this was how her ancestors said yes. I actually wondered if Lisa would survive. Then, everything, the sound, the creatures, and the moon beam shot like an arrow into Lisa, and it was over. There was no more breeze, no more chant, and no more dust. Just as they came in, the teachers stood up and filed out, with the students following them. Lisa was last.

From behind Mrs. Tenderschott, I tried to look at each of the girls' faces. They were terrified, like I was, chins quivering, and tears flowing. Gwen was the worst of all. Her make-up smeared down her cheeks and her entire body trembled. Lisa, on the other hand, was actually smiling.

I held it together until Lisa left through the curtain. Then I fell to my knees, thudding on the hard black stone floor. Tears had been streaming down my face, and I hadn't even realized how badly I had been crying until that moment.

"You're okay," Mrs. Tenderschott said as she knelt down next to me. She draped an arm around me and pulled me close.

"What the hell was that? Will Lisa be okay?" I squeaked between sniffs.

"Yes, dear, she is fine. The answer was yes."

"Yes? That was a yes?" I asked, wiping my nose on the sleeve of my robe as I tried to stand.

Mrs. Tenderschott nodded.

"But those creatures... that noise... That..." I beseeched her for answers.

"Larissa, magic is both good and dark. True witches find a balance between the two, and control it, but not all are an equal balance and lean more one way than the other. You know what Lisa is, right?"

I nodded, kind of already seeing where this was going.

"Then you shouldn't be surprised to hear she has to tap into one side more than the other, and that side had to be provided to her. So..." Mrs. Tenderschott's eyebrows raised under her hood.

"That is what I saw? The dark magic coming to her?" I asked, almost afraid to know the answer.

She nodded and helped me up to my feet, and we started to walk out together, but she stopped. "Many ascension ceremonies involve dark magic, and I have been part of more than I could ever count. They are happy rites of passage, seeing a witch come into her own, and fully joining our community. But, I have never seen the dark entities react like they did tonight." She turned and looked right at me, stunned. "I believe they felt you, and knew what you were. If it wasn't for the runes, they probably would have come out after you."

"The runes?" I asked with a heap of curiosity while wondering if I needed to apologize for causing an issue.

"The writings on the floor, they are called runes; magical charms of protection that established a boundary that they can't cross. A kind of magical fence," she said as she walked around the room, stopping at each one of them pointing each out of the floor. "You were never in any real danger. Mrs. Saxon put these here herself. She is a powerful witch, and these are powerful runes. So pretty unbreakable."

"Runes, charms, spells, ascension..." I rolled my eyes. My mind had started to settle down from what it had just experienced, which created space for the constant feeling of confusion to set in again. Of course, I was starting to get used to that feeling.

"You have a lot to learn," she said as she returned to my side. A single brush of her right hand along the top of my head pulled the hood back. "Let's get this thing off of you. It's not you." Then she paused and looked down at herself, and yanked hers open and slid out of it, exposing a bright red dress that hung down to her ankles. "It's not me either," she laughed.

Seeing her return to herself brought a smile to myself, even in this room of darkness. I felt better as soon as my robe was off, leaving me in my jeans and t-shirt.

"Better?" she asked.

"Better," I responded joyfully.

She took my hand, and we walked out through the black curtain. Just passing through, I felt my spirit lift, though one image stuck with me. The expression on the girls' faces.

"So, all witches have to go through that?" I asked when we closed the door behind us.

"Yes," Mrs. Tenderschott started. The inquisitive look on her face told me she shared the same thought I did. Then she said, "You are a big mystery, aren't you?"

I am sixteen and will forever be trapped in the body of a sixteen-year-old, but I am almost a hundred years old. Have I already been through this, or will I never have the chance?

17

"Come on! You have to tell us!" Apryl screamed. She all but leaned over in my face when she did it. I got it. I was the spy, unofficially, since I never agreed to go and report back to any of them. They, all of them, looked at me like it was some sort of obligation. Probably because I was one of them.

"It's because you are one of them, isn't it?" Brad accused, which was rather shocking and ironic, considering what I was thinking. Not that it wasn't true, it was completely true. I was a child of two worlds, three in reality. Those worlds didn't seem to be getting along at the moment. The shock was in who it came from. Brad had always seemed so prim and proper, above all this petty teenager stuff.

"Look, just like I wouldn't tell them about anything we do, I can't tell you about this. It is very personal to them," I explained, or tried to. They met it with a chorus of sighs and people turning their backs on me. Even those I thought my closest friends, of course it had been just a few days. The movie they had paused turned back on, and attention went right back to that. I didn't exist to them, and to be honest, I was okay with that.

Actually, that was stupid for me to even think that. I wasn't okay with it. I still didn't remember anything from my life pre-Nortons. That is what I had decided to call the life I couldn't remember. What I could remember was post-Nortons because I had to assume they were the ones that turned me, and at this point I wanted to assume they did so for some righteous reason. I couldn't really bring myself to accept anything else. I remembered my life with them. It was great. We were a family, and I felt like I belonged. That was something I needed to feel, more than well... I can't really say air itself, but let's just say it is a necessity, and now I sat here, not belonging.

Mrs. Bolden stroked my hair as she passed the chair I was in, and sat in the one closest to me, which had appeared to be no-man's-land before. She smiled at me gently, with almost compassion in her black eyes. "Give them some time," she whispered just above the sound of the air moving around us, but just loud enough for me, and only me, to hear. "You did what was right." The hand that had stroked my hair reached over and gripped my own. I wondered if she meant it, or if this was all just one of the reactions she and her husband tried to teach us to appear more human.

My isolation lasted most of the night. Make that all night. I don't believe Mike letting me know, "Sun's coming up," as he walked by was a sign of forgiveness. Back down in my room, I didn't have many choices available. Either watch something on the television, or flip to chapter two in Spells and Witchcraft 101. I hoped it was something more than how to set things on fire. I felt I had that pretty well mastered already. I mean, look at what I had managed to do with the circle of friends I thought I had. A smoldering pile of something.

Chapter 2, Moving the World. That was quite a lofty title for how to move an object, or telekinesis. Lucky for me, I kind of already felt I had this understood. Exhibit number one, Jack Nash. Of course, there wasn't a lot of control there, it was more of an outburst. If I could learn to control it, that would be great. Past attempts never worked out too well. The tally, or at least the tally I could remember was, about a half a dozen glasses, two picture frames, a lamp, and a ceramic figurine that wasn't really the object of what I was trying to move, but the picture frame hit it and knocked it off my dresser. I told my mother, Mrs. Norton, that it fell when I pushed a drawer closed too hard.

The first few pages of the lesson matched the previous chapter. All about visualization. Where before it said we needed to visualize the air getting warmer, now I was to imagine a hand pushing to push an object, or a lasso or hand grabbing to pull back. That sounded simple enough, and being I already had some experience, I didn't feel I needed to read the remaining twenty-three pages and closed the book. So, which to try first?

I looked around the room for an opportunity and spied the closet door that I left open after I came down from the deck. This should be easy, I thought to myself, and visualized a hand pushing it closed while repeating the word suggested in the instructions, "Mot," which was Latin for move. The door didn't mot or move. It didn't even budge. It moved more when I created a breeze by closing the hallway door. Another attempt, and not a creak. The next attempt I decided to more than visualize it, and held my hand out, moving it as I visualized. "Mot." Nothing. Not until I slammed my hand down in frustration. Then the door slammed shut enough to rattle the mirror hanging on the wall. Well, I would call that a partial success.

Now, for my second trick, I will open it. I envisioned a rope lassoed around the door handle. In my mind, I gave it a little yank, "Mot." Nothing. A frustrated yank, and I fell off the bed, dodging the door handle that flew back at me and embedded itself in the wall behind my bed. Maybe a little less of a success. The door then fell in on the floor. My yank had broken the hinges. Of course, in just a few moments, everything was back the way it was supposed to be. If only my old room had been like this.

Control. I had to find a way to control things. Somewhere between nothing happening and pulling the place apart would have been a nice happy medium. Of course, control was the one thing that didn't seem to be around much at the moment. My control and focus meter was on empty.

I made a few more attempts to close the closet door and realized something rather important. The level of focus and concentration needed to walk the fine line needed to make things work was more than taxing. I felt a small amount of respect for Gwen and her posse, not that I would even admit it. I gave it one more try with my concentration on the edge of exhaustion and the image of an invisible hand pushing on the door in my head. As the imaginary fingers pushed forward, I felt the muscles in my own forearm flex, and the door moved. It didn't close, but it moved, and strangest of all, I felt it. I felt the wood on my fingertips. I felt the resistance of it against my hand as I pushed. The book slid off the bed with a thud when I collapsed backward against my pillow, both exhausted and elated. Like when I learned to light a candle, I wanted to show this to someone too, but I was fairly sure no one wanted to see this. Instead, I rolled over on the bed, disappointed, and looked out the window at the overcast day. The perfectly beautiful overcast day.

I strolled out to the pool, not exactly sure why I was out there, other than it was just where everyone was. As soon as I emerged out the door, that extra feeling we all had told me every set of eyes was now on me, and not a one of them was welcoming. Everyone was separated out like yesterday, with only one exception. The empty lounger I had occupied was no longer next to my friends. It wasn't even close to them. Instead, it was now halfway around the pool, about as far away from both sides as possible. I knew I was something different, and now I knew what it was called, a leper.

Instead of making any attempt to talk to Apryl or Laura, I went the other way, walking past the invisible line that separated them from the witches. Why I thought this would be better, I wasn't too sure. The contempt filled coughs and murmurs of "fake witch" and "blood sucker" didn't hurt. I knew they were aware I could hear the whispers as I walked by.

Only when I walked past Mr. and Mrs. Bolden did I receive a friendly greeting of "Hello Larissa." Even Mr. Markinson and Mr. Stevens, the two faculty werewolves, welcomed me with a "good day."

Of course, their students were slightly less polite, with the wolf whistles as I walked by, and a "looking good there stiff," from Martin, but I would take it. He stood on top of the waterfall, water dripping off of him. Nice looking and fit. I was sure all the long runs they go on at night made sure of that. An overly white smile glistened against his tanned skin. Unlike the witches, the werewolves didn't seem to have any animosity toward us, contrary to what Mrs. Saxon had said regarding vampires and werewolves. They didn't seem to have any toward anyone, even Gwen and her posse. Just some good-natured ribbing they sprayed around at everyone. But it was something in how he looked at me. Like I was a piece of meat.

"Down boy. You smell like a wet dog," I shot back as I sat down on the chair.

"Oh, that hurts," he said just before Rob, the second member of the dog pack, shoved him into the pool and then leaped in on top of him. If I had to put up with this for the rest of the day, I could tolerate it. At least it wasn't the stares of evil daggers. I sat back and placed the headphones that just happened to appear on the dresser, over my ears and turned on the music and closed my eyes. It was nice to just be out of the room, and out here.

My choice of music for my listening pleasure, jazz. I was from New Orleans, so I might as well explore my newly found roots. It wasn't bad. I could learn to like it. I was about three songs in when I heard a scrap of metal on concrete over the music, which I had extremely loud. That sound could only mean one thing. Someone had forgiven me. The only question left, who was the first. I sat up and opened my eyes, completely prepared to deliver some cheesy smug one-liner like, "I am ready to accept your apology," but instead I realized there was a second, unconsidered explanation for the sound. I scrambled to yank the earphones out of my ears. I didn't mean to send them skipping half-way across the pool.

"This seat taken?" Nathan asked, smiling down at me with that perfect god-like grin framed in his granite like features.

"Ah, yea... I mean no... I mean yea," I stammered. Not exactly sure what to do with my hands, they just waved around as erratic as my words. I stopped, didn't take a deep breath since I don't breathe, and tried again, with my hands clamped to the edge of the chair. "I mean, it is now. You took it." Inside, a little voice was telling me it was time to go inside, but so much of me wasn't listening.

He laughed and laid out a towel on the chair. Even overcast, the sun glistened off of every ripple of his muscular frame. The heavy dose of suntan oil that covered him just added to it. My black eyes were lost in his bottomless blue eyes as he laid back, and a gentle breeze blew a few strands of his hair out of place.

I wasn't sure how much time had passed since he laid down, a few seconds, or weeks. Time appeared to stand still while I was lost in his presence. When I finally realized what I was doing, I forced myself to settle back, and tried to act normally, which meant reaching up for my headphones, the headphones that were now floating in the pool. My empty hands lowered, and I laid back, closing my eyes to die a million deaths from embarrassment.

Across the pool, Gwen was giving me a complete death glare. I didn't need the ability to read thoughts to know what she was thinking. On the other side, my friends were doing their own gawking.

"So, what's it like? Being both a vampire and a witch?" Nathan asked. I turned my head to look at him. He was lying there with his eyes closed.

"Confusing," I said, and, using something I had picked up in Mrs. Bolden's class, I forced out a small amount of air with the words to produce my best attempt at a sigh.

"I bet. I figure you are kind of like me, and don't feel like you fit in anywhere. Gwen will never let you join her little club, and I imagine you are getting some grief from your tribe."

"You could say that."

"Don't be too impressed. I didn't reach that conclusion after a sociological study of the cliques in this place." He smiled widely, reminding me of what heaven felt like. "You were sitting over here by yourself, an easy conclusion."

Duh, it was. "I guess that makes this misfit island," I said, and then laughed after I realized how stupid it sounded.

The good news was, Nathan agreed, and laughed as well, which settled my thoughts and nerves. This was stupid. Why was I feeling this way when I knew I shouldn't, and more importantly couldn't? Then I remembered, I was almost a hundred trapped forever in the emotion and hormone driven body of a teenager. A teenager that couldn't feel her breath quicken or pulse race in response to being around someone she found attractive. Okay, make that mesmerizing. That was too weak of a word. The lack of physical sensation was made up for by the loops and laps my brain made.

"So, just curious. What was the ultimate betrayal with your tribe?"

"Well, I wouldn't be their spy," I said flatly.

"They wanted to know about the witch's secret handshake and all, and you wouldn't tell."

"Kind of. I attended Lisa's ascension ceremony, or whatever it is called, and I wouldn't tell..." I stopped as Nathan sat straight up, startled. "What?" I asked, just as startled, and now more than a little worried.

"You can stop there," he said. The joyful bounce that had been in his voice was gone. "My mother once explained what it was to me, but wouldn't tell me anything about what really happens. She said it was very personal to those participating. You can never tell anyone about it. If that is what they are mad at you about, let them be mad."

"Okay," I said, not sure what else to say.

"Don't worry about all of them. Everyone here is pretty nice. Once you get to know them, they will come around. Until then, you have me. Any time you need to talk I am here."

If my heart beat, it would have fluttered at hearing that. When he reached his hand toward mine, it would have skipped a beat. I pulled my hand back, remembering the warnings, "Sorry, it's dangerous, and I heard your mother doesn't want us really around you." I noticed at that moment, every set of eyes were on us, even the instructors. Each watching not out of curiosity, but a collective worry that you could have cut with a knife.

He reached further and grabbed my hand before I could pull back. Something that shouldn't have been possible, but he caught me off guard while my attention was on everyone else. Their attention was on me.

"I think I am safe. You seem different from the others."

I yanked it back in a panic, just before a splash of water hit us both. A football followed, and I caught it before it hit Nathan.

"Nice catch." I tossed the ball to Nathan.

Martin hopped up out the pool and smugly asked, "Did I splash you? Are you melting?" Then he shook off like a dog, spraying water on everything within ten feet of him. I glared back at him and bared my fangs with a hiss.

"I got some of those, too. Want to see?"

Nathan stood up, football in hand. "Slow down there. Martin, catch!" He tossed the ball toward the center of the pool, and Martin jumped in, catching it with a big splash. "I'll be back," Nathan said, and then went and joined the dog pack in the pool.

I sat there, and pretended not to watch for a little while, but I watched. I couldn't help myself, and from what I saw, he couldn't either. After each throw, after each catch, there were little looks in my direction. I was intent on sitting there the entire day waiting for his return to the chair next to me, but life always had other plans, and this time those plans arrived in the form of Mrs. Tenderschott standing at the door waving for my attention.

The path to see what she wanted was littered with more looks and comments, but I didn't care. I felt the best I had in days. What I did care about, though, was the hitchhiker I picked up when I left the pool deck. I could smell Gwen's fruity perfume from over a hundred yards away, but didn't need to this time, since she was just a few steps behind me. I hoped this was just a coincidence, and she had had too much sun for the day and was heading in. When she stepped inside and started with, "Hey you soulless wench," I knew it wasn't my lucky day.

"I want to get two things straight with you." She grabbed my shoulder and spun me around; stronger than I expected her to be. I stared right at her with a grim expression and a flat smile. I had seen myself do this before in a mirror, and with my black eyes, I looked evil. She looked back, unshaken. "First, you are not one of us. So whatever illusions you have in your head about being one of us, it will never be. You shouldn't have been there last night at all."

I interrupted, "Mrs. Saxon invited me."

"I don't care," she warned with the wag of a glossy red fingernail. "It's not for you, and second, stay away from Nathan."

She stewed for a few seconds before I asked the question that hung between us, "Or what?"

"You know the rules. All of us, especially a blood sucker like you, are to stay away from him," her voice trembled.

"Oh, like I haven't heard that before." I turned to leave, but she grabbed me again, and this time I spun around on my own, and hissed, "If you like that hand, you might want to take it back."

"Watch it, I would hate for a wooden stake to fly into you," Gwen fired back, with a surprising amount of venom. Before now I thought she was just a harmless little, well, witch, but now I knew to be wary of pushing her too far.

"Larissa, come on," Mrs. Tenderschott called from the hallway.

"Saved, for the moment," spat Gwen.

She turned and pranced back out to the pool, and I went to join Mrs. Tenderschott, who greeted me with, "Young Mr. Saxon is rather dreamy, isn't he?"

18

Mrs. Tenderschott giggled like a schoolgirl for a few steps before she noticed I wasn't laughing with her. Nothing about my little conversation with Gwen was funny, and she was more than a little on my bad side. Of course, I really had done nothing to her, other than just be me.

With a pull here and a tug there, Mrs. Tenderschott pulled herself together and out of her attack of the giggles. "Well... now that we know what you are, I have an idea. I want to try to see if we can figure out what was chasing you, if you are up for it?"

"Sure," I reluctantly agreed. Each of my so-called trips took something out of me. The more I found out, the more questions I had, and the more it made me emotionally frazzled. This was one we had to figure out. I had kind of hoped something Edward would find would answer this, but he hadn't come back yet.

"Come on in," she said, leading me into her classroom, or what I had started to think of as the mad scientist's laboratory. Every time I had been in here, I was asked to drink something. I had a seat in my usual spot, which had an empty vial sitting in front of it. I slid it forward, and humorously said, "Fill'er up barkeep."

"Not this time. Come on around here," she motioned for me to join her on the other side of all the tables where I found another door, which was opened. Walking through landed me in what I could only describe as grandmother land. Take every cliché about a grandmother and put it under one roof, and that was what Mrs. Tenderschott's residence looked like. Doilies on top of every table. Slippers on the floor next to an easy chair with a pattern that was not of this century. A crocheted Afghan blanket was folded over its back. I wouldn't even bat an eye if someone told me she had made it herself. Pictures of people, all young, covered every wall, like they were her grandchildren, which they might be. I didn't know much about her, but seeing all this made me almost sure she had a family somewhere. The smell of fresh-baked cookies, chocolate chip, wafted in from the kitchen.

"Get comfortable on the sofa. I am going to have you lay there while we do this," she called from another room, which I assumed was her bedroom. I looked around and saw the sofa against the other wall. I then realized she missed a cliché. Its outdated pattern matched the easy chair, but there wasn't a plastic cover over it.

I sat and waited. She came back into the room holding a black crystal in one hand and dragging an old wooden chair in with the other. I held my hands out for the crystal, but she never attempted to hand it to me. Instead, she pulled it back. "Oh no. This will let me join you. You already have what you need. Now lay back and close your eyes." I did as I was told and heard the wooden chair creak as she sat down on it next to me. "Repeat exactly what I say while thinking of that moment when you believe you saw it."

"Alright." My voice only sounded about as half as unsure about all this as I felt. Then, not wanting to cause any problems, I let my mind drift to that moment when I believe I saw it. The chills and fear came first before the vision. Once I had it, I weakly said, "Ready."

"Family of my past, help me see," she said in a very monotone voice.

"Family of my past, help me see." I repeated exactly like she said.

"Family of my past, help me hear."

"Family of my past, help me hear," I repeated.

"Family of my past, help me know."

"Family of my past," I started, and then noticed I felt weird and the darkness I saw had changed. There were little flashes of light around the edge.

"Larissa?" asked Mrs. Tenderschott.

"Family of my past, help me know," I repeated quickly to catch up.

"Family of my past, show me."

"Family of my past, show me."

Whoa, what the hell? Images flashed at super speed, like the slide show from hell. My mother. The house in New Orleans. New Orleans itself. An orchard somewhere. Fights and screaming. More images of my mother. Some with a man standing next to her. Was that my father? Then the Nortons. Afternoons in the library while it rained outside. The woods behind our house. My old room and the window I stood at often. All of them life-sized and zooming past me. It wasn't just the images, either. The emotions and feelings, comfort and safety, fear and anger flooded in. Many of the moments were foreign to me. What wasn't foreign was the final image, the one I landed in. That same street scene with me jumping over a car. I felt that fear again. I also felt the evil presence of whatever was chasing me closing in.

I wanted to look back to see what or who it was, but couldn't. Not because this, whatever I was in wouldn't let me. I had already moved a little to make sure I could move, but I was frozen with fear, just like that night. My mind already knew what it was. A dark, large, lumbering monster, with glaring red eyes of fire, and teeth dripping with blood. It had to be that. That was what my mind saw. It also saw a single claw just the width of a hair from grabbing me by the shoulder. If my mother hadn't yanked me down the alley, it would have had me. Or at least that was what my mind was telling me.

Another attempt to look back, and the feeling of fear crept up with every degree I turned my neck. By the time I was around far enough for its shape to start to appear in my vision, I felt the cold fingers of death closing around me. I had no heart to stop or breath to take away, but that didn't stop my mind from ramping up my emotions to the brink of overload.

The image began to take shape the more I turned my head. It was not right on top of me, as my fear led me to believe. Instead, it was on the top of the buildings on the other side of the road, leaping from rooftop to rooftop. It also was not a seething monster with red eyes and blood-stained teeth. It was one of us. A well-groomed man, with black eyes, slicked back dark long hair, and skin as pale as the moon. He wore a black robe or cape that flew behind him.

Frozen there, he didn't appear to be all that menacing, but seeing him filled in the blanks that were just all a black blur during the attack that killed my father, Mr. Norton. Most of the black blur I saw was the cape whipping around while his hands ripped my father's head around, breaking his neck. Then standing over him while his body turned to ash. To my horror, just thinking about that instance took me back to it. I was standing there, my mother's hand yanking mine while I watched the dark figure that now had a face. A face that had a satisfying smile on it while the first particles of dust that used to be the man I believed was my father rose up in the wind. I yanked free from my mother's hand, which hadn't really happened, and stepped toward him. His head pivoted in a single movement and leered at me, which I didn't remember happening the first time either, but it was possible that I had blocked it out with other, less impactful moments of this traumatic event.

"I see you, Larissa," he growled in a deep drawl. The sound of it sent waves of fear through me, and again I couldn't move, but he could. He walked perfectly fine, and almost strutted toward me, with a finger pointed in my direction. The only thought I had beyond those inspired by pure fear was that this guy was an arrogant bastard. "I see you right there, Larissa. So nice of you to come find me."

I screamed, and came out of it, waking up on the sofa in Mrs. Tenderschott's living room. "Tell me you saw that?" I yelled as I sprung up from the couch. "Tell me you saw that?" I screamed again.

She only nodded.

"That voice." I clenched both of my fists. "Ooooh," I seethed. "It was evil, and oh my god, that smile. He enjoyed what he did."

"Yes, dear," Mrs. Tenderschott said in a calm tone. I knew she was trying to calm me down, but it was going to take more than that to even make a dent in what I was feeling. "Did you notice the accent?"

"Yep," I answered shortly.

"New Orleans, which tells us something."

I stared at her blankly, still thinking about that evil smile and wanting an opportunity to rip it wide open for him.

"Larissa, it means whoever it was is from where you were born," she said, again in a calm and soothing voice.

"What?" I had heard just a little of what she had said over the furor that steamed inside.

"He is from New Orleans, so I think this is from your life there," she explained.

Then it hit me, a collision of two worlds, my two worlds. I had only realized recently that there were two worlds to me, and I wasn't talking about the witch and vampire worlds. These were the Nortons and Dubois. Once I realized that I had two lives, I had thought there was a brick wall separating them, but now that wall seemed to be a little flimsier, or not existent at all. They were all linked in some way, and then a more astonishing thought. "That long ago?"

I had whispered it to myself, but in this room that was small and cozy, there was no such thing as whispering, and now it was Mrs. Tenderschott's turn to look at me blankly. That was a detail I hadn't told anyone about after I learned it. There was no time like the present to let them in on the one secret I had. "I am older than you."

This drew another look of confusion, so I clarified. "I am almost a hundred. Born June 17th, 1923. At least that is what my mother told me, but I figure she would know, and seeing the house and the old Model-T kind of confirmed it."

Her jaw dropped.

"Yeah, I'm old," I grinned.

"Well, you don't look bad for your age," she said, still stunned.

19

The last little trip gave *me* an idea, but I was afraid to ask Mrs. Tenderschott or anyone else really. I wasn't sure if there were limits on what I was allowed to try on my own yet. The book Mrs. Saxon gave me covered what I thought were the basics. How to move things, and how to set things on fire. Both of which I could do. Control was the remaining piece of the puzzle. This was neither of those, nor was it any of the variations of either covered in the rest of the book. This was beyond that, but something I knew I had the ability to do, seeing that I had just done it, but I didn't exactly know how. The only place I could think of that might tell me was some place I had only gone once.

I pushed open the door of the library and walked to the row of tables in the center. I sat, not knowing how long this might take, and then did as I saw Mrs. Saxon do during my first visit. "Edward?"

His head appeared in just a matter of moments with a very polite. "Good evening Miss Dubois, what can I do for you?"

"Any update on the research you are performing?" I asked. Hopefully, he had some answers, but hadn't had a chance to report back yet. Of course, how busy could he really be. There weren't many students here, and again, just like before, no one else was in the library.

"Not yet. I am still going through the various records. It shouldn't be too much longer though. I have identified the correct time period," he reported.

"Okay, I do need your help with something else," I started very tentatively as I realized I wasn't really even sure how to ask for what I was looking for.

"Of course, I am at your service."

"I just used a spell to go back to a memory. Are there spells that will let me connect or talk to those in a memory?"

"Miss Dubois, there are books here with spells to pretty much do anything you can imagine," Edward said, dignified, almost snooty as he leaned back a bit, allowing him to look down his nose at me. I resisted the temptation to look to see what was under his neck. "Are you looking to relive a memory, or connect and talk to those involved in the memory?"

"The last one. I want to connect and talk to them."

"Family or stranger?" he asked and turned to watch for my reply with his left eye.

"Family," I started and then corrected, "Step-parents."

"One moment," he said, and then disappeared.

Throughout the library, I heard the echo of whistling and the rustling of the books on the shelves. I craned my neck to look up and around in the sound's direction, but I never saw a book move, or any sign of Edward. Books, one at a time, plopped on the table in front of me. The stack stopped when it was seven high, and Edward reappeared. I sighed at the thickness of some of the books in the stack. I had a feeling I knew what Edward was about to tell me.

"These are the best seven books on ancestral projection. Miss Dubois, this is rather advanced. Are you sure you want to tackle these on your own? Might I suggest Mrs. Saxon or one of the other instructors."

"How advanced?" I asked, knowing that really anything was very advanced for me at this point.

"The act of visiting a memory is simple. It is all in your head and anyone can pretty much master that on the first attempt. To connect and then talk with someone from a dream, which requires mastery of several techniques, some of which not all can do," he said with a cautious look in his eyes. "First you need to master time and location, to pick the specific moment of the memory, which is not just remembering the memory. You have to find that memory in time and space. That is in books one and two. The next three books are about tracking. Using the memory location to then trace and track all the individuals that were involved. That will tell you where they all are now, so you can reach out and talk. Those are difficult to master, but a rather common skill set for an experienced witch. There are many uses. The last two books cover astral projection. Are you familiar with that terminology?"

With my head already spinning from the last two topics, I shook it, which only scrambled the topics more.

"Astral projection, the ability to separate your spiritual form from your physical. You can then send your spirit to go talk to anyone you located, but I would be remiss if I didn't warn you about how dangerous this is. Your body can only live for a few moments without the spirit, so your trips have to be short."

"How short?," I blurted out as I was thinking about the question, not really expecting to ask it out loud.

"Shorter than an hour. Anything longer is too dangerous," then Edward paused for a moment, and his eyes squinted. The books separated out across the table. The fourth book, a large book with a green cover and gold inlay, opened, and the pages flipped wildly, and then it shut with a thud. The books re-stacked, and he said, "Let's stick to the hour limit to be safe. There is nothing in there that covers your specific condition."

"Condition?" I asked, almost offended, as it sounded like he implied I was sick.

"Your being immortal. You will find many things have dangers and I don't know how *that* affects those dangers, so it is best to keep to the rules."

"Got it." I nodded.

"The second warning, you will be vulnerable while you are visiting. Your spirit can't cast spells, nor can your body. Only the whole can. I assume they have explained to you the dangers that we all face."

I nodded again. The dangers were something I was well aware of with firsthand experience.

"Good. Are you going to read these here, or shall I have them sent to your room?" Edward asked as he turned and looked at the pile.

There was no way I could read all of them in one sitting, and I wasn't exactly sure I still wanted to. The warnings Edward provided still played in my head like a siren. "You can do that?"

"Yes, Miss Dubois, I can do anything," he said with a little smug tone. The books disappeared. "They are waiting for you in a stack by your bed. When you are ready to return them, just call me and I will retrieve them. Is there anything else?"

"No, Edward. Thank you."

"My pleasure, Miss Dubois." Edward disappeared, and I did the same. My exit took a little longer though, as I had to walk to the door and out.

That night, I stared at the stack. I knew what I wanted to do, but some of Edward's warnings gave me more than a few second thoughts. Who was I to start messing with those kinds of things when I couldn't even control the couple of spells I had learned so far? I imagined little toddler witches, all dressed like mini-Gwens, lighting birthday candles and unwrapping presents using those spells. I would set the whole cake on fire and throw the gifts against the wall.

I flipped through the 101 book and then slammed it shut. I had had enough of being a witch for the day, and I needed to be me, or the old me, and my eyes looked toward my closet door. Behind it was the staircase that led up to where the others like me sat. Of course, right now, they didn't accept me either. That didn't matter. It's a big deck and I could stay at the other end and maybe hear some music and just enjoy the night air.

With it settled, I headed up, and just like the first two nights, I saw them all gathered at the other end in the furniture. I heard the murmurs of conversations below the music. If I wanted to join in, I would have to move closer, but I didn't, so I didn't. Instead, I walked to the railing, looked out at the woods, and had my own conversation with the moon and the woods, letting the music be my background.

As I stood there and watched the serene scene, I saw Martin, Rob, and another young boy emerge out on the pool deck with Mr. Markinson and what were obviously two other instructors I hadn't met. After a quick conversation, they took off running and morphed into huge wolves before they hit the grass on the other side of the pool.

They sprinted out into the woods, another patrol, and another reminder of the danger out there. Not being able to go anywhere else, I imagined I would see them return in a few hours. There was a funny irony to all this. The world, popular culture movies and all, saw us as the danger.

Even several songs into the night's party, I couldn't pick out a specific genre. It was random. Everything from modern pop music, old classic rock from the fifties and sixties, and even some club dance mixes which had everyone but Brad, up dancing. I kind of thought he would be the dancer of the group. I wanted to be down there dancing. Anything to distract me from where my mind was, but I wasn't. I wasn't even dancing where I stood; not a sway or an attempt to even move to the groove. My mind was still stuck on one image; that arrogant smile, and the sound of the smooth Cajun drawl under his growl as he spoke. His words played over and over. "*I see you, Larissa.*" Each syllable of my name in his voice caused a chill down my body. Over and over, he said it.

Then the second phrase. "*I see you right there, Larissa. So nice of you to come find me.*" My stomach retched at the sound each time I heard it, with that smug expression on his face. I wanted to rip it off, but how could I if his words had me frozen so bad. The harder I tried to pull my mind from it, the more it maintained its hold on me. Almost like I was back under that spell, and I was there again. He repeated it more times than I wanted. Once was enough. Two dozen were torture. It was in the last time he repeated it that I screamed and fell back on the deck. The words were different this time. "*I see you right there Larissa. I am coming to find you.*"

I sat up, tears streamed from my eyes, and I noticed the cavalry heading my way, with Brad and Apryl leading the way. Brad was the first to flash to my side and helped me back up to my feet. "You okay?"

"I think so, just going through a lot lately," I said, feeling a bit embarrassed, and a whole lot disturbed. There was no way what I had heard could have really happened. It had to be my mind playing games on me, fueled by the stress of everything.

"I know I would scream too if I learned I was a witch," joked Apryl. She threw an arm around me and walked me to the other end. "So, music, even Pam's bad mix, will make you feel better."

20

I spent the rest of the evening sitting in a chair on the edge of my circle of friends. They were in and out of their seats all night dancing, but I didn't. Not because I didn't feel like I belonged with them. In all appearances, they seemed to have accepted me back in, leading me to believe that maybe I overreacted, and this was just a little tiff, and not as huge of a falling out as I had believed. Not that it much mattered at this time. The feeling of belonging was nice to feel again.

The ominous and threatening feeling delivered by his voice restricted my dancing, or any attempt to relax, for the rest of the night. I knew it was just my mind messing with me, but it packed a punch that took the proverbial wind, and any sense of safety I felt, right out of me. So much, most, of the night I kept my focus out on the woods to make sure that figure wouldn't come out of it after me. To my relief all I saw were the werewolves returning and then making another pass just before daybreak.

When the first shimmer of sunlight splashed off the bay to our east, we headed back downstairs to dress and get ready for classes. Today I had somewhat of a schedule change. After the morning of the normal math, science, English, and history—not my best subject by any means—I had my first day of witch's school to look forward to. *Go me!*

The prospects of having to spend the morning and all afternoon in a classroom with Gwen was not pleasant after our little conversation yesterday. It was clear she hated me, and I could deal without being around her. The good news, Mr. Bolden said we could spend some of our time out on the deck at night to go over what I missed in their how-to-fit-in-with-humans class. I wasn't sure if my little secret had gotten around, and I had noticed myself doing little things here and there in the mirror that made me look more human without even thinking about it. My advanced age might make me more experienced at this than they were.

Showered and dressed, I headed down to class. Pam and Laura were waiting for me at the stairs. Laura said Apryl wasn't done with her hair yet. Which I didn't get. My red hair was longer, and I didn't really have to do much to it on a daily basis, it just naturally fell into a perfect flowing frame around my face. Instead of waiting, we walked on down to class, and I told them I would be missing the afternoon classes, which both appeared to be a little disappointed about. Either that, or they were practicing the outward signs of that emotion. Two steps from the bottom, I felt something like a little string grab my ankle and yank, throwing me off balance and sending me falling. Mike and Brad were both there in a flash, ready to catch me, but I didn't need them. My own enhanced speed allowed me to get my feet under me before I reached the floor. When I landed, I found myself face to face with a third rescuer, Nathan.

I knew he wasn't that fast, so he must have been there waiting to begin with. His pulse raced, either from the quick move to extend his arms to catch me, or he was anxious to see me. Having a split-second left before most would realize I had landed safely on the floor, I decided to run a little test and let myself fall gently into his waiting arms, now for the second time.

Ha, I knew it.

His heart fluttered and his blood rushed. He was waiting for me. I lingered there for longer than was really necessary. I liked how his arms felt around me and how my cheek felt on his chest, but I also knew what was behind me. The glaring stare of Gwen, who both Brad and Mike were looking up at.

Nathan *helped* me steady myself, and then I turned around and glared up the stairs too. Gwen stood midway up with Lisa and Tera in tow. Both Lisa and Tera looked astonished, and Gwen looked furious. "I must have tripped. Clumsy me," I cooed, and then headed toward the classes with Mike and Brad on either side of me.

"You know Gwen did that," Mike whispered. "I saw her finger doing something just before you tripped."

"I know. It kind of backfired, didn't it?" I whispered. I had planned to brag more, but it was interrupted by the shriek heard around the world that sent all three of us rushing back toward the main hall, which was now full of ruckus laughter, and one scream.

When we arrived back at the scene of the scream, we saw everyone laughing. Pam and Laura sat on the stairs laughing. Steven and Stan were both bent over, laughing. Martin and Rob were howling from their landing on the stairs. Up our side of the stairs was an image that might take a while to get out of my head. Apryl, full curls, and makeup, wearing a hot pink outfit with a mini-skirt that made her look like Gwen's twin. All I could say was, "Oh my god!"

Gwen stormed off with Tera, Marcia, Lynn, and Lisa following her. Each was doing their best to stifle their giggles. We let the other groups go on. Each gave an amused look in Apryl's direction as they passed.

"Nice legs," commented Martin. Apryl responded with her normal single finger gesture.

Once everyone else left, Apryl made her way down the remaining stairs with the grace of a drunken giraffe. We could all see it. Her quick reactions couldn't hide it from us like she had the others.

"How the hell does she walk in these things?" she squawked. "They're like a torture device." At the bottom of the stairs, she pulled it together and strutted down the hallway.

"Work it girl," shouted Mike. In reply, he received a deep throaty growl from Apryl and a slap on the arm from Laura. I just followed her, doing my best not to laugh as we walked into the classroom and to our normal table in Mrs. Saxon's class. English was first today in the rotation.

When Apryl sat, she leaned toward me, and complained, "How does she sit in this? My ass is about to fall out."

In my opinion, I was doing good controlling myself until that point, but that was the comment that opened the valve on my laughter. The quick explosion that escaped my mouth before I slapped my hand over it finally got Mrs. Saxon's attention. She hadn't looked up from her notebook yet, but one look in our direction and she knew everything.

I expected her to admonish us, or at least ask about it, but she didn't. All we received was a curious look before she stood up in front of the class and asked us to hand our homework forward.

The one good thing about never sleeping. You had plenty of time to do your homework. I finished my character analysis on Tess of the d'Urbervilles, around four in the morning while the others danced. Luckily, I had read it several times over the past few years while sitting in the Norton's library. That familiarity made it easy.

The morning went exactly like my first morning. I assumed these classes and how the morning went were like any other school, though I hadn't attended a traditional school and didn't have anything to compare it to besides what I had seen in movies and on television shows. From that vantage, it looked like any other classroom full of teenagers. Even our Gwen look-a-like would have fit in to the storylines of those shows.

The afternoon was something altogether different. Nathan walked with me to the first of three classes in the afternoon before he disappeared to do homework and then head to the gym, something I didn't think his Adonis body needed, but I wasn't going to argue. He offered to meet up later to listen to some music or work on our history assignment together. The offer was more than a little enticing. I had already had my fill of listening to music after the last several nights on the deck, and I hated history with a passion, but being around him was my new drug, not that I had ever had a drug before. His presence was intoxicating. All the confusion I felt about who I was, and the fear about what had happened, melted away when he was around. The bad part, how he made me feel also clouded my judgement about him. I knew I shouldn't, couldn't get involved with him. It would never work, would it? A vampire and a human. Of course, there was another problem. The warning, which I promptly brought up.

His reply, "Don't worry about that, you seem different from the others." Then he hugged me before walking off. His pulse raced as he pulled me in, and its fast pace was beautiful music to my senses.

Gwen and the others saw it, earning what had become the traditional dirty look from her, and some smiles and giggles from the rest. I guess that was why what happened in all three classes that afternoon didn't really surprise me.

First up, Mrs. Tenderschott's potion class. Having read a little too much popular fiction about witches I had developed certain opinions that I quickly realized were, well, tainted. I expected we would be using ingredients such as toad warts and eyes of newts. In truth, this was more alchemy than anything. Copper, resin, silver, and even substances as toxic as mercury and arsenic were used in the potions. What the potion did was controlled by the ingredients, the mixture, and the bit of magic we added. Volumes after volumes of cookbooks contained the exact mixtures and instructions, as well as the incantations for each exact purpose. Both parts had to be exact. Even the slightest error in the mixture, or misspoken word, and you were left with a concoction that ranged from a foul smelling and tasting liquid to liquid death, or worse. The worst was something Mrs. Tenderschott didn't go into much other than pain, suffering, and possible deformity. Today's lesson was about the natural world, and we were creating a growth formula. Each of us was given a sprig of green vine, and Mrs. Tenderschott showed us what to do first. She mixed together silver, phosphorus, and iodine in the proper portions and then said the words, "Growus maximus." Instantly the vine tripled in size and sprouted beautiful white flowers.

After answering a few questions about what we just saw, she paired everyone up. Gwen and Marcia. Tera and Lisa. Mrs. Tenderschott teamed with Lynn. Not that she was playing favorites, she explained. Lynn was an elementalist. Causing a plant to grow came natural to her, and Mrs. Tenderschott wanted to make sure she truly used the potion, and not just her ability.

That just left Jack and me. Neither of us appeared too thrilled to be paired with the other, but when Jack looked at me, there was something else. A fear. I could sense his rapid pulse as he moved over to my table. When we set to the work, each helping the other to measure each ingredient exactly, his eyes kept darting up at me. That was strange, but what he wasn't doing was even stranger. There were no snide remarks. Not that Gwen left any room for him in that department.

"Mrs. Tenderschott, don't you have to be alive to give something life?" cackled Gwen.

Mrs. Tenderschott looked at Gwen and noticed her looking back at me. She gave me an unamused look and then reminded Gwen, "Gwen, just worry about your own potion. This potion is the manipulation of the forces of life itself. Anyone can screw it up if they aren't paying attention."

Lisa and Tera worked together at their own table. I saw each of them give their leader a disapproving look. Not that she noticed. She was too busy leering back at me, and I was too busy watching her while she did.

"Focus," Jack barked at me. It was a harsh command, not at all his normal snide style, but he was right. I needed to focus. I had already poured too much iodine in one bowl. Luckily, we had decided to measure everything out first before combining them. Jack's idea, not mine. Too much iodine was my fault and not his. I poured all of it back in its original jar and re-poured, being more careful this time.

"Growus Maximus," Lynn's voice said in a calm, and almost fantasy tone. Like something out of a movie. Everyone in the room stopped and watched. Then I did something I never did in mixed company. I let my mouth drop wide open in amazement as the vine spread out over their table and sprouted beautiful white flowers.

There I was, watching a witch make a vine grow the equivalent of several years' worth of normal growth in mere seconds, shocked, amazed, and with my fangs out for all to see. I realized it when Jack turned back to our own experiment and stared at me, alarmed. I snapped my mouth shut and then asked, "Where were we?"

"I need to sift the phosphorous over the silver, then we can mix everything together."

Then it happened again, "Growus Maximus," cried Tera. Just like for Lynn, the vine took off across the table and the white flowers appeared.

Jack carefully sifted the yellow powder over the silver. He was slow, maybe too slow. In the time it took him to do that, Mrs. Tenderschott had already given Lisa and Tera another plant; now it was Lisa's turn. This wasn't a competition, but that didn't matter to me. I didn't want to fall behind Gwen.

"Okay, now pour the iodine while I mix," Jack instructed with a metal rod in his hand ready to mix it all together. I reached for the bowl, and it lurched from my grasp, sliding across the table where it teetered on the edge before falling. I caught it before it hit the ground and had it back on the table before Jack could blink. All he saw was it falling, and the look on his face told me he expected the worst. Over his shoulder, I saw Gwen taking it all in with a devious smile on her face. Jack followed my gaze around and saw her. I saw his shoulders fall when he reached the same conclusion I had as soon as the bowl moved.

"Gwen, knock it off," Jack yelled sternly. She put on her best face of innocence and held her hands up.

"Miss Michaels, stay focused on your own work," warned Mrs. Tenderschott. She watched everyone like a hawk until all heads were turned back to their own tables. Slowly, I poured in the iodine and Jack stirred it. When it reached a lavender color and a crème like consistency, matching Mrs. Tenderschott's example, Jack stopped stirring. I completely expected him to pick it up and pour it on the plant first. He had measured most of the ingredients and stirred it, but he hesitated and motioned toward the potion. "You first, it will burn her," he whispered.

In both spite and curiosity, I picked up the glass bowl and let a few drops fall out on the plant. Then I spoke the magic words, "Growus Maximus." The vine took off, spreading across the table. Gorgeous white flowers. I almost screamed, but held it together. There was a shriek. It was at the table in front of us where Marcia was stirring the concoction for her and Gwen. In a huff, Gwen grabbed the bowl, yanking it from Marcia. The metal rod she used to stir it clanked on the side of the bowl, and Marcia exclaimed, "it's not ready!"

I couldn't see Gwen's face, but her jerky movements told me she was fuming as she shook out a large dollop that almost smothered the vine, and then uttered, "Growus Maximus." Nothing happened for the first few seconds, then smoke rose from it before it burned the vine down to nothing but a pile of dust.

"You screwed it up!" The blame was aimed right at Marcia, who attempted to defend herself.

"I said it wasn't ready. It was not thoroughly mixed yet."

Gwen slammed both hands down on their table and looked back over her shoulder at me. Happy or pleased did not exist in her vocabulary at the moment. This was disdain.

Mrs. Tenderschott gave them a new vine and Marcia went back to stirring. Then she walked to our table and took our vine away before bringing back a new one for Jack. I mouthed to him, "Thank you." He nodded, but still seemed distant. I figured that distance was just something I was going to have to get used to in this company. I wasn't really one of the 'club.'

21

The second class of the afternoon was defensive spells, taught by Mr. Helms. I hadn't had the opportunity to meet, or even see him, before this class. Heck, until this class, I didn't even know he was here. Something I later asked Apryl about, and she hadn't even heard about him either. Must be a private person, I supposed. Of course, it was quite possible he was around the other witches and instructors, and our paths just hadn't crossed.

Upon introductions, which Tera handled, the bald-headed, red-bearded man in a tweed sports coat seemed leery of me, but then again, his specialty was defensive spells against hostile magic attacks, and his number one principle, as clearly painted above the chalkboard was, "Your enemy is everyone and everywhere." It struck me as a little extreme, but I understood the sentiment. My enemy was at the next table, which created a bit of concern when he directed everyone to an open area in his very spacious classroom with cobblestone floors and walls and asked them to pair up for exercises. The hint of delight in Gwen's eyes lasted until Mr. Helms told me to sit this one out and just watch, and watch I did.

The show that was put on in front of me was better than anything Hollywood could have dreamed up. Fireballs flew across the room. They were either batted away with another fireball or bounced off some kind of invisible shield put up by the target. Lisa summoned spirits which appeared as grey humanlike figures that flashed in and out of existence. Each appeared more than happy to throw themselves in the way of anything heading for Lisa, which allowed her to focus on her offensive spells.

The most amazing to watch were Jack and Lynn. She was something else. Jack would throw balls of fire in her direction only to have them dowsed by water she pulled from a bucket nearby. Jack would then send another fire ball or some other object her way, and a gust of wind or a column of water knocked them out of the way before Lynn returned the favor, sending Jack dodging to the floor. During one attack, a plant in the room reached out and grabbed Jack's arm. Something I knew for sure Lynn was behind. Jack's defenses reminded me of what I believed mine might be. A fact Mr. Helms pointed out to me several times. "Your speed and strength will give you an advantage here. If you learn to use your magic along with it, you will be formidable."

"Unbeatable?" I asked, which was a mistake that he communicated rather clearly with an admonishing frown.

"Unkillable," he corrected me with a lecturing tone. "I do not teach offensive skills here. I give you the skills to defend yourself against those that will try to harm you, and Miss Dubois, there are many people out there willing to bring harm to any one of us."

"Understood," I replied sheepishly, with my eyes locked on the two of them. Then a sight off in the distance caused me to drop my jaw for the second time today. Gwen had produced a swirling black disc in air right in front of one of Marcia's attacks. The fire ball entered into the disc, and then it closed. No sign of either was left as they continued their exercise. I was sure Gwen would be happy if I fell into one of those discs and disappeared like the fire ball.

The third and last class of witch school for the day was Mrs. Saxon's spells and focus class. It was really just called her class of spells, but she emphasized focus during each lesson. "Focus is the source of power," she reminded everyone.

That was a conclusion I had already reached on my own, much to my disappointment. Control was not something I had much of, and my mind was anything but focused. Mrs. Saxon's reminder also gave Gwen fuel for my continued torture. Today was about levitation. Being in a room with people that I knew couldn't tolerate me at best, hated me at worst, with objects floating around the room under their control, made me feel like a long-tailed cat in a room of rocking chairs. The only question was, when was something going to rock down on my tail?

The question was never who. I knew that blindfolded, and when a rubber ball hit me in the back of the head, I wasn't shocked to hear Gwen's voice claim, "I guess I lost focus."

She did it twice more, each time a little harder, before it drew a look from Mrs. Saxon that the entire class noticed. Others were losing control of their ball, but none were flying in anyone else's direction. Most just fell down to the table or bounced to the floor. Mine stayed mostly planted to the surface of the table, with only a little hop here and there. I had to make sure my mind never thought about firing the ball at Gwen. Based on what I had seen with the fire and the closet door, I would have probably taken her head off.

By the time class was over, most of them had good control of their objects and could move them around obstacles and land them down softly. Jack and Lisa moved on to larger and heavier objects, and I left with a promise to keep working on my focus.

I was closing my notebook and about to get up when Mrs. Saxon asked me to hang back. Of course, that drew looks from everyone else as they walked out and caused a lump to develop in my throat. I knew what this was about, Nathan. The rule Apryl told me was clear, yet I still talked to him. More than talked and had plans to meet with him later this afternoon. This would be either a warning from the Head Mistress of the school or his mother. I wasn't sure which would be more painful to hear.

I sat at my table and waited. Once everyone had left, Mrs. Saxon came over and sat at the table across from me. Her face concerned as she addressed me, "Larissa, I need to talk to you about something. Something concerning."

Great, the mother speech, I thought.

"Jack talked to me before class, and as you know, he can read people's thoughts."

The lump in my throat became a boulder, and I wanted to sink right down into the ground below me. Jack probably told her about my feelings for Nathan. Luckily for me, I could play it cool. My body wouldn't sweat or become flushed because of embarrassment, so Mrs. Saxon would never know that inside I was dying.

"Jack said you had a pretty traumatic and emotional vision last night. It was powerful enough to wake him up."

So much for private thoughts, I fumed, but forced myself to calm down before I spoke. "I thought he could only read thoughts. He wasn't even around me." I was stunned, and now rather embarrassed.

"Usually, but think of emotions as a form of energy. It radiates from all of us. The stronger the emotion, the stronger the energy. We can all pick up on it, but to someone like Jack, it's a loudspeaker that screams at him. Sounds like your energy was strong enough to wake him up." She leaned forward and braced her arms on the table. "You have been through a lot, so having a nightmare would be almost expected."

"Oh, this wasn't a nightmare," I said. "Remember we don't sleep."

"Very true," she said flatly, as if not surprised by that correction. "So, this was a vision. Care to talk about it?"

I looked across at Mrs. Saxon, the teacher now turned therapist, and opened up completely. There was nothing to hide about, and if anything, maybe this would help. "It was a vision of the night my father, Mr. Norton, was murdered." Using that word almost hurt as bad as my now second nature reaction to clarify who I was talking about every time I used the word mother or father. It was almost as if I was referring to strangers, and they most certainly were not. They were family, a loving family that I had great memories with. "Mrs. Tenderschott helped me go back to that moment and see the vampire that did it." A shiver passed through my body as I thought of that moment again. "I will admit seeing him, seeing what he did was upsetting." I sugar coated it a little. "Seeing him and then hearing his voice... I think all the emotions in my mind caused it to play a trick on me and put some words in his mouth."

She jerked forward, further across the table. "Like what? What did he say?" Her tone was alarmed, with a hint of a quiver.

"At first, it was just - I see you Larissa. He said it over and over, like he did earlier with Mrs. Tenderschott, but then last night it changed to -I see you right there Larissa. I am coming to find you."

Mrs. Saxon was normally pale, but what little color there was had now drained away, giving her a gray appearance. The features of her face trembled as she sat back in the chair, but that was just for a second, or even less. Her body erupted forward, her hand grabbed mine from across the table, and then rushed out of the classroom, dragging me behind. This felt frightfully familiar.

Down the hallway we rushed without a word between us, and I knew in that instant she was right. Emotions were energy, and I felt hers. It was fear. She didn't even knock when we reached Mrs. Tenderschott's door, and just went right in. There were no pleasantries or greetings. I didn't even see Mrs. Tenderschott in sight when Mrs. Saxon yelled. "Why didn't you tell me?"

"Tell you what, Rebecca?" Mrs. Tenderschott emerged from the door that led to her residence. "Oh, hi Larissa." she said, and acted surprised to see me.

"You should have told me about it seeing her during your spell!" she roared, finally letting my hand go. "It saw her."

"I know," admitted Mrs. Tenderschott.

"Wait!," I interrupted. Now it was my turn to be the one who was trembling. Of course, that was only on the inside, and no one else knew. "That wasn't part of my memory? That was real?" The words scraped my throat raw, coming out.

"Yes," answered Mrs. Tenderschott, still as calm as she always was, but then doubt crept across her face, "sometimes. It depends on who the other person is. It won't with a normal human, but with others it can."

Mrs. Saxon scowled at her colleague.

"But there is a block. Neither side knows where the other is." Mrs. Tenderschott paused abruptly and put her finger to her lips and turned and walked a few steps away before turning back. She was a woman lost in thought, and that more than concerned me. It absolutely petrified me. "Or should have," she croaked. Then she blurted out an explanation that passed by me so fast my head spun. "I don't know. I did the best I could with what I know. We have never put anyone who was a vampire under that particular spell because it is a witches only spell, and now we have someone who is both, which I don't know what that means to the spell or really anything. How it would react with a vampire, or a witch that was a vampire, seeing another vampire in the memory, I don't know? It's never been done." She was exacerbated and threw her hands up.

"Well, she had another vision last night!" Mrs. Saxon exclaimed, upset, but she wasn't the only one who was upset. I was now seeing a different side of Mrs.

Tenderschott that I hadn't seen before. The normally calm grandmotherly woman was now disturbed and traumatized. "Go on Larissa, tell her."

The spotlight was now on me, and I re-explained what I just told Mrs. Saxon, "I saw him again last night while I was standing up on the deck, and he said 'I see you right there Larissa. I am coming to find you.'"

"You should have told me," Mrs. Saxon chastised Mrs. Tenderschott.

"I know. I know," she apologized. "But I don't think he knows where she is."

"We hope not, but we need to tell the others."

"The others?" I asked, more curious and scared of the prospect of others knowing. Everyone else already knew I was weird.

"The other instructors," she said, turning to face me. "We like to think of this place as a school, but it is also a sanctuary from the evil that exists in the world. We will protect it and anyone in it. That is our responsibility. We view each of you as our own children and we will protect you all with our own lives if it comes to it.

"This place is hidden, but it doesn't mean others like us can't find it. Come, Mrs. Tenderschott, let's go talk with the others, and you.." she looked into my eyes, the tension that was there just seconds ago, now gone from her face, "if you have any more visions or encounters with him, tell me at once."

"Yes ma'am," I said as they both left the classroom, leaving me in there alone with the smell of cookies coming through the door to Mrs. Tenderschott's residence.

22

After I composed myself, which was harder than I thought it would be, I rushed out to the pool deck. I was supposed to meet Nathan after class. Thanks to this little issue, I was now over an hour late. At the door, I stopped running, brushed the hair back out of my face, and pulled open the door wondering if this was a mistake. Was I entertaining something that would backfire, and lead me to more heartache? I walked through the door doing my best to convince myself I was just out here to talk with a classmate.

Night was setting in. The small landscape lanterns that surrounded the pool cast the entire deck in a magical orange glow that matched the last glimmer of daylight disappearing over the top of the trees to the west. I did my best to walk out in a way to match the Hollywood movie setting that was all around. While nature gave me the fantasy setting I didn't ask for, my mind was still in a disaster movie.

The confident strut I made toward the second table on the deck was all for show. It wasn't how I normally walked, or had ever tried. There was a part of me that thought I might actually look ridiculous from the outside. A terrifying thought considering Nathan sat at the table watching me walk toward him. He had a book open at the table, but wasn't reading. His focus was on me, and seeing that, feeling that, and feeling his pulse quicken made me uncomfortable. It was a primal and a burning type of uncomfortable, but it wasn't in my throat. Again, I had to remind myself that I was just here to talk with a friend, nothing else. I could say it over and over as many times as I wanted, but the way he looked at me put other thoughts in my mind.

"Hey there," I said, and then cringed. I sounded perky, almost like Gwen.

"Have a seat."

I pulled out the metal chair and sat down across from him. My butt hit the arm of the chair, but I recovered before he noticed. I had been paying more attention to his eyes than what I was doing.

He reached up and turned on the light that was inside the umbrella. It showered us both with a magical glow. I wasn't ever the type that was a romantic novel or movie softy. Maybe a romantic comedy with my mother, Mrs. Norton-I needed to stop that-, here and there, but never the straight on romance. That wasn't me, but now this was getting to me. I was that girl, in those movies, and I felt my mind running with it, and the possibilities that could be, which really couldn't't.

"So, should we get to it?" he asked with a smile that mesmerized me. This wasn't just any smile. This was a spell within itself. I must have been lost in it because I never heard him ask the first time, the second time, or really the third time until he said again, "history?"

"Oh yea," I stammered ridiculously. "The Ottoman Empire." I opened my book, which was a first, and flipped to the chapter. When I found it, I stared at the picture on the top of the page of an old guy with a full beard and something on top of his head. Why exactly I needed to know about things that happened almost seven hundred years ago, I didn't know. Then I did something that shocked myself. Both arms jerked up and collapsed, crossing themselves on top of the book. My head fell down to them, letting my chin rest on my arms, and then I did it. An act that I couldn't believe I even knew how to do. I pouted, "I am terrible at history."

Where the hell did that come from? A very human reaction. A very embarrassing human reaction that I had carried out quite well without having to think about it. I had obviously done this before, and that thought embarrassed me. That was not who I was. Then again, there was so much about me I didn't know. Was I really who I thought I was?

"Some people like history, and some people don't," he said. "It's mostly just reading. This isn't my favorite subject, because of the reading, but my mom stays on me."

"So, what is your favorite subject?" I asked him, and sat up, leaning in like I was interested. I was, and I hadn't even thought about it.

"You're going to laugh," he smirked.

"I won't," I promised. Crossing my silent heart.

"Math," he said. "Call me a nerd, but it makes sense, and so much of what I have seen in my life doesn't. It's nice to have something that does."

I didn't laugh or call him a nerd. I understood. It made complete sense, and my pondering took longer than it needed to, leading to an awkward silence that I was oblivious to until he spoke.

"You're laughing on the inside, aren't you?"

"No, I promise you I'm not. It just makes so much sense," I said, looking past him at the building that housed so much that wasn't normal, which included me. He smiled at me, and I let my guard down for just a split second and returned the favor without even thinking about it. A shock of panic hit me and forced a hand up to cover my mouth, and my exposed sharp fangs. I looked away, and said, "Sorry."

"You don't need to hide around me." His expression never changed from the pleasant and comfortable smile he had shared that got me in trouble in the first place. I still hid. It was my natural reaction.

"Can I ask you a question?" he asked, but his voice trailed off and he looked like he was embarrassed.

"Of course."

"What's it like?" He stammered, and then rushed to apologize, "I'm sorry. I'm not sure why I blurted that out like that, and it was probably rude of me to even ask. I've never asked anyone that question before."

"You haven't?" I asked to clarify, but I didn't give him a chance to answer before I added another question driven by more emotion and logic. "Why me then?"

His hand reached up and rubbed the back of his neck before returning to the table. "Well, there is just something different about you. You aren't like the others."

I laughed. "Of course. I am both a witch and a vampire. A vitch, or a wampire. You can go with either term." I let the laugh continue and hoped it wouldn't come across as a nervous one. What I had just said sounded better in my head than coming out of my mouth.

It was a good thing he laughed too and flashed that smile again. I wondered what I had to do for him to let me just sit and stare at that every moment of every day. "It's not that. You are just different from the others, and I'm sorry if it was too personal of a question."

"Oh no. It's fine." I rushed to reassure him and found my hand reaching across the table and touching his. Just with that light touch, I could feel the pulsation of every capillary in his hand. He didn't pull back like most who knew what I was would. "What is what like? Ask me anything."

"Being a... well, a... vampire?" He gulped.

This was the first time he ever acknowledged what I really was, and he seemed mildly uncomfortable. The question made *me* more than mildly uncomfortable. Not because of the question, but because I didn't really know how to answer it. I had never thought about it before. I sat and pondered it for a few moments while his gaze studied me. Not that I minded in the least.

As I thought about how to describe being a vampire, I decided to describe the differences between humans and us, filtering out all the gross and dark parts. Those filled me with a fear that he might run away from the blood sucking monster that sat on the other side of the table from him. Especially if he knew that monster could feel every thump of his heart, and the swish of his blood in his veins.

"Well, there are the obvious things that you probably already know. We are immortal and never age. Which can be a bit of a bummer, depending on what age you are turned at. We have our super speed and strength, which is all because our muscles aren't driven by a heart and the flow of blood. Don't ask me how that works. I honestly don't know. Oh, and then there is that. Our heart doesn't pump anymore, and we don't breathe. Which creates more problems than you might think. We have to remember to pretend like we breathe and blink and stuff like that to avoid sticking out when around humans. Rather annoying for us. That is even what one of the classes Mr. and Mrs. Bolden teach-"

"Wait, you have to act like you breathe?" he asked with a curious gaze.

"Yep, like this." I sat up straight and raised my shoulders just a quarter of an inch or so slowly, at least for my speed, and then let them drop again slowly. "See?"

"Umm," he coughed, "That looked rather natural, and they teach you how to do that?"

"Well," I hesitated, feeling I was about to brag, but found I couldn't help myself. "They teach them. Someone else taught me a while ago, and now it comes naturally, but that is not all. They teach how to blink. Walk without going too fast. How to react emotionally to situations. How to..."

"You don't feel emotions?" he interrupted my gushing.

"Oh, we do." Boy do we ever. "Our bodies just don't show it. We don't flush or sweat. No big sigh, because like I said, we don't breathe. No beating heart, so none of the normal physical responses that come from emotions like embarrassment, sadness, hate, loss, and even love and lust." I almost bit through my own lip when I realized the last two I had thrown in.

"Wow, and you learn, how?" he asked, and I was thankful he let those slide.

"By watching movies and shows, and then mimicking the reaction to various situations," I said in an attempt to make the explanation sound as clinical as possible to avoid stepping into anything.

"So, you are actors?"

"Yep, some of the best," I agreed with a laugh, and what I hoped was a flirtatious smile.

He leaned back in his chair and appeared lost in thought while his eyes studied me. The look wasn't a critical one. It was friendly and warm, and if my body responded to these sensations that were floating through my mind, I would be sweating and red. "So, acting? So, we won't ever know when a vampire is being real."

"No," I screamed, horrified. "Yes, I mean. We are being genuine, we just..." Then I paused and calmed my thoughts down and set my mind to explain it in the best way I could. "Remember, we were all once human, and we each remember how important physical cues were to knowing how someone felt. Once we change, we lose that, and have to force ourselves to keep it up to restore that connection with those around us. It's one way we try to remain human, though we aren't. Understand?"

"Actually, I do. So, these are honest emotions. You are just forcing the reaction so we know what you're feeling?"

"Exactly," I said, relieved. "Not to say some aren't being deceitful like some humans are, but I am always honest with everyone, like you." Why did I say that? I had to break that promise instantly, just to hide the embarrassment I felt.

"Can I ask one more question?"

"Of course," I said, relieved he let that go.

"Does it hurt when you are turned?"

"Are you sure you want to know about that?" I asked, hoping he wasn't the squeamish type.

"Yes, as long as the question doesn't bother you."

I shook my head and looked at him. He had the same kind eyes his mother did. I was sure the question was a curiosity, but I picked up something more. Something more personal, almost a worry, that I had been hurt. Whoa, slow down there, girl. My head was making leaps that logic didn't backup, but logic had no place here. I leaned forward, bracing myself against the table with my arms, and brushed my red hair away from my face, tucking it behind my ears. Then I swallowed. Not that I needed it, and this wasn't any cooked up reaction that I felt humans would have done. This was a genuine response to what I was feeling at the moment. "Yes, it hurts. It hurts a lot," I said grimly. As much as I didn't want to, I let my eyes wander away from his. I didn't want to see his reaction to what I was about to explain. "Imagine the worst pain you have ever felt, then ramp that up by a hundred, and set it on fire. Then, you die from the inside out, slowly. It drags out for hours that eventually turn into days. One by one, you feel each muscle die, then your internal organs. Which hurt more than the muscles. Toxins build up and your stomach bloats. All of this happens while your heart beats out its last beats, slowly, but still enough to keep you aware. Then it all stops, which you are aware of for several minutes until the brain runs out of oxygenated blood and finally shuts down."

"Whoa," he said, his voice wretched like he swallowed something disgusting, and it was coming back up.

"That's just the start," I said with another nervous brushing of my hair by my hand while I gave whether or not to continue with the horrifying details half a consideration. "When the venom kicks in and does whatever it does, it sets you on fire again from the inside, and then bolts of lightning shoot through every cell. That's it bringing you back alive or whatever this is. Then the world explodes on you. Every sound, scent, and color brighter than before. Wait," I finally looked up at him. The shocked expression he had wasn't as bad as I expected, and I hadn't heard him run from the table. "Before you think that is great or anything, you need to think about it like this. You can see everything more spectacularly than you ever remembered. Every sound clearer and more beautiful than before, but that is it. There is something missing, something deep inside that you can't put your finger on, but you know isn't there anymore. It's an emptiness you can never shake."

The hand that kept brushing my hair was now playing with the chain around my neck. His eyes followed its movement as my fingers traced the links down to the vial of red liquid. I mostly kept it hidden inside my shirt, like most of the others did. Not that I was trying to hide it, just a habit. His eyes stopped and stayed stuck on the vial as my fingers tracked back up the links. He was mesmerized, and I moved my fingers back to it and held it out so he could get a closer look.

"This is a blood charm. Your mother told me what it is called. Before that I didn't know much about it." I paused and gave a nervous laugh. "In fact, I didn't know anything about it until she told me what it was. It contains the last drop of my blood and represents the gift of immortality I can pass along. It stays red until I turn someone and then it turns clear. Once that happens, it becomes an antidote that can reverse the venom if given soon enough after the initial bite. or can temporarily turn one of us back to human. That is what had happened to me that night you first saw me." My voice trailed off.

"Oh, so you turned back and then turned back to this?" Nathan leaned forward and asked.

"Yep, about two days later," I said quietly, not wanting to have to explain that yes, turning back the second time was as painful as the first.

"That had to be both horrible and confusing." He got up and slid his chair around the table next to mine. The warmth of his body bathed my own. I knew he wouldn't feel the same. I had the warmth of an ice cube."Can I ask another question?"

"Seeing as I have already shared very intimate details, why not. There is nothing left to hide." I had nothing left to hide at the moment, except how I was feeling, but I felt relatively sure he wouldn't ask about any of that, or I hoped he wouldn't.

He reached his hand over and brushed my forearm. I felt it. The warmth and the shock waves it sent through me were intoxicating. There was no denying it. "They say you can't stand being around someone like me. That just our presence around you is so tempting it is torture."

If he only knew.

"Is it really that bad?"

It was torturous, but not in the way I knew he meant. "You mean what some call the blood lust, right?"

"I guess." He nodded. His hand now caressed my arm down to my hand. Was he tempting me? Trying his luck?

"Some find the thirst uncontrollable and insatiable. It's so bad, it controls them. I have never been that way. I have pretty good self-control over it." I wasn't bragging, just stating a fact. Not once, except the morning I first turned, had I ever felt it as an uncontrollable urge. There was a possibility that I was feeding enough to keep it at bay, but I felt it was more than that. That was why I could sit here while he titillated me with his touch, and even though I could feel his pulse quicken, I never felt the need to devour him, or even take one bite for a taste.

"How good is that control?" he asked. There was an evil smile on his face. Not evil like a murderous or horrific evil, but an innocent, devious type. He leaned forward toward me. I felt his breath on my cheek. Was this really happening? The better question was, would I let it happen? My body gave the answer and betrayed my better judgement. I leaned in to meet him.

"Get it, Larissa!" called a voice I recognized as Mike.

I pulled back and glanced up. There was everyone, and I do mean every one of my friends, standing along the railing on the deck. If I was human, I would be more than a few shades of red, like Nathan was. Instead, I just hid my face in my hands, not a forced response. My emotions were embarrassed, and my mind relieved.

The whistles from above continued for a bit, as did the embarrassment. Then, seeing the dog pack come out to start their first patrol for the night, was the cherry on top. Martin, Rob, and Dan passed by. Each gave their approval. Well, they gave Nathan their approval with comments like, "Nice, Nate." When Mr. Markinson passed, it was just a simple, "Evening guys."

We both turned and watched the four morph into large wolves and head out. "Not sure about you, but it doesn't matter how many times I see that, it never gets old." I had to agree with Nathan. Some things around here never got old, and I was okay with that. Everyone here was like me. While I may have thought I only belonged with those like me, I was also starting to feel a belonging with everyone in some way. Well, everyone but Gwen.

"Why don't we head back in? We can talk about the ottoman empire in there," offered Nathan. I accepted.

He led us back in, and as we walked through the doors, I noticed something had changed. There were white symbols everywhere. On the floor, the walls leading up the stairs, and ahead on the door that I first came in. When I turned around, they were on the door leading out to the pool and all around the windows. I had seen something like them before. "Runes," I mumbled.

"Yea," Nathan started to say, but before he did, I blanked out and found myself standing in that alley again. Nathan's voice was gone. My own sobs and screams had replaced it. Its dark eyes stared right at me like it had in my last vision. Seeing him looking at me like that for the second time was no less terrifying. In fact, it was more so this time because I now knew this wasn't a memory or my mind messing with me. This was real. He took two fast jerky steps toward me, and then growled, "You have slipped our grasp a few times, Larissa, but we know where you are, and you won't slip through this time. Your gift will be his."

"Larissa. Larissa. Wake up." I was on the floor. Nathan held me firmly in his arms while he called my name, and I shook and sobbed. I may have not had a soul, but this vision shook me to whatever was left.

"I saw it again," I bawled. "I saw it again."

23

"Well, we knew this would eventually happen," Mrs. Saxon announced frankly, her arms crossed tightly across her chest.

"You did?" I asked in disbelief of what I heard, but tried carefully to avoid any emotional outburst. I was now the animal under the microscope in front of all the instructors at the school, many of whom I hadn't met before now. *My problem* was now their first impression of me. Not the impression I wanted to make, and I didn't need to make it worse by crying or screaming, though it was hard considering what I felt. Control was not one of my strengths.

"Yes, we did Larissa," Mrs. Tenderschott said. She was seated next to me on the sofa, holding both of my hands. "With or without the spell, it would eventually happen. He was seeking you out." She looked up at Mrs. Saxon and said, "She needs to know."

I looked at Mrs. Tenderschott's kind face and then back up at Mrs. Saxon, whose expression was more tense, with pursed lips and an intense stare. All that was missing was the rapid tapping of her foot.

"Know what?" When I scanned the faces of everyone in the room, I got the feeling I was the only one who didn't know this little secret.

"Rebecca, it is her history, and we may not be around to help her when he finally finds her."

Mrs. Saxon didn't break her intense stare.

"She's right Rebecca," Mrs. Bolden agreed. She walked back around the backside of the sofa and rubbed my shoulders. Mr. Bolden nodded in agreement with his wife. Many of the others nodded as well, but not Mrs. Saxon. She was a stone statue that just stared at a spot that was a few feet in front of her.

"She needs to know," Mr. Markinson said. He stood next to Mr. Helms and a Mrs. Parrish, a beautiful blonde with striking model like features, but who knew if that was really what she looked like? She was a shapeshifter. It was an easy deduction. I knew for a fact she wasn't vampire, witch, or werewolf; that only left one option left. I also surmised there was some kind of relationship between the two of them by the way she hung on his arm when they walked in.

Mr. Markinson's agreement didn't appear to sway Mrs. Saxon into any action. What seemed to move her was the person sitting on my other side. "Mom, what is it?" Nathan's question drew a look of disdain from his mother, which she followed with the order, "Leave us." How quickly he got up and left the room told me this was not the first time he had heard that request, or that tone.

"All right." Mrs. Saxon turned to look at me. "Larissa, Edward finished his research just moments before Nathan brought you to see me. Some of this you might not want to believe, but these are all part of our records, so they are facts. These records are never wrong."

She paused and even though she didn't ask me for my agreement, I felt everyone in the room looking at me for my acceptance of this absolute, even though I was never a person who liked absolutes, I didn't feel I had a choice. "Okay."

"You are Larissa Dubois. You were born in 1923. The daughter of Maxwell and Susan Dubois. One of the oldest families of witches in New Orleans, and a member of the Orleans' Coven. Both your father and mother were highly respected members of the coven and the city. That home you saw during Mrs. Tenderschott's spell was your family's plantation on the north side of the city. According to our records, your mother died on June 19th, 1939, as a result of injuries suffered at the hands of members of Jean St. Claire's Coven. Have you ever heard that name before?"

"No, never."

"Edward," Mrs. Saxon called, and right on cue he appeared. "The St. Claire roster please." Without a word, a thick red book appeared where Nathan had sat. It opened, and the pages flipped quickly and then stopped. The book spun around to face me. "Larissa, do you see anyone on that page that looks like the person in your vision?"

There were six rows of six pictures. Each black and white, or brown and white due to what appeared to be some fading, but they were remarkably detailed. I scanned them, starting with the top row. Each man was dressed like the others. Each had dark hair that was fixed the same way, which acted like frames for their pale faces, which weren't really all that different from picture to picture. When I hit the fourth picture in the third row, I felt a sharp stab through my head. There he was. He even appeared to leer at me from the picture like he did in the visions. I pointed to the picture, and both Edward and Mrs. Saxon leaned over to look.

"Reginald Von Bell," Edward read from the name below the picture.

"He wouldn't do the dirty work himself," Mr. Bolden said.

"Agreed," Mrs. Saxon said. "Larissa, what you are looking at are the pictures of the oldest and most powerful vampire coven in New Orleans. A ruthless man named Jean St. Claire runs it. He came over from France to set up his empire in the New World. He is not a fan of witches, and our coven in New Orleans has been in conflict with him for centuries."

"The list of witches that he or one of his goons has killed is quite extensive," added Edward.

"Edward's right. His name is known well in our world as someone you stay away from, and I believe it does in your world too." She looked back at Mr. and Mrs. Bolden, and both confirmed her thought with a nod.

"Larissa, if there is a devil in our world, he is it. His only loyalty is to himself and those that help elevate him. If you cross him, or don't pledge your support to him, he will have you killed," Mr. Bolden said gravely.

"Your family, being who they were in our Orleans' Coven, crossed him on more than one occasion," continued Mrs. Saxon. "Your father and he had more than a few run-ins, according to our journals. Based on our records, he took his revenge by killing your mother, and believed he killed you as well. An act he celebrated and gloated about to build the specter of his power in both communities."

"What about my father?" The question seemed to take the air out of the room. Even Edward appeared upset by it. It prompted several looks back and forth between everyone in the room. "What about my father?" I asked again with a hint of desperation in my voice, and the feeling they were hiding something from me growing in my head.

Uncomfortable looks were abound, and no one appeared eager to answer my question. I looked around and searched all of them with my eyes, damning the black orbs that replaced my natural green eyes, robbing them of the ability to convey deep emotion. Though I didn't doubt everyone in the room was aware of what I was feeling. Especially after what control I had finally let go, "My father?" I cried. My hands and voice both begged for information.

Mrs. Bolden was the first to break ranks of the statues of grim looking adults that stood around me and walked toward me. She pushed the book aside and sat. I turned toward her. She sighed, and her eyes glanced at her husband first before returning to me. Whether this was a natural reaction, or learned, I wasn't sure, but it seemed fitting. As did the tear that ran down my cheek.

"Larissa, Jean St. Claire took your father during the attack that killed your mother. He held him for a while before turning him into a vampire himself. Our journals say when he realized your father kept his magical abilities too, he became obsessed with finding a way to become like your father, both a witch and a vampire, even resorting to keeping him chained in a room and feeding off a diet of your father's blood, until he finally killed him in frustration from his failure." She mouthed I am sorry, as her hand landed on my shoulder.

"Larissa, that is the key to all of this, I'm afraid. If he, or one of his supporters, were able to become both, they would be more powerful than any creature I have ever heard of, and now, there is only one way for him to get it, and that is from the one who is what he wants to be," Mrs. Saxon said coldly as she pointed at me.

"That is why he wants me," I whispered, thinking it was only to myself, but the room was quiet enough to hear a pin drop. So, a whisper was just a normal conversation.

"Not you, Larissa," Mrs. Saxon corrected. "Your gift to pass on. Your blood has both abilities, so anyone you turn, or anyone who drinks the contents of your charm should become both. He was already a vampire so your father couldn't turn him, and I seriously doubt they captured any of your father's blood at the time he was turned, that makes you the only source of what he wants and explains why nothing he tried ever worked. I still have doubts that it would work for him since he is already a vampire, but that doesn't mean he couldn't use it to turn someone else who would be loyal to him."

My hand reached out for the object of his desire, and instead of tracing the chain and caressing the vial as I had done more times than I could remember, many of which were subconscious acts, my hand now gripped it tightly, protectively. Anyone who wanted would have to rip it from my cold dead fingers. Not that I felt that prospect would really stop the person they were describing.

"How dangerous is Jean St. Claire?" I asked, though I already knew the answer. He killed my mother, thought he killed me, and imprisoned my dad until he killed him. I guess somehow he found out I was still alive, and then came after me, killing the man I felt at the time was my father.

"He is evil," Mr. Bolden spoke up from behind Mrs. Saxon. "Jennifer and I have never met him or anyone in his coven, but we know some that have and have heard the stories of others. He and his coven are well known by all of us, and considering your age, I am a little surprised you haven't heard of him before now. I don't want to scare you, but he is someone you don't want to cross or become the attention of. He is the type that doesn't usually do his own dirty work and has an army of those that will, without hesitation. Reginald is one of them, but there are others. Many others." His voice trailed off, and his wife reached back for the book she had pushed out of the way, and then put it in my lap.

"I am sorry," she said and flipped the page. Her voice sounded as devastated as I felt when I saw the center two pictures on the top row of the next page. Marie Norton, and Thomas Norton, my mother and father.

24

"Try to just listen to some music and relax." That was the advice I got from Apryl when I joined the others up on the deck. Neither was going to happen. Relax was not a word that meant anything to me in my current state, and music may have been playing, but I couldn't hear a beat of it, no matter how loud it thumped. My thoughts were thousands of miles to my south, and almost a century ago.

I still didn't remember anything on my own, but looking at the journals Edward had brought out from the Orleans' Coven started to fill in the Grand Canyon sized gap. References to my parents, who seemed to really enjoy the social life in New Orleans and threw the best parties for both members of the coven and normal mortals, told me who they were as people, and who they were as witches. Both were extremely powerful. My father was an elemental. My mother though, was like Laura had described Gwen, just a plain witch, but there was nothing plain about her. She was a spell-slinger. There wasn't much she couldn't do with the right spell, and her spells were powerful. They were both offered the role of Supreme in the coven, but neither wanted that responsibility, but it was well documented they were never far from the Supreme and always supported them.

Everything I learned were facts, dates, and events, but not a one of them felt familiar. I didn't feel an emotional connection to any of it. It was as if I was reading something about complete strangers. The more I thought about it, the more I realized I was.

Even reading about myself. My own birth announcement was just a date and weight. I was a hefty baby at almost eleven pounds. There were a few other entries that were a little more detailed, but most of those were simple notes where I was mentioned, along with others as part of a class. It made me wonder if it was a school like this, hidden inside some magical void away from the rest of society. On some level, I might feel a familiarity with this place because of it. That might explain why I didn't spend several days wondering if I was on some kind of drug induced trip, or constantly having one oh-crap moment after another. Those entries categorized my ability as above average capability and control. That tickled me a little, considering what little control I had now. Of course, it had been how long since I tried to use it, and obviously it wasn't like riding a bike.

I did find one entry that was more detailed than the others, if you call two paragraphs detailed. My own debutante ball, held on my family's plantation. With the focus on the list of people that attended, I got a sense that anyone who was anybody was there. Of course, I didn't know who any of them were, so they could have been nobody. I was mentioned in both paragraphs, and as brief as they were, they were the most detailed accounts I had read so far. I wore a large light blue dress, with a hoop skirt, white ruffles, pearls, and elbow length white gloves, and I was a beautiful sight, like a younger version of my mother. That was it. I tried to remember back to that moment, and even laid back on my bed and tried what I did with Mrs. Tenderschott, but nothing. Just a blank canvas of darkness, like the rest of my memories. I had hoped to find some connection, some solace, but instead, it left me feeling emptier than before. I didn't believe that was possible.

The same couldn't be said when I read what the coven had about Jean St. Claire and his coven. Every word chilled the spot that used to be my soul, causing my fear to bubble. He was ruthless. Fully enveloped in the creole black magic of the region and looked upon as almost a god by some of the old voodoo practitioners; a fact made more chilling when I read it was still true today. He and his coven preyed on anyone and everyone, and it wasn't as simple as a blood war. No, it was just whatever they wanted to do, and when they wanted to do it. The Orleans' coven had no doubts that the thousands and thousands of people reported missing and never seen again didn't succumb to the swamps and the creatures that lived within, except in the cases where Jean St. Claire and his coven were those creatures. It even seemed that the local humans knew of their existence; they just learned to stay out of the dark shadows of the old streets, and to look the other way.

In so many ways, I wish I were like them and could look the other way. As frightening as learning about what was after me was, there was one detail that was haunting me even more. Normally something like this would set my temper into overdrive and I would be stomping around up here fuming and looking for a fight, but seeing those two pictures sent me into a tailspin that shattered everything that I thought I knew. There was only one explanation. Well, there may be others, but only one made sense. Edward said in the history of Jean St. Claire it was rare he did his own dirty work. It appeared those that I loved most were just his tools, and killing my real parents was their job. The people I loved like parents. The people I thought were my parents. They were nothing more than dirty-vile-vampires that killed my mother, captured my father, and stole me. That was the only word that seemed to fit. They stole me and stole my life from me. Then, even worse, they hid who I was from me for years. I thought it was only a few years, but no, it was longer, much longer that I spent holed up in that house in Virginia, never knowing who or what I really was, but they knew. My waves of anger ebbed and flowed in a sea of denial as the emotions of my feeling for them, and the longing to be with them again, ran hot and cold.

"How are you holding up?" A hand brushed the hair on the top of my head.

I looked up and saw Mrs. Bolden gazing down upon me. "Fine," I breathed.

"You're not, but that is fine. I know there is a lot going on in your head, but I don't want you to be afraid. What Mrs. Saxon and Mr. Helms said was right. You are safe here, and we will protect you."

"We all will," stated Laura from two chairs away.

Mike cracked his knuckles and flexed his huge chest under his t-shirt. "We got your back."

"Covens are family, and a family protects and takes care of each other," added Brad. There was a similar show of machismo from him, though he sat there with a blue sweater tied around his neck.

Jeremy let out an elongated and very country sounding, "Damn right." His head never stopped bobbing to the music.

"It's true," Mrs. Bolden said. "Covens are family. This isn't the first time someone has come after one of our own. We defended them then and we will defend you now."

"Mr. Helms said the enemy is everyone. Even your husband told me about the dangers of the world. Are there..." I started, still reeling from everything, struggling to create a logic thought. "Is the world really that dangerous?"

Mrs. Bolden sat down on the arm of the chair I was sitting in. Her hand brushed my hair again and then landed on the back of my shoulder. "Yes, and no." she said, with a tilt of her head back and forth. "There are dangers out there for us, just like anyone else in the world. Evil has no boundaries. Just our evil is a little stronger than your average mugger or murderer. You have those motivated by fear that seek us out. Vengeance in some cases, and power in others. Either to force us to comply and help them, or eliminate us as a threat to stand against them. Same stuff that is everywhere else, just on our levels. And yes, there have been threats against members of this coven before, many threats. There isn't a coven in the world that hasn't dealt with threats or attacks on their members, and there isn't a coven in the world that didn't stand together to try to defend them."

I knew she was trying to make me feel better. They all were. It might have helped a bit if the dark cloud that was over my head hadn't intensified into the storm of the century, and that storm came with a side effect, an eroded feeling of trust. Everyone that meant anything in my world, those that I cared about the most, and those I trusted beyond question were not who I thought they were. They were the opposite. They were the ones that killed me. The only person I could truly trust was myself. I wouldn't turn against myself.

I mouthed, "Thank you," to each person. I didn't want to seem ungrateful, but I wasn't feeling very magnanimous at the moment. I was sitting there with a large group of others like me, but in my mind, I was on a desolate island all by myself, void of people and hope.

My hearing picked up a knock from my door below and my body cringed. Knowing the charmed locks on each doorway kept anyone but vampires or one of the instructors from entering. I concluded it was Mrs. Saxon. I cringed when I heard the second knock and pushed up from the chair. Mrs. Bolden's hand slid from my shoulder. As I passed Laura's chair, she reached and gave my hand a squeeze and said, "We got you."

Jeremy got up and stepped toward me, before standing there uncomfortably just a foot or so away. I paused and looked at him. His body leaned, and I thought over and over, don't hug me. It looked like he wanted to try, but either had never actually done it, which was completely possible—vampires weren't the most emotionally connected creatures in the world, especially new ones — or he was scared to get that close to me, which was fine by me. I rescued him from the moment with a "Thanks Jeremy." Relief was evident in his eyes.

I trudged to my door, knowing that there was bad news behind it. Why else would she come up here at this hour of the night? My hand lingered on the doorknob for a moment while the thought of not even answering it danced in my head. Doing that would only delay hearing the news, and not stop it from coming, I turned the handle and slowly opened the door wide open before I looked up from the floor.

I looked up and collapsed forward into Nathan's arms at the same time. Our eyes only met for a moment before my head was in his chest and his arms wrapped around me. "Are you okay?" he whispered.

"No," I said, being totally honest as I sank into the rhythmic sound of his pulse. I had found my moment of solace.

25

I spent the rest of the night thinking about ten minutes. The ten minutes that I stood there in my doorway, being held. Something I can't say I had a lot of experience with. I wasn't someone that ever really sought out physical comforts. In fact, I avoided it most of the time, but this time I needed it, and didn't even know I did until it happened.

During those ten minutes, there was no big conversation or spewing of my problems. Just the simple question Nathan asked when I opened the door, and my single word response. I wasn't sure if he expected me to spill my emotions out there for him, or what he already knew. The way his arms pulled me in tight, seemingly not concerned about who or what I was, told me he knew enough about what I had just learned. There were serious doubts in my mind that his mother would have told him anything. She seemed to want to keep him separated from this world, but the fact that he was able to pass through the lock on the door leading to our rooms told me something about that. The possibility that he was so concerned about me that he listened through his door and then came to find me told me more.

I wasn't used to someone caring about me, and especially someone who didn't have to. Not that anyone ever neglected me. The Nortons didn't. At least not that I remembered. Knowing they were probably who killed my mother and then stole me kind of changed that feeling, but there was nothing I could actually remember where they did anything wrong. They were my parents, and I was their daughter. I guess I just accepted they would care about me as a default, so it never seemed like anything special. We stayed isolated from everyone else, never really seeing anyone, so no one was around us close enough to develop any kind of bond. There were no cheek pinching aunts or crazy uncles, or friends of my parents that were like members of the family. It was just them.

Of course, I felt, or hoped, Mrs. Saxon, the Boldens, Mrs. Tenderschott, and the other instructors cared about me. They had shown it in their own way, but that was different. I felt they had to. They were the adults—ignoring my true age, which most only now found out about—and caregivers to the students in this school, coven, or whatever it was.

Nathan was the first person that didn't have to care about me that did, and to be honest it kind of scared me. Okay, it more than scared me. It was nice and frightening, and confusing, all rolled up in a big wrapper of comfort. I liked it. I wanted it. But I didn't understand it, and was scared to accept it, and knew I couldn't. We were different, and that would eventually cause a problem. No matter how much I thought about it, I couldn't make any logical sense out of it. When he finally let go, it hurt, but I sucked it up and said, "Thanks." He departed after saying, "See you in class."

The next time we saw each other was in class. I didn't wait for the others to be ready before heading down to class and found myself the first person to arrive, which was fine with me. I enjoyed the moment of silence. Though the silence was only what was around me. Inside, I was anything but. Thoughts and emotions rolled like an evil storm, and I was in a dinghy being tossed around by the waves and the wind.

The door opened behind me, and a different type of storm came in. There was talking and chatter that sliced through the silence, but only for a moment. What replaced it was a painful and deafening silence. I felt set after set of eyes gazing at me as they walked past. Each went to their normal place, but each kept their eyes on me as they passed. Word had gotten around. I didn't have to be like Jack to be able to read everyone in the room. When my friends, at least I thought they were, sat next to me, there were no greetings. Each looked down the table in my direction, but I kept my focus straight ahead, and only saw them out of the corner of my vision. Laura sat next to me, instead of Apryl, who normally did. She gave my back a simple pat, and then a rub before she opened her notebook. I knew they meant well. We had spoken about everything most of the night. Well, not everything. I hadn't mentioned the Norton's role in things, and don't believe either Mrs. or Mr. Bolden would have broken any confidence and said anything either.

Even Mrs. Saxon cast me a long, almost woeful look, and it was not without notice. Most followed the direction of her eyes, looking back over their own shoulders at me. When Gwen looked back, she appeared to have a smirk on her face. I never thought someone could be so cold.

Once Mrs. Saxon started the lecture of the day, my brain zoned out. Not the best way to keep my grades up, but it didn't really give me a choice. It had a mind of its own, or really, it had my mind. It even forced me to glance back over my own shoulder to my right. Nathan was sitting where he always did. His blue eyes were focused on his mother lecturing the class on, well... I didn't really know. I was about to turn around when his eyes cut to meet mine, and he smiled. It was just a moment, but that moment felt like an eternity, and was exactly what I needed. We both turned back forward, he listening to the lecture, and me finding that Laura had slid her notes close to me so I could try to catch up.

For the next several hours, my brain played hide and seek with reality. Thoughts flashed in and out. Brief sections of my classes or conversations I heard between Pam, Apryl, and Laura stuck. One of those was Brad suggesting I tell them I am too sick for witch school and take a break this afternoon. Something I thought about, or I think I did, though I still went to class as I normally did.

I must have been moving in slow motion that afternoon because I was the last to reach Mrs. Tenderschott's potion class, and I had to walk through the crowd gathered by the door. Just like when they entered Mrs. Saxon's class in the morning, silence took hold. This time, it only lasted until I passed. Once I was at my table, the chatter resumed. I wasn't sure if any part of the education around here taught one another the characteristics of each other. If it had, they would know I could hear them as if they were whispering into my ear. Yet, they spoke openly about the rumors that involved me, and not a one appeared nervous or anxious. The pulse and heart rate of each felt very normal and relaxed. I was sure if mine still beat, it wouldn't be.

Mrs. Tenderschott called class to order, and Jack Nash took the seat next to me at the table. There was room with the others, and any number of free tables he could have chosen. I found it a little easier to concentrate on Mrs. Tenderschott's nurturing voice as she covered the variations of sleeping potions and how they are different from sleeping spells. Spells sounded more temporary and only put the target out, where a potion could be made to last longer. You could also, depending on the variant, wipe their memory and give them new memories or dreams. At the moment, those seemed rather appealing for my own consumption.

Jack slid his notepad toward me, and I pushed it back. I didn't need or want his help. I was actually paying attention now. With a little flip of his wrist, it moved back toward me. Somewhat of an impressive trick, he had obviously done his homework from Mrs. Saxon's class.

I pushed the notebook back again, and this time he used more old school methods and pushed it with his hand, pointing at something written in the corner. *I can feel what you are going through. I got your back in class today.*

I knew he could feel what I was going through, but him reminding me of that fact burned me. My thoughts were my thoughts, and so were my feelings. Plus, I had a hunch, one that I didn't hesitate to write down in response.

I know you are the one who told everyone what is going on. Thanks, but no thanks.

I pushed the notebook back and saw him immediately start to scribble, while I flipped my potion textbook to the part Mrs. Tenderschott was going over. Using these to self-medicate seemed like a good option for me. Of course, there was the question if they would even work on me. We don't sleep.

Jack pushed his notebook back again. In big letters was the word *NO* followed by, *Look, I know I screwed up out by the pool and made a bad joke. It's a common one. We are all orphans. That is why we are ALL here. I never tell anyone anything I sense unless I feel Mrs. Saxon or an instructor needs to know, and that is only so they can help.*

I looked at him and saw a stone like steadfast expression. It was almost convincing, but not entirely. I wrote back, *Nice try. They all know. I can hear you all talk.*

There was another moment of furious scratching of his pencil on his notepad. Mrs. Tenderschott had started with her list of ingredients explaining what each did as part of the potion, and Jack's scribbling went on as long as mine did as I copied down the list with the detailed information; he was probably making similar notes. Everyone was. "Knowing what each element does will let you one day develop your own potions," she stated several times, interrupting her list.

She was on the ninth element when Jack pushed his notepad back over again, and sat up, his pulse calm.

They only know someone is after you. Another vampire who killed your parents. Think about it. We are all orphans, which means our parents are dead, and the runes that went up are specific to blocking and alerting us when a vampire crosses them. They don't know anything beyond that. Nothing about the Nortons or what happened to your real father, or who is after you, and I won't be the one to tell them. I may be a jerk, but I am not that type of jerk.

"Thanks," I whispered, and pushed the note back.

"Everyone has secrets, and I know them all. Even what people think of me, and I can't stop it or say anything about it. If I did, no one would ever trust me. That is my burden," he whispered just above a breath.

Much to my disappointment, this was just a lecture session on the ingredients, amounts, and methods. We weren't allowed to try it on anyone in the class, and there I was all ready to volunteer. I was sure Gwen would have jumped at the chance to put me under, and I wasn't sure I would have resisted too much.

Mr. Helm's class was the same, and again he asked me to just observe instead of taking part. His decision this time was driven by my current lack of focus, which could get me hurt. That made me feel like a weak little child. So much for helping me.

I watched, or I thought I did. I didn't remember much until everyone started packing up to leave. Mr. Helms walked up to me and asked me to stay after class. Inside I sunk, expecting either more news, details, or anything else that might feel like a gut punch. How much more I could take was the biggest question no one seemed to be concerned with.

After everyone else left, not without giving me a look as I waited, Mr. Helms closed the door and then walked back over to where I was standing. I braced myself for what other morsel of great news I was about to hear. My insides shook when he opened his mouth. "Larissa, we need to prepare you for anything. You have your abilities as a vampire. I am going to show you how to use your abilities as a witch with those. Come with me to the front?"

I followed him to the open area of the class. "Stand here?" He pointed to a spot on the cobblestone floor, and then walked to a spot about thirty feet away, just in front of one of the large stone arches. The door opened, and someone I had only seen once, during Lisa's ceremony, walked in. He was one of the cloaked figures that entered behind the students. A tall and slender man with a gaunt face and a pale complexion. An eerie frame for his dark beady eyes, which glared from under a mop of stringy black hair. As with everyone I saw around here, I tried to make a guess of what they were. Vampire was high on my list of possibilities, but I hadn't met him yet. He silently took a seat in the back, and Mr. Helms didn't even acknowledge him.

"Let's talk defensive first. I am going to send some simple fire balls your way. Let your instincts take hold."

Without delay, he unloaded three volleys of fireballs that shot out at me faster than any I had seen fired in the class before. Their speed was surprising, but I managed to move out of the way of most. One got close enough where I felt the heat and smelled singed hair. It was then I realized he fired one right at my head, and looked at him, surprised.

"Remember, your enemy is everyone and everywhere," he shouted. When I looked back at our silent observer, he sat there with his hands crossed in front of him on the table.

Another barrage came, and this time I didn't watch them approach. I was out of the way long before they reached me, or so I thought. One seemed to follow me. I backed up and slammed into the cobblestone wall behind me. On instinct, I turned and climbed it, flipping off it and back to the floor. The ball of fire blasted into the wall with a small explosion. I looked back over my shoulder at Mr. Helms. My hair still moving from the flip. "My enemy is everyone and everywhere," I seethed. That was too close, and a little personal.

Before another arrived, I wanted to give him a taste of his own medicine and focused on the air on the floor around his feet. The molecules moving faster and faster until a large column of fire erupted up from the floor. Taller and more intense than I wanted. I pulled it back, snuffing the flames out until they disappeared as Mr. Helms jumped away from it. This time it was his turn to look across at me surprised.

"Sorry," I apologized, sheepishly. I just wanted to warm the floor, not melt it.

"Don't apologize. Your enemy never will." I looked up at our observer, who was now leaning forward. "That was good. Now I want you to learn how to throw one. It's the same as you just did, except imagine the air as a ball in front of your hand, and when it ignites, send it with a column of air in my direction."

I stood straight with my right hand hanging down. In my mind, I pictured a ball of air in front of it getting hotter and hotter. I felt the heat and knew it was close to igniting. I figured now it was time to send it. A column of air is what Mr. Helms said.

To me, that sounded like a strong breeze, and as I imagined it, I felt it gathering behind me and rush past as I threw my right hand forward.

Both of my hands shot to my mouth as a wave of flames launched forward and filled the room. I ran behind it to see if I could push Mr. Helms out of the way, but he threw up a shield that the flames blasted against. The heat as it deflected off was intense, and now our observer was standing.

Mr. Helms stood untouched while the moss and ferns that littered the gaps between the stones in the wall smoldered. He was also looking in the direction of our observer, who now had walked around the table he was seated at and strode, very upright, down toward us.

"Great power requires a greater focus," he said. His voice had a hit of an old English professor to it. Sharp and short. My first impression, he was a mysterious guy with a saying.

"Another proverb of this class?" I asked, remembering the first rule, and wondering if there was a third rule that said we don't talk about the first two.

He was not impressed as he continued until he stood between us. His hands behind his back, and upright straighter than any board that existed. He turned toward me in a single and rigid move. "No Miss Dubois. You have great power, which requires even greater control. Instead of imagining a ball, try imaging the head of a pin. When you try to move things, they slam around, don't they?"

I nodded.

"Larissa, meet Mr. Marcus Demius. Our expert in the dark arts."

I looked at him and felt a little fear with this new knowledge. I hadn't even considered that someone here taught dark magic.

"Don't imagine a hand pressing them, imagine a molecule. Tighter focus. Tighter control." He stepped forward and out of the line of fire. "Again!"

I went through the process again and attempted to focus my thoughts with a ton of everything else spinning around in my head. Again, a large mass of fire streaked across the room, but it never reached Mr. Helms. The mysterious man swiped his hand forward, absorbing the fire into his palm. "Focus!" he demanded.

"I am trying. There is just a lot on my mind." I readied myself to start again.

Mr. Demius stormed toward me and stopped just a few inches from me. The point of his narrow nose protruded forward and made me feel the need to lean back a little. The fear of him made me lean back a little further. "Miss Dubois, life is chaos, attacks are chaos, magic is chaos. Your mind will never be clear. It will be a cloud of worry, emotions, and self-doubt. You cannot let your magic be driven by any of them, only focus. When I said imagine the head of a pin, I wasn't being metaphorical about your focus, I was being literal. I have read about your family, and you were powerful witches. Your abilities are untrained and have been under-used for decades. I feel the dark energy in you from your other state has further amplified your capability, which requires a greater focus and makes you dangerous when emotions control you. You and I will discuss that after you master the simple. Now I want you to try it again and focus all of your thoughts on to the head of a pin, and let's see what happens."

He cocked his head sideways while waiting for my response, which was just a simple and not too sure sounding, "okay." He then stepped to my side, but never took his eyes off of me. I could feel their glare watching my face. If my body had the ability to show emotions, I would probably be soaked in sweat.

I started again, but immediately he spoke up, "The head of a needle."

The head of a needle. The head of a needle.

I repeated it over and over in my head, attempting to clear everything out. Then I picked a spot in the palm of my hand the size of the head of a needle. That spot became warmer and warmer. Just before it became too hot to hold, I threw it forward, and a ball of fire about the size of a softball flew across the room toward Mr. Helms, who hit it with one of his own. When the flash was gone, he was standing there smiling at me. I was smiling as well. I couldn't help it. Something I had tried actually worked rather well. Something had finally gone right.

26

I spent an hour, or maybe longer, in my room that night just lighting the candle and shutting my closet. The single tip seemed to be the key. I even managed to send a flame dancing through the air from my bed to the candle, where it settled perfectly on the wick. Then I tried to stretch myself a bit. I shut two doors at once, quietly. To say I was proud of myself was an understatement. I wanted to bound up the stairs and tell everyone, but I knew they wouldn't understand. The only ones that would were floors below me, and I wasn't exactly welcome there. Plus, I didn't really have time; I had another date, or so the note slid under my door said. Maybe I could impress him.

The momentary successes had cleared some of the doom and gloom from my mind, and also helped me feel more connected with my real mother. I had a few moments before I needed to head down to the pool area, so I laid back on my bed and imagined my mother's kitchen. It wasn't a real memory. Not of the real place. Just of the place I had seen when I had visited there with the help of one of Mrs. Tenderschott's potions. I hoped this would work.

"Family of my past, help me see. Family of my past, help me hear. Family of my past, help me know. Family of my past, show me."

The world around me melted away, and the thick humid air of the deep south surrounded me. This felt familiar to me. Of all things for me to finally find familiar, the sticky and suffocating mugginess of the swamp laden area. It was at least something. My visit didn't take me right into the kitchen, as I had hoped. Instead, I found myself standing on the front porch in front of the screen door. This time, there was no hesitation to enter and follow my nose down the hall and back into the kitchen. When I entered, I expected to find my mother, but she wasn't there. I left and went back down the hall, thinking perhaps she was in another room of the house. As I turned off the hall through the next door, I entered the kitchen again. This wasn't a different door into the kitchen. I found myself standing in the same place as if I had entered the normal door to the kitchen. I backed out and crossed the hall to the closed door on the other side. When I twisted the handle and pulled it open, I found myself again, standing in the same spot in the kitchen. Confused, I ran back down the hall and up the stairs to where I assumed the bedrooms were. The long hall ended just off the stairs, with only the door at the very top there. With it being the only choice, I opened it, and again found myself standing in the same spot in the kitchen. Now I was more than confused. I was completely perplexed and concerned. Had I made a mistake and found myself now stuck in my own personal twilight zone?

I remembered Mrs. Tenderschott telling me to return I just needed to shift my thoughts to the current time. So, I let go of the memory and returned my thoughts to my room, and in no time, I was lying on my bed with my eyes opened. The candle on my dresser still flickered with the flame I sent over to it, with the plant I am supposed to freeze sitting next to it. I sat up on the bed and let my feet hang over the edge while I tried to figure out what I had done wrong. It didn't take much before I remembered, and realized I was most certainly confused. It was the hot coffee like potion that sent me back to see my mother. What I had just tried was what I had done to revisit my memory of the day Mr. Norton died, so I could see who the attacker was. One took you to your ancestors, the other took you to a memory. Then a chill of horror and clarity came across me. Just days ago, I didn't know there were such things as witches. Then I found out I was one. Now I am here repeating words as if I am some kind of expert, and I didn't even know what they did. How stupid I was. I needed to be more careful to avoid a deadly mistake, and the stack of books Edward had placed next to my bed seemed full of bad opportunities.

I headed down to the pool right at five minutes to eight. The time the note asked me to meet him out there. On the way down, I passed Marcia and Tera. Each gave me a pleasant look; not the normal sneer I had grown used to. I was a few steps below them when Marcia spoke. Until now I had wondered if she was mute. She had never spoken to me before, nor had I heard her talk to anyone else or even in class. Of course, most didn't talk when Gwen was around. She didn't give them much of a chance. "Hey Larissa, you should stop by some time. We can help you with your spells and such."

I thought for a minute about the reaction my presence might cause and then found an excuse to decline without appearing rude. "I don't think I can get through your door."

"You are one of us too," Tera said. She stepped aside on her landing and pointed at the door. "Why not give it a try?"

Tera had me curious, and I could tell by the squint in her eyes, she was too. A quick try wouldn't hurt. Or maybe it would. Mrs. Saxon only told me the doors were protected by charms to not let us cross into each other's space. She didn't say what the charm would do if someone tried.

I stepped back up to the landing and stood at the door with Marcia and Tera standing to the side watching intensely. I felt their gaze increase in intensity when my hand touched the door handle. Not feeling any pain or major jolts of any type was a good sign. Enough of one to allow me to give it a turn and push. It opened to a hallway that looked exactly like the one on my floor. Was this it? Or would the door open for anyone but stop them from stepping through? I didn't know. Again, realizing how little I knew about any of this stuff. What the hell was a charm anyway? I used to think it had something to do with social graces and being polite and such.

There was only one way to learn, and this time I wasn't doing it unsupervised. Both Tera and Marcia were there watching. Maybe I should have asked them before I stepped across and into the hallway. Nothing happened, except Tera and Marcia rushing in to join me and grabbing me by the arm.

"Let us show you around," Tera said. Her pulse had increased, and she seemed generally excited.

"I really need to go," I said, trying to decline politely. I didn't want to keep Nathan waiting, and more so, I felt really uncomfortable. Like I was invading enemy territory. *Your enemies are everywhere and everyone.*

Before I could try to decline again, I was pulled toward another open door where Tera let go and bounded inside. "This is my room. What do you think?"

"Wow, nice," I said with a big grin while my mind screamed — *too much pink.* Pink walls, pink bed, even a pink floor. Jesus, it was like someone drank hundreds of bottles of Pepto-Bismol and then threw up all over everything. But this did match her personality and how she dressed. Always in pastels. Everything from her skirt to her hair tie.

"Mine is across the hall. It's not so bright," Marcia snickered, catching me a bit off guard. It was only a few moments ago I heard her talk for the first time and now she was cracking jokes about her friends in front of me. What was this? I gave a nervous laugh at the joke, while considering why the acceptance all of a sudden.

"We have a commons area down the hall. Want to see it?" asked Marcia.

"Of course she does." Tera rushed out of her room, grabbed me by the hand, and pulled me down the hallway. I stumbled after her down the hall another several doors. Then she stopped, and told me, "Wait here."

I stood there as Marcia and Tera went around me and through the door. Now I was alone across the border in no-man's-land. My head was on a swivel, looking up and down the hallway. The door opened again, causing me to jump a little. Tera poked her head out and said, "Come on."

I entered into a large room with tables, a large couch, a big screen television. "This is our hide out," Tera explained. "We hang out here to just relax or work on things together. Through that door over there," she pointed to one on the wall next to the door we just came in through, "takes you straight to the library. The one on the other wall takes you out to the balcony that overlooks the pool."

"We have something similar, it's mostly a deck on top of the roof. Outdoor furniture, large television, and music." Both looked at me with wide eyes.

"That sounds amazing," said Marcia. "We just have the balcony, but it is more of a quiet zone. Let us show you."

We started toward the balcony, but Tera was the first to the door and then turned around, waving her arms wildly. "We need to go." She grabbed me by the arm and pulled me out of the room back into the hallway. There had been a lot of people grabbing me and dragging me lately.

"What's wrong?" I asked, both curious and alarmed.

"Gwen was out there," she said as we rushed back down the hall to the door. "I thought she had gone to bed. Sorry about that."

"It's not a problem. I get it."

I stepped back through the door and out onto the landing. Tera stood inside the door. Her arms and shoulders had gone limp, and she avoided looking me in the eye. "It is a problem. One we all hope will get better." Then she finally looked up. "Larissa, we like you. Marcia, Lisa, and me, and we are serious about our offer. We would love to help you get caught up. Just Gwen...," her voice trailed off as did her eye contact.

"Thank you," I said, and genuinely meant it, as I felt she genuinely meant what she had said. "Maybe we can meet somewhere else to work on things without her knowing."

"Perhaps. I think she will eventually come around. Gwen just likes being the center of attention, and you have stolen some of her spotlight being new and all. She will get over it in time."

"Or someone new will arrive," I said, partially in jest.

Tera laughed, "Yep, until then, we can probably meet in the kid's area. She never goes there, and they love it when some of us teenagers come down there."

"Wait? What?," I stammered before I was able to properly phrase the question. "There are kids here?"

"Yep, quite a few. They have their own rooms and area down in the other wing. I can show you sometime."

The image of an entire class of little girls in dresses and pointy hats on sprang into my mind. Of course, I knew that wasn't what I would find, or was it? Nothing at this point would surprise me.

"You have a lot to learn, Miss Norton," Tera said. "See you in class." She closed the door, leaving me standing there dealing with the realization there were more students, and probably more instructors, in this place. What else was there that I didn't know about. The possibilities were endless, especially how this space adapted itself to your needs and wants.

The first few steps down were slow while I pondered this place. At the bottom, I continued my zombie like walk all the way out to the pool and up to the table where

Nathan waited again. I didn't even see him, as I stood there, not attempting to take a seat.

"Penny for your thought?"

"Huh?" I responded.

"You seem lost in thought," he said. "What is it?"

"Got one hundred years. I just found out there are more than us here. There are little kids."

Nathan got up and walked around the table, pulling out the chair across from him. Then his hands gently guided me to the chair and gave me a little pressure down to encourage me to sit. When I did, he removed his hands from my shoulders, and I felt the coldness of the world that his touch had chased away. I looked up, just in time to see Gwen turning on their balcony to head back inside. I would be lying to say that didn't give me a little warmth.

"Yes, there are little kids here. About twenty or so, if I remember right, and they are all witches. It is rare to find a vampire at that age, since you aren't born like that. Werewolves don't hit the age of passage until about age sixteen, or sometimes later. Shapeshifters," Nathan paused his report and appeared lost in thought before he shrugged. "I am not sure. I just know we never have any younglings."

"You seem to be an expert in all this," I said, and relaxed in the chair, thanks to his smile that I finally saw when he admitted he wasn't sure about the shapeshifters.

"You can blame my mother," he replied, and flashed me another smile.

"Ah."

"So, what's new?"

"Oh, not much. Being chased by an old vampire from New Orleans that wants my blood. The people I thought were my parents actually killed my parents. Oh, and I am ninety-eight years old."

"Want to talk about it?" he asked, extending his hand across the table. Mine met his halfway. Feeling his warm fingers intertwine with mine and then rub the backside of my hand, was something I had craved since the last time we were together. It did make me wonder what it was like for him. Most consider warm a comforting feeling. Few seek out the cold, but that is all my touch could give him.

"Not really." Which was the truth. I didn't. I was already on overload after all the internal conversations I had with myself over the last few days. Talking to someone about everything would only put me through another round of torture, and there was enough of that going on as it was. "I do have a trick to show you though." I grabbed his notebook and tore out a blank piece of paper. I twisted it long-ways and handed it back to him. "Hold it up and out away from you." I didn't really trust myself completely yet. With a single finger, I sent a little flame across the air slowly. It danced in the night breeze until it reached the paper, where the tip ignited. I let it burn for a second and enjoyed the amazed look on Nathan's face. Then, I closed my hand and squeezed it shut, snuffing out the fire from across the table.

"Getting better, I see," he said with a smile.

"I am sure you aren't that impressed. You have been around this all your life, but I am pretty proud of myself." Then, without a movement, I sent his notebook sliding back in place. I even lifted his history book so it could slide underneath. This produced another amazed look from him, and a smile from me that I tried to hide.

"So, if you don't want to talk about that, what would you like to talk about?"

"Well, that is a good question." I had to think for a minute, and then decided to forget about what his place was, and return to the core of who we were, or at least who he was. "What would normal teenagers talk about?"

"Oh, I know what teenagers talk about, I just don't know what people over ninety talk about," Nathan said, amusingly.

I didn't laugh, instead I pouted, "Ouch!" I turned away from him, but kept cutting my eyes to see his reaction. He was still laughing at himself when the dog pack came by with Mr. Markinson for their nightly patrol. Each greeted us with a simple "hi," or a look or a wave before they headed out. Again, we both watched as they morphed into large wolves and ran out into the woods. I doubt that will ever not amaze me.

"I was joking," Nathan said. "I would imagine they talk about music, movies, and other teens. That is when not complaining about their parents." I let that hang in silence for a minute, hoping he would start. Partially so I could learn more about him, he sure seemed to know a lot about me. He actually knew exactly the same amount about me as I did. Kind of a hard fact for me to accept. "I hear you guys have some really wild parties up there at night."

I turned back toward him and felt myself melting in his smile and eyes. He had leaned forward against the table and seemed really interested. "Depends on your definition of a wild party. We listen to music and dance most nights. Other nights are movie nights. We will watch a few movies all night long."

"Okay then Larissa. If you were to invite me to watch your favorite movie of all time, what movie would you pick?"

I didn't find that question fair. I wanted to learn about him, not have him learn more about me, and I knew the answer right off, but I hesitated to say it, not wanting to scare him off. "Dead Break," I said very tentatively.

His face cringed at my response. "a horror film?"

"Yea, I love them," I said, still holding back my normal enthusiasm.

"Not a rom-com, or something sappy?" he asked.

Now it was my turn to cringe at his response. I curled my lips and wrinkled my nose while I shook my head. "No way. I am not that kind of girl."

"Good," he said. "I am not much into that stuff either. I fall asleep when my mother watches them with Mrs. Tenderschott."

"I can't really imagine your mother watching any movie."

"She does have her down time. She just doesn't let the students see anything but her prim and proper image."

"It must be hard going to a school that your mother basically runs?"

He laughed. Not just a little snicker or jerk, but one of the hardest laughs I had ever seen anyone do. He even wrapped his arms around his chest as he did so. "Hard," he started through the laughs. "Try impossible. There is no privacy, no freedom, and everyone acts like they are scared of me. Not to mention the unwritten rule about me." he stopped laughing but still sat back in his chair where he stared right at me. "So, who gave you the warning?"

"Someone."

He threw both hands up and ran them through his hair, then leaned his head back, looking up at the night sky. "My mother?"

"No, Apryl and Laura told me about it, and they also told me about Gwen..."

"Gwen?" he interrupted. "Well, you can stop right there. I wouldn't believe anything that comes from her. If you listen to her, she has us already married with three kids and her in position to take over as the Supreme in this coven when my mother steps down. All part of her master plan." He put air quotes around master plan and said it all with a tone of contempt.

"So, I take it you guys were..." I started, and felt myself choking on the phrase. I didn't want to say it. I didn't want him to give me some story that they were, and just broke up, or even worst that they still were. "An item?"

"An item?" he asked with a snicker. "Who uses that term? I forgot you are old." He winked, and I figured I better get used to these kinds of jabs from him, though I didn't really mind. "And no, we weren't and aren't an item or anything anywhere except in her mind. She constructed a whole fantasy the day we first met, and she realized we were the only ones here the same age. That was it."

"Why not?" I asked, then wondered why I did. I didn't really care.

"You have to be joking. She is too into herself, her makeup, and all that. I don't like girls, or even people, who are nothing more than just what you see on the surface. I like people with depth, makes moments like this better when you have something to talk about."

In all that, I only heard him say moments like this. We were having a moment, the first of many, I hoped.

"So, you never told me what your favorite type of music is to listen to up on your deck?"

"Not country. That is Jeremy's. I like most anything but that, but if I had to pick, nineties grunge, but I recently started listening to some old New Orleans' style jazz music, it's not bad."

"Doing a little research?" he asked.

"I guess. I felt like checking it out to see how I like it. It's not too bad."

"I am with you on the nineties grunge. That is what me and the dog pack listen to a lot. We get a little wild ourselves. Listening to music, watching sports, watching slasher films, just being really loud and rowdy. You should stop by some time; I have a feeling you would love it." I had a feeling I would too, no matter what was happening, as long as Nathan was there.

We spent the next several hours talking like teenagers. Music, tv shows, movies, and stupid things our, I mean his, friends did. Listening to several of those stories really did make hanging out with the dog pack sound like the place to be. Of course, it also sounds like it was a good thing the building adapted to what was needed. More than one story ended with something smashed, or a few body-sized holes in the wall. Not from wrestling, but more from dancing. Hearing everything convinced me that if this were a normal high school like I had seen on television or the movies, Nathan would be stud athletic star. He already was in my eyes.

We went back in just before midnight, we shared another comforting hug at the bottom of the stairs. I didn't want to let go, and it felt he didn't either. Even when he released me, he kept his arms around me for a few moments looking at me, and then asked, "Why did you ignore the unwritten rule?"

"I don't know," I said, not wanting to confess how I really felt around him. How the only comfort I felt was when I was in his presence. How nothing made sense to me except when I was around him, and even that didn't make complete sense.

"Good answer," he said, and leaned down. My mind entered a panic state. How do I respond? Do I come to meet him?

A cough from up the stairs stopped the moment, and Nathan stood up straight. His arms lingered around me for a few seconds before releasing me. I already knew what was up the stairs and didn't bother turning around.

"See you tomorrow?" he asked.

"Yep, good night." I stood and watched him walk away before I turned and glared up the stairs. There she was, the queen of pink, standing there in pink sweatpants, pink shirt, and pink bunny slippers. Top that off with perfect hair and makeup at this hour of the night. *Good god, did she sleep like that?*

I walked up the stairs and didn't even look at her. I expected some comment, warning, or hate filled explosion, but there was nothing. Just the glaring. When I passed the landing she stood on, I kept on going. Her pulse had quickened, and I heard her inhale to start to speak, but I stopped her with, "Nice bunny slippers, princess." She stood there glaring up at me until I went through our door.

27

From inside my room, I could hear disco music coming down the stairs in my closet, and I found myself in the mood to dance, even to disco, and ran toward my closet. My foot hit the first step of the stairs, and I felt odd, but couldn't really put my finger on what it was. So, I continued up, but when I stepped out on the deck, I hit the ground. It was soft, moist, grass covered ground in the middle of a dense forest.

I was disoriented about where I was, and when, as this didn't seem to match any memory I had, but I knew what this was. This was another vision, and I leapt up to my feet and looked around for Reginald Von Bell. He wasn't there leering at me like he had been the first time. The best I could tell, I was alone. I couldn't hear anything besides the wind, the sounds of an owl off in the distance, and the crashing of waves. The waves had a familiar sound; they sounded like... our cove. Another look around at the trees, and I realized where I was, and that sent a shiver through me that even made me feel cold.

I crept back toward the coven, being very aware of my surroundings. I didn't have to think about this too long before I realized what this meant. He was here in the woods. I kept listening for anything, but heard nothing except the waves. Even the owl had left, and no other animals were scampering through, disturbing the leaves or limbs. I couldn't even feel the pulse of anything here, but I wasn't sure if I could in a vision or not.

"Larissa, it's just a matter of time. You will finally be ours." His voice, as creepy as ever, came from just behind me and froze me where I stood. I wanted to spin around, but my legs disagreed. Then I found the wood of the deck below my hands, and I screamed, causing a rush of others to my side.

Mike and Brad were the first to arrive and knelt next to me. Each tried to help me to my feet, but my hands swung around in a frenzy, pushing them away. Laura and Pam were next. "Larissa, what's wrong? Where are you hurt?" Pam asked. My hands still pushing everyone away. Over their heads I saw Mr. Bolden stop his rush toward me and head to the railing of the deck. Then he sped past me, down the stairs, causing everyone to stop where they were and watch. Mrs. Bolden, pushing through them all, and knelt down in front of me. My hands had stopped when I saw Mr. Bolden run by. She asked "Vision?" I nodded, and a grave panic draped over her face as her hand grabbed and said, "Let's go."

She pulled me down my stairs and out of my room, down the hall, and to the stairs. We emerged out on our landing to a chaotic scene. Horrifying wails filled the entry, and everyone was out on their landings looking down at a now empty hall. When Mrs. Bolden and I started down the stairs, all eyes fell on us, watching each step as we rushed down. At the bottom, she ran, pulling me with her. "Back to your halls!" she barked before we ducked into the side hall that led to Mrs. Saxon's room. Screams and wails swallowed our path.

Mrs. Bolden didn't knock at Mrs. Saxon's door. She just yanked it open. An explosion of painful wails greeted us. Mrs. Saxon had her back to us, as did who I recognized as Mr. Markinson, Martin, and Mr. Helms.

"Rebecca, Larissa had another vision. I think they are close," she said.

"In the woods behind the coven," I added before she turned around. It was a good thing too. The scene I saw when she turned around would have taken my words away. Mr. Bolden was knelt down beside Rob. He laid on the floor, blood pooled around him as Mr. Bolden and Mr. Demius tended to his wounds, some still squirting blood as they attempted to tend to it.

"We know. They jumped werewolves, and injured Rob," she said, strikingly unemotional considering the scene behind her. "They are going to break through the entry. I saw it."

I gasped and put my hand over my mouth. I felt Mrs. Bolden's grip tighten on my own hand. "This is all because of me," I whispered, and I honestly believed that. If I weren't here, they wouldn't be out there, and Rob wouldn't have been hurt.

"Stop it, and hold yourself together," Mrs. Bolden whispered at me harshly.

Her hand squeezed me, let go, and then squeezed again. It felt odd, and I turned to look. I had seen that twitching of the jaw and empty stare before. The scent of all the blood was getting to her. It wasn't that I couldn't smell the metallic odor in the air, but my mind had other things in focus. I turned and ordered her, "You hold yourself together."

Her mouth twitched, and her muscles stiffened even more. I was quite sure I still benefited from my rebirth and would have the strength to hold her physically if I needed to, but this was not the time. "You need to leave," I whispered quietly enough so we were the only ones to hear it.

Well, us and Mr. Bolden, who turned his attention for just a split second from Rob and yelled, "Jen, Larissa, get out of here."

Her head snapped toward his direction, and the animalistic expression on her face broke, leaving an uncomfortable shell of who she was. "You need to go." I pushed her backwards toward the door, and then shut it once she was outside. Then zipped to Rob's side, startling Mr. Bolden, who grabbed me with one hand, "No!"

I looked at him reassuringly, but still very concerned. "I'm fine. Is it the venom?"

He released his grip, and Mr. Demius said, "No, vampire venom does not affect werewolves. It's just the bites."

I then looked back at Martin and Mr. Markinson. "Did you see them? How many were there?"

"Six," said Mr. Markinson. "One is wounded, and one is your Reginald. I didn't see Jean St. Claire."

"Not surprising. From what I have read, he rarely leaves his own coven, and never leaves New Orleans," said Mrs. Saxon.

"I think I have stopped the bleeding." Mr. Demius held his hands on two large bandages on Rob's chest. Each appeared soaked in blood, but as I watched, their color changed from red stained to white. Mr. Demius noticed me watching the transformation and smiled. "Dark magic," he mouthed. "Werewolves have unbelievable healing abilities. His body is already repairing itself; we just need to support it until it does."

Mrs. Tenderschott came in the door with a vial of yellow liquid. "And there is the support he needs," Mr. Demius said. The magic elixir she carried never reached Rob.

"The entry!" screamed Mrs. Saxon.

The ground shook, heaving up and down beneath us, and then the walls shook violently. The crash of shattering glass drowned out Rob's screams. I looked up at the wall of windows in Mrs. Saxon's residence. They shook, but held. A few cracks crept across them. The room was so silent you could hear their progress. I watched it stretch across the wall when the others ran out. Mrs. Tenderschott remained and knelt down next to Rob. There was concern in her eyes, but with how she kept looking at the door, I didn't think it was because of the state Rob was in. From what I could tell, most of the bleeding had stopped, and I could feel his pulse was strong.

I didn't ask or wait to be told and hurried out. To where? I had an idea, but what I was going to find, I had no clue. On the way, I heard large thumps, bumps, and slams. I kept my eyes down the hall toward the source and picked up the pace, but slid to a stop on the carpet when I saw Martin rolling head over tail in full werewolf across the opening. He recovered though and stalked whatever had thrown him. His throaty growl vibrated down the hall. When he disappeared past the entry, I started again, this time as fast as I could, and slid to a stop out in the entry.

What the hell had I just run into?

That was the only reaction that seemed to match the image of the wall of windows that lead out to the pool and woods, smashed by the largest boulder from our waterfall. It now sat in a crater made in the tile floor by its impact. Its entrance destroyed the frames, door, and the runes that adorned them. A flurry of fireballs and bolts of lightning flew toward six black clad targets, each managed to jump out of the way. Witches, both instructors and students, lined what remained of the stairs.

In the middle, an all-out melee of vampires jumping and clawing at the invaders. Mike threw one against the wall with a thud that cracked the wall itself, but it did nothing to his attacker. The thick individual with a head of flowing blonde hair and black eyes just stepped from the hole his body created in the wall and jumped back only to be caught in the jaws of the black werewolf, Mr. Markinson, but he even escaped that, and then picked him up tossed him into the pool behind them.

"Larissa!" a voice seethed. That voice. That voice that I knew belonged to Reginald Von Bell. My eyes jumped to its source, and there he was, climbing up to the top of the boulder. Our eyes locked as he stood there like a conquering hero, while the madness of a war zone continued around him. He stepped down, and I felt my legs tremble.

"Child, we have been looking for you for a long time, but you will elude us no longer." He smiled madly and walked closer.

I couldn't move. My legs were going nowhere, even when I yelled at them. I was again, that girl that stood in the alley just a week ago watching him kill the man I believed to be my father. The girl that was so frozen that the woman I believed was my mother had to pull me away by the hand. She was not there this time. It was just me and him. For the second time, he stared me down.

He was now close enough to reach out and touch me. His bony finger reached under my chin and pushed my head upward toward him. The touch was cold and evil, as were his eyes. "Finally," he growled. Then I felt a sense of familiarity. I had been here before, but I was younger, much younger. I was a little girl, looking up into his dark and dastardly face, with the icy touch of his finger forcing my head upward to look into his eyes. Around me was screaming and yelling, with several familiar voices with creole accents yelling.

Then, out of nowhere, a blast of fire threw him to the ground, and I was back in the destroyed grand entry. Gwen standing at my side. She barked, "Wake up Larissa, we have work to do sister!" She put an exclamation point on her statement with a few more shots at Reginald. He fled away, dropping the black coat he wore to smolder on the floor. The chaos of the moment didn't stop him from adjusting his black suit before leering back at us with a hiss.

Jeremy took a run at him, passing Mike, who had one of Reginald's party in a headlock. I saw him give it a twist that was reminiscent of what I had seen happen to Mr. Norton. His body fell just as limp. Reginald swatted Jeremy away like he was just a mosquito. Then he turned his attention to his fallen friend. Mike stood over the body until it turned to ash.

While that may have been a win, what I witnessed over the next few moments told me it was actually a mistake. Five vampires hissed in unison, and then rushed at anyone and anything close to them. Witches, wolves, and vampires alike. They ran through fire, lightning, columns of water, and objects thrown at them. Two vampires, which included the thick one that had deposited Mr. Markinson in the pool, ran up the walls, as if the laws of gravity didn't apply to them. Tera, Lisa, and Marcia were sent flying through the air. Brad caught Tera, and Mr. Bolden caught Lisa, but Marcia hit the floor with a scream. Gwen and Jack were both on the offensive until another vampire flashed through them with a tackle any all-pro linebacker would be proud of.

While I stood there and watched all that I lost track of where Reginald was, and barely noticed out of the side of my eyes another vampire, a girl, short and blond with black eyes, in a black cape rushing at me. I lunged in her direction, and then ducked, sliding under her reach on the floor. She stopped, turned, and hissed at me, baring her teeth. I returned the favor. The shock and fear of the moment had worn off, and anger had taken its place. I wanted blood, but not for feeding. I just wanted to spill their blood like they had Mr. Norton, and like they were now trying to do to my friends. I crouched down and threw myself at her. I was there in a flash. Both hands grabbed her by the shoulders as I passed and threw her into the wall in front of me, but that wasn't good enough. I was there when she landed and punched hard into her chest. I knew it wouldn't do any mortal damage to her, but the explosive thud of the impact was satisfying to me and shocking to her.

"The head!" Brad exclaimed from the other side of the room. I turned, and he was looking at me, and before the shock of my punch wore off, I reached up and gave her head a twist, like I had seen Mike do and like Reginald had done to Mr. Norton. I popped it off like an old twist top bottle.

When I turned around, witches were everywhere on the floor. They were no longer on the offensive, but on the defensive. Marcia appeared hurt, and Apryl and Laura were guarding her. Tera and Gwen were doing their best to defend Mr. Demius. Mr. Helms was still on the offensive and moving rather spry for what he appeared on the outside, but that was until I found Reginald again. A single punch and kick sent an unconscious Mr. Helms sliding across the floor. I ran to the center of the entry, looking for someone to help.

"Larissa, no. Get clear!" someone yelled. It was Lisa. She stood with her arms out. I saw her eyes roll back, giving her a freaky appearance, and then spirits, the ones I saw during her ascension, exploded out from around her. They hung in the air for a moment as if they were getting their commands and then went after the closest vampire they could find. The spiritual mass spun around them and through them, but didn't seem to have any effect other than to distract them, but that was enough. Mr. Markinson had pulled himself out of the pool and appeared to take pleasure as he ripped the head off the closest vampire. Brad and Jeremy had the pleasure of taking the other one.

A female vampire with short dark hair was affixed to the wall like some kind of insect. Reginald pointed at her and then directed her forward with his hands. She crawled like a spider along the wall, attempting to get behind us, but I fired a few fireballs of my own at her to discourage her. She brushed them off, hissing with each impact. When she found herself above Mr. Demius, she pounced from the wall for him, but met a fate that I couldn't even comprehend. Gwen produced one of her discs above them, and the vampire disappeared through it before it closed.

Steven and Stan had now transformed themselves into a wall to defend the injured. Most of the witches were down. Martin and Mr. Markinson were both limping, with bloody bite marks all over them. Apryl, and Mrs. Bolden were tending to Marcia, who appeared to have fractured her leg in the fall. Pam was lying in a corner, battered, and bruised, but brushed off any attempt by anyone to come to her. "Just deal with them."

The spirits cleared, leaving two very angry and hostile vampires surrounded by the rest of us. Reginald's gaze never left me. I was his target, and everyone there knew it. The other was there just to clear the way; a task he was surprisingly efficient at. In a single pass, he had knocked Brad and Mike both out of the way and sent Gwen and Mrs. Saxon scrambling. I was so busy watching them, I never saw Reginald lunge for me, or Nathan sprinting into the entry, tackling him. I didn't even know he was there until I turned and watched Reginald sink his fangs into Nathan's shoulder. Nathan dropped to the floor in front of him, and his body started to twitch. I knew that look. I thought my rage was at the top of its scale, but soon found out it hadn't even come close. Everything inside boiled, and I saw red when I rushed at Reginald. The fury I hit him with appeared to even startle him. I was about to pop his head off when his friend knocked me away. I made another attempt, and this time the other one hit me and knocked me to the ground before I made two steps. He stood over me, glaring down at me. Dark eyes under his short spiky blonde hair, and his charm dangling as he bent. It was clear. He never saw the shard of broken wood until it pierced where his heart should be. As he fell, I stood up, yanking the charm from around his neck. I threw it to Mrs. Saxon, and then turned my attention to Reginald, who appeared a little less arrogant now. Maybe it was what he had just watched, or the hundreds of burning wood splinters I had hovering behind me. I wasn't focused on the head of a single needle. I now had hundreds of them, and they followed me as I walked toward him.

I felt great satisfaction as each of them thrust into Reginald. His body fell, and burned right there in the entry, and I basked in the warmth of the fire until I remembered Nathan and ran to his side. Mrs. Saxon had already administered the vial, but he was still losing consciousness.

"Is this normal?" I asked, looking right at Mrs. Bolden with a tear running down my face. It hit me what had happened, and that it was all my fault.

"I don't know. I have never done it."

I looked around from face to face of those now gathered over us, pleading for someone to tell me he was going to be okay. Each returned a concerned look, and most shared the same tears that now rolled down my face.

"He needs rest, I believe," Mr. Demius offered, but he was not convincing.

I gathered Nathan back in my arms, much like he did that first night, and carried him back to Mrs. Saxon's residence. Mrs. Tenderschott exploded into tears as well when she saw how pale he had turned. I stood there, holding his massive frame in my small arms, and begged, "Help him." My words barely audible over my crying.

"I wish I could honey, but I can't."

"Larissa." I turned to face Mrs. Bolden. "You are the only one we have ever known who has taken the antidote from the vial. You are the expert here."

I straightened myself up and sniffed. "Rest it is," I said. "I slept for a while after I took it."

"Come right this way." Mrs. Saxon led me through to Nathan's room.

I sat there every moment of every day for the next three days, thankful that I didn't need to sleep. This was also a curse since the time crept by, and I couldn't even close my eyes to make a few hours pass here or there. Nathan tossed and turned most of the time, which concerned me. In my mind, I could see the black venom making its ways through his veins and sinking into his muscles. Luckily for me, my imagination was worse than reality. His pulse never stopped or slowed. It was a steady and comforting beat. When no one was looking, I leaned down, letting my head lay on his chest just to be closer to it. Each pump helped him heal and get stronger, and gave me a reason to be.

I wouldn't be lying if I said life happened one beat at a time. In the simplest form it does. One beat, one moment, leads to the next, which is another beat. That beat leads to another. One after another. Each giving you the chance to make your life worth something. Something that matches the miracle of life itself. Some of us do just that, and make the most out of it, making their lives and the lives of those around them better. Which in the end is really all that matters. Each beat of Nathan's heart gave him another chance at that. Each beat made my life better, and I wasn't even sure he knew it yet. My problem was, my beats stopped years ago, but that didn't mean I wasn't going to do all I could to find my moments to make his better too.

"Well, that sucked. Please tell me you haven't been there staring at me the whole time," Nathan groaned, his eyes squinting into the sunlight coming in through his windows.

"All five months," I said, forcing myself not to giggle.

"Five months? I have been out five months?" he asked. This time, he attempted to open his eyes completely, but then clamped them shut. "Am I a... you know?"

"Do you crave raw meat and blood?" I asked. My face pinched to hold in the laughter.

"No, but I could go for a hamburger." A smile crept across his face.

"Then no." I finally let out a giggle that caused him to open his eyes again and reach for my hand with his. Nathan groaned when he did. "You took quite a beating, not to mention I am not sure how far you turned before the vial took hold."

"I feel like I was hit by a truck, and then he backed up and took another run at me."

"Not far from the truth." Now he opened his eyes fully. They were bright blue and full of life and filled me with the same life.

"So really five months?" he asked.

"No, just three days, but I would have been here if it was five months, ten months, or ten years. However long it took." His hand rubbed mine, and the warmth felt nice. I had held it many times over the last three days, but it had never returned the favor.

"I know you would." Nathan let go of my hand and sat up in his bed. A groan or grimace followed each movement he made. I reached to move the pillow up behind him to cushion his back against the headboard of his bed.

As I was doing this, we found ourselves face to face, inches from each other. This time, there was no audience high above looking down on us. As he moved in, I said, "Be careful, I bite."

"Wouldn't be the first time." Then our lips met.

We pulled apart, my eyes opening before his giving me a glimpse at the smile on his face. "Kind of like kissing my grandmother." He flinched backward, expecting to be hit, but I let him have that one. There was no playful slap or slug. I didn't want to cause any more bruises. Instead, I reached behind his neck and pulled him in for another kiss. His hands did the same, gripping the side of my face. This was no kiss one would give to his grandmother.

We were only separated by a short, but loud cough, "Ahem."

I didn't look back at its source. I didn't need to. I had my suspicions of what I would find and feeling Nathan's body tense up as he looked over my shoulder, I knew I was right. "Hi mom."

And for the third time in my life, I felt like I was going to die.

Up Next - Coven Cove Book 2—The Shape of Things to Come

1

Ever notice the switch to turn on your nerves was someone telling you not to be nervous? That was the on switch for mine, and Mrs. Saxon threw it into the on position when she told me Council of Mages would be visiting tomorrow. She told me several times to not be nervous, which, of course, caused me to worry like hell about what I had to be nervous about. Yes, our coven had been attacked by some two hundred-year-old vampires, and yes, technically, it was my fault... and that is where my mind stopped, and the mental gymnastics took over.

I spent the rest of the day asking anyone I could find about the council. My mind had already created an image of twelve people walking in wearing black robes with their noses held high, ready to pass judgement, and sentence me to some horrific magical punishment. None of the other students had ever met or seen them. Not even Gwen, and even she seemed concerned when I mentioned they were coming for a visit, but I couldn't be sure that she wasn't just messing with me. We had a rather tenuous but unspoken truce since Reginald Von Bell's attack. She had stepped in during the attack and defended me, and even called me sister, something that I thought of a few days later while watching over Nathan. Was it just a comment or exclamation, or was she referring to me as a sister witch? I never asked. I didn't want to push things and threaten our peace. There were still the little jabs here and there, but no more than anyone else, and she no longer tortured me during our classes. Well, at least not as much as before. We even sparred once in Mr. Helm's class, and it never became heated or out of control. There was a still an icy glare from her when she saw me with Nathan, but I didn't let that bother me. Why should I?

"Oh dear, you have nothing to worry about," Mrs. Tenderschott said when I asked her about the council.

"I really wish people would stop telling me that. It makes me think I have something to worry about." I let my head collapse down on the table with a thud.

"Nonsense. I have met with them many times. A few of them are full of hot air that they like to blow around to make themselves seem important, but the rest are just like us. Nothing to worry your pretty little head about." She reached over and gave the back of my head a soothing rub.

"But you once called them witch hunters." I said muffled, and then picked my head up to see her response.

A nervous smile crept across her face, and her eyes ran away from mine. "Don't worry about that. That is old history."

The lack of conviction in her voice sent my head back to the table with a thud. "What do they want?" I asked, muffled against the tabletop.

"I imagine they want to make sure everyone is okay and find out everything they can about what happened." I felt her hand on my head again. She stroked my hair first and then gave it a little tug. I lifted it off the table and looked up at her. "That means they will want to talk to you. Just tell them what you know, and tell them clearly what you don't know. You will be fine. Now, are you ready to try again?"

I rolled my black eyes up to the ceiling and sat back in my chair. Another day, another potion. "Sure, let's do this." I held out my hand, and Mrs. Tenderschott handed me a vial of green liquid that had flecks of orange in it. I made the mistake of asking a few times what the contents were. Something I instantly regretted. Now I don't ask. I just down the concoction and hope it doesn't kill me or cause my body to grow hair all over the place. I wasn't ready to become a part of the dog pack.

It tasted worse than it looked. The orange specks were chunky and hard; and they scraped my throat on the way down. If this were meant for witches, I wasn't sure how their sensitive human systems would be able to handle it. Like every time before, the room dripped away, leaving me in darkness before that dripped away too. What appeared were the steps leading up to the front porch of my childhood home. I went in and immediately headed to the kitchen. My mother was there. She wasn't sitting at the table like she was the first time. This time she was at the sink, washing dishes while looking out the window. The sunlight that came in the window caught her red hair just right, making it almost glow around her. She turned when I stepped in and caused the floor to creak.

"Larissa!" She rushed and hugged me. I hugged her back. "You are still so cold."

"It's fine, mom," I said. My voice still sounding like a much younger version of myself. I still didn't want to discuss what I really was, not yet. It was something I knew I would have to tell her. How? Now that was the big question. I was still getting to know my mother. I wasn't ready to break her heart yet. Not that anytime would really be the right time to tell her.

She let go of our embrace, but grabbed my hand and led me over to the kitchen table. I sat down while she took off her white apron and folded it neatly over the back of her chair before she sat. For someone was was washing the dishes, she was dressed rather well. White short-sleeve shirt, grey skirt, and wide black belt. "I am glad you came back to see me."

"I promise I will make more of an effort to visit often. There has been a lot going on, and right now I still have to use a potion to come see you."

"Because you still can't remember your life here? I see." My mother's brow furrowed as she looked down at the table in front of her. "And you can only do one potion a day. Even that frequently can have side effects."

"No kidding," I said out loud, causing my mother to cover her mouth with her hand as she let out a reserved giggle.

"Enjoying the nightmares?"

"Not really." I gave her my best face of dismay. I remembered the nightmares from when I was human again, but since the antidote had worn off, I hadn't slept, so no more nightmares. Having to explain that to my mother would mean explaining the other detail I didn't want her to know about yet. To me they were, I guess, daymares. Little flashes of hell while I was wide awake.

"There are various spells that can create a memory block. Unfortunately, breaking them is not as easy as putting them on. Is that wise witch that showed you how to visit me the first time still around?"

"Yes ma'am. In fact, there are many wise witches around me. I am part of a coven up in the northeast. They are teaching me all the things I need to know." Hearing this appeared to bring a smile to my mother's face. At least I was able to give her some good news. "I know we were part of the Orleans' Coven. I have been reading through some of their records to learn about our family. Things are coming back to me." I lied. Nothing was coming back to me. Not yet. Mrs. Tenderschott and Mrs. Saxon had already tried a few reversals for memory blocks, and every cleaning spell they knew. Neither were hopeful they would make a difference. Memory loss wasn't common in the turning process, but it happened, and at the moment that was the leading theory of what my problem was. The best I could do was read the records, which I had, and come back to visit my mother. If something clicked, I could handle these trips all on my own.

"In fact, mom, there was something I read about, a party, my debutant ball."

"Oh my," her hand again went up in front of her mouth, but I could still see the edges of her wide smile on either side of it. "I hadn't thought about that in years. You were so beautiful in that light blue dress." Her voice cooed.

"Yea, I read about that."

"I still remember you dancing with Todd Grainger. He was in a tuxedo with a bow tie, and you wore that dress. You both made such a cute couple. Have you seen him recently?"

"No ma'am. Not in a few years." *Try ninety years.*

"I had so hoped you would have stayed in touch with him, but you didn't really seem to enjoy yourself dancing with him. He was such a nice boy, and his family…"

"I am sure they were a fine family. He just wasn't my type." I wasn't sure if he was or wasn't. By now, he would be long in the ground and definitely not into dating. Not to mention I had Nathan, I hoped. "Mom, do you remember anyone with the last name Norton?"

I watched my mother pinch her lips together and her eyes searched her memories as they floated by, giving a little shake of her head. Then it became more pronounced. "No, that name is not familiar. Why do you ask?"

"It's just a name that keeps coming up in the research of our family. I was trying to understand the significance." I watched my mother again, as she pinched her face and appeared lost in thought. Maybe I was reading too much into her expression, but to me, it looked like more than just someone trying to remember something. Did she know the name? She had to. If Jean St. Claire were as much of a nuisance in the New Orleans area as I had been told, and my parents were who I heard they were, there was a good chance she would have known members of his coven.

"No. That's not a name I am familiar with," she answered. Her voice wavered. There was a question in there, maybe to ask why I was asking about them, but I wasn't ready to open that can of worms yet. Of course, it could just be my mind playing with her response. I knew the truth of who they were and what happened, and I didn't doubt my mother still viewed me as her little girl and might hold something frightful back.

"Okay," I answered, letting it drop. "I do have another question for you, more on the magic side."

She sat up straight, but still not as straight as Jennifer Bolden. That was a vampire thing. "That I can handle. What is it?"

"Two actually. You said there was a way for me to come back and visit you on my own. That I could just drift back and forth. Can you show me how to do that?"

"I can tell you, and then you can try later. You need to focus on memory that you have of this place, but you have to more than see it. You have to feel it, like you are there in that moment-" Her voice trailed off as my mood declined. I had to assume I projected that depression on my face.

"That's the problem. I remember nothing, so there is nothing to focus on. I tried remembering back to the first time I came here, but that didn't work."

"No, it wouldn't," agreed my mother. "It has to be a real memory. That is why they need to work on breaking through that memory block. Once that is gone, you will have what you need to come back to see me anytime you want. No more yucky potions." She said as if she were talking to a six-year-old who just took her last spoonful of medicine. "What's the second question?"

"This one, I hope, is easier. Did I have good control of my magic when you were—alive?" I gulped.

"Oh yes," she beamed. "The best of anyone your age. You developed superb control at an early age and progressed beyond simple to complex spells before anyone else. Why?"

"I have been all over the place lately. For a while, anything I tried to move either didn't move or flew across the room violently, almost killing someone. I was told it was a question of focus and that I needed to concentrate everything on something the size of the head of a pin, but that is exhausting to have to remember to do each and every time."

"But it is good advice." My mother pointed at me when she said it like a lecturing parent. "You have a powerful gift, always have. That requires a stronger focus to control. That rule applies to everything from moving objects to even your spells and potions. Most think the potion is really just the combination of ingredients, but it is much more than that. We are the ones responsible for enabling the potion with our gift. The words we say, the thought we have in our head when we say it, give the potion the power to do what we want. The ingredients are just vehicles for our magic. It's not the other way around. Not having good control and focus then can lead to disastrous outcomes."

"Gotcha," I said, trying to sound sure of myself while inside I was again realizing how dangerous I really was.

"How much time do you have?" she asked hopefully.

I looked down at my watch, which wasn't there. What I saw beyond my arm was the edge of the straight black skirt I was wearing. My hand slipped down under the table and explored the fabric up to my waist, where I found the texture of a thick leather belt, much like my mom's, bordering a white blouse. This must be one of the last outfits my mother remembered me in. I thought about it, and knew I hadn't been here too long, maybe twenty minutes, and had a couple of hours until my date with Nathan. "I have a bit. Why?"

"Let me show you a few things."

The Shape of Things to Come – Available as paperback on Amazon and Barnes and Noble

Stay in Touch

Dear Reader,

Thank you for taking a chance on this book. I hope you enjoyed it. If you did, I'd be more than grateful if you could leave a review on Amazon (even if it is just a rating and a sentence or two). Every review makes a difference to an author and helps other readers discover the book.

To stay up to date on everything in the Coven Cove world, click here to join my mailing list and I will send you a **free bonus chapter** from "The Secret of the Blood Charm".

As always, thank you for reading,
David

A big thank you to my beta reading team. Without all your feedback, books like this one would not be possible. Thank you for all your hard work.

The Secret of the Blood Charm © 2022 by David Clark. All Rights Reserved.
All rights reserved. No part of this book may be reproduced in any form or by any electronic or mechanical means including information storage and retrieval systems, without permission in writing from the author. The only exception is by a reviewer, who may quote short excerpts in a review.

This book is a work of fiction. Names, characters, places, and incidents either are products of the author's imagination or are used fictitiously. Any resemblance to actual persons, living or dead, events, or locales is entirely coincidental.

David Clark
Visit my website at www.authordavidclark.com

Printed in the United States of America

First Printing: January 2022
Frightening Future Publishing

Printed in Great Britain
by Amazon

38655956R00089